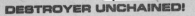
DESTROYER UNCHAINED!

She was the sand, the wind, the struggling life. She was also the storm, her anger rising in her need to bury, to destroy. She looked out of the whirling chaos of storm, and she also watched herself looking out. She saw her face, as if in a mirror, indigo against dirty magenta, bridgeless Dushau nose, hate-filled indigo eyes, sickly white teeth—Desdinda's face. She was Krinata and hated Desdinda, and was Desdinda and hated the human intruder and Jindigar, the Aliom priest who had befouled an Archive with his Inversions. Destroy!

Krinata felt the ravening madness reaching out to shake the very sky, and everything in her denied it. Then, another presence was attracted to the turmoil, a presence that stretched her brain and distorted her mind as if to rip her identity apart. She didn't even hear herself scream...

"No one writes about cultural symbiosis with a more sensitive voice than Ms. Lichtenberg, who has created a fascinating set of relationships between ephemeral Krinata, eternal Jindigar and computer simulacrum Arlai. The action is continuous and exciting, leaving the reader anxious for more."

—*Romantic Times* on *Dushau*

BOOKS IN THE DUSHAU UNIVERSE:
DUSHAU
FARFETCH
OUTREACH (to be published)

BOOKS IN THE KREN/FIRST LIFEWAVE UNIVERSE:
MOLT BROTHER
CITY OF A MILLION LEGENDS
LAST PERSUADERS (to be written)

BOOKS IN THE SIME/GEN UNIVERSE:

by Jacqueline Lichtenberg:
HOUSE OF ZEOR
UNTO ZEOR, FOREVER
MAHOGANY TRINROSE
RENSIME

by Jean Lorrah and Jacqueline Lichtenberg
FIRST CHANNEL
CHANNEL'S DESTINY

by Jacqueline Lichtenberg and Jean Lorrah
ZELEROD'S DOOM (to be published)

by Jean Lorrah
AMBROV KEON

NONFICTION BY JACQUELINE LICHTENBERG:
STAR TREK LIVES! (with Sondra Marshak and Joan Winston)

THE DUSHAU TRILOGY #2
FARFETCH
JACQUELINE LICHTENBERG

POPULAR LIBRARY

An Imprint of Warner Books, Inc.

A Warner Communications Company

POPULAR LIBRARY EDITION

QUESTAR® is a registered trademark of Warner Books, Inc.

Cover art by Ken Barr

Popular Library books are published by
Warner Books, Inc.
75 Rockefeller Plaza
New York, N.Y. 10019

Ⓦ A Warner Communications Company

Printed in the United States of America

First Printing: September, 1985

10 9 8 7 6 5 4 3 2 1

To Tom Baker, who portrayed the Fourth Dr. Who and reawakened my sense of wonder by juxtaposing depth of understanding of the universe with *joie de vivre*. He has given me new aspirations, new definitions of the art of drama, creating, among many things, this series of books. May each reader of this book say a special blessing for this man. May each writer among you aspire, as I do, to create a part that could be played only by Tom Baker.

ACKNOWLEDGMENTS

I must thank the people who helped by commenting on the first draft of this novel: Jean Lorrah, Judy Segal, Roberta Mendelson, and Susan DeGuardiola. In addition, the staffs, contributors, and readers of the three fanzines dedicated to the Sime/Gen universe have been indispensable, particularly Karen Litman, editor and publisher of *Companion in Zeor;* Kerry Schaefer, who is now the editor for *Ambrov Zeor;* Anne Pinzow, *Ambrov Zeor*'s executive editor; and Katie Filipowicz, editor and publisher of *Zeor Forum;* all of whom can be reached through the post office box below.

I'm already working on the third novel in the Dushau Trilogy, and the quick help and encouragement of these people has been vital to this project. But I'm still most eager for comments from the readers—those who have read my Sime/Gen novels and can compare them with Dushau and Kren, and those who have not yet read any of my other series. I write primarily to entertain, but I can't know if I've achieved that unless you tell me.

So here I want to acknowledge and thank each reader who will write to me about this trilogy. What do you want to see in the next book?

For information about forthcoming Dushau novels, or on any of my other series, send a legal size, SELF-ADDRESSED STAMPED ENVELOPE to:

Ambrov Zeor, Dept. D-2
P.O.B. 290
Monsey, N.Y. 10952

It may take several weeks to get a response, but be sure that each note, each inquiry is treasured. Writers, too, have bad days, and it could be that your question or criticism will spark the answer to a plot problem or bring you a free copy of a fanzine and a flood of new friends when it's published.

If I should ever move, you may still find me through the Scott Meredith Agency in New York City, or through any of my publishers.

Contents

ELEVENTH OBSERVATION OF SHOSHUNRI

"The Third Law of Nature is vigilant cognizance of the purpose behind action."

SIXTH OBSERVATION OF SHOSHUNRI

"Fidelity is the most demanding Law of Nature, thus the most highly rewarded."

From: *Purpose and Method*
By: Shoshunri, Observing Priest of Aliom

ONE

Crash Landing

The computer was moaning to itself, dribbling sparks onto the twisted and buckled bridge deck, dying in agony.

By the glow of those blood-red sparks and the faint emergency lights Krinata Zavaronne could see a small puddle of her own red blood spreading to mix with the deep purple blood of the warm Dushau body she sprawled against. Dying.

No! Not dead yet! We survived the crash!

Driven by sharp urgency, she fought for consciousness, fastening on the nonhuman rhythm of Dushau breathing, groping for the scintillating thrill of the curious psychic resonance she'd once shared with two Dushau.

But her eyes drooped shut, and she slipped back into darkness, swept into what seemed only a dream.

Dazzling sand dunes marched away into the mauve-hazed distance. An unforgiving copper fireball of a sun beat from the bare magenta sky. A small metal sliver lay half buried in a large dune. She became every grain of sand in the desert. She was the metal sliver, and the sky and sun, air and sand, balanced in ecstasy, celebrating within herself, the perfection of the Celestial Artist.

Then, subtly, the vision changed.

Death baked the hollow sliver and the protoplasm within. The huge dune ached to swallow the sliver and heal the wound the foreign thing had made in it.

In the far distance a sinister dirty haze smeared the horizon. A vibration in the sands identified it even as vision expanded to encompass it: sandstorm.

But it was veering away from the metal sliver. The rage of the dune, which was herself yet separate from her, reached out and dragged the scouring menace toward the helpless sliver that was also herself, anticipating a vicious satisfaction, a healing triumph. For a moment she fed all her energies into the dune's effort to cleanse itself, and the hissing, seething wind that moved mountains swerved toward the sliver.

Within the turbulent wall of sand, a face appeared—a Dushau woman, young, elegant, bitterly hostile. The face withered with illness before her eyes, becoming suddenly familiar. It was the face she'd seen on the viewscreen as she'd fired on the Emperor's flagship, Desdinda's face, come to life to wreak her sworn vengeance.

Krinata squirmed and wrenched and beat free of the nightmare, pursued by the rising howl of the anguished winds, a howl of betrayal. "How could you!"

The keening wail of storm faded to the electronic sound of the computer's agony. She put one hand to her forehead and found a bruised slash. *Head injury. That explains it.* The helpless fear and rage had nothing to do with her real self. Already the details of the nightmare were gone.

She wiped blood from one eyelid and focused her eyes on the whirling kaleidoscope of colored shapes—the bridge monitor displays and control stations of *Ephemeral Truth*. It all began to come back to her. They had outraced the Allegiancy Empire's Squadron, found this system, and crash-landed the orbit-only ship. *And we made it!*

She pulled herself up, holding her breath against the pain in head and ribs, and found the bleeding gash on her arm. Gripping the pressure point of her left elbow with her right thumb, she twisted free of the torn crash webbing—meant only for Cassrians, not strong enough to hold a human—

and staggered to the mangled console that had been her station during their mad flight across the galaxy.

The answer to her inquiry about this planet was still etched faintly into the screen, mocking her. THE DUSHAU OLIAT TEAM, RAICHMAT, DECLARES FOURTH PLANET OF XB333291MS NOT FIT FOR HABITATION, COMMERCIAL EXPLOITATION, OR DOME COLONIES. SYSTEM FILE CLOSED.

Clinging to the warped edge of the console, she turned to look at the only other person on the bridge, Jindigar. He had lied; this was no safe-haven. He'd surely known that. Centuries ago he'd been a member of Raichmat, the exploring team that had evaluated the planet. But he had told her the planet was marginally habitable and had never been reported because it was not commercially useful. So, according to Jindigar, this official record did not even exist.

As the shock of betrayal swept through her, she had to fight off a dizzy wave of déjà vu.

The computer's wails became barely articulate pleas for relief. It was a Sentient computer, a half-protoplasmic brain plugged into the ship's circuits. He had named himself Arlai, and had been her friend. But clearly they'd never repair him now. Tears in her eyes, Krinata turned to tug loose Arlai's power cable. *Put him out of his misery.*

The blood on her hands made her grip slippery, and as she struggled to perform the act of mercy, she didn't hear Jindigar gain his feet. She gasped as his warm, finely napped skin brushed her. He gripped her wrist with his seven-fingered, nailless hand, stopping her. "Not yet," he said.

She desisted. It was his ship, and Arlai his oldest friend.

Limping, blood flowing from a ragged hole in his thigh, he climbed the tilted deck to the astrogator's station, which he had been covering for their dive into atmosphere. In a velvety voice as midnight-deep as his eyes, he crooned to his computer as he worked the controls. "Arlai, I'm sorry. You did your best. I must ask one last service, then I'll give you peace. Please—we must know."

Through his agony the computer responded, "Serving."

"Thank you, Arlai. Can you show me your previous display—the one just before we entered atmosphere?"

"This is the best I can do. Too many circuits out."

The screen before Jindigar flashed. Krinata scrambled up the canted deck to look around the tall Dushau's elbow. Despite the blurs on the screen, she identified the stellar array that had been on their rear viewscreen for days. But near the edge of one blur there was a new symbol—a massive hyperdrive trace—the Allegiancy Squadron!

"We didn't outrun them!" she groaned. A single ship had traced them as they fled the Emperor's flagship and had called the Squadron in on them. They had crossed the galaxy in short dashes to elude the Squadron and had finally lost them just before entering this system.

But they'd known the Squadron would search every system in the quadrant for any trace of them. So they had voted to try for a landing, Arlai insisting he could get the ship and its cargo of colonization materials down safely, though *Ephemeral Truth* would never make orbit again. When she accused Arlai of volunteering for a suicide mission, he had pointed out that he'd meet a worse end left helpless in orbit.

Arlai had planned for his passengers to take to the landers while Arlai brought the ship in empty, but while they were loading, Jindigar had suddenly called them to strap in and had Arlai take the ship down immediately.

Krinata had been looking for a good colony site when she'd found the official report on the planet. Before, she'd only studied Arlai's other files on the place, coded under the name Phanphihy, confirming Jindigar's statements. If Jindigar had lied to her, if she'd been wrong about him, it was way too late to change her mind. The crimes against the Allegiancy Empire they had committed together had already condemned her to be executed with him.

"Arlai," whispered Jindigar, "can you show us any sort of scan of this planetary system?"

"Atmosphere distorts, and—"

"*Anything*, Arlai," begged Jindigar.

The monitor cleared and another view sketched across it, one corner of the screen whited out by the planet's sun, for they were on the dayside. The rest was a blurring haze that shifted as Arlai struggled to find functional sensors and circuits. But the hyperdrive trace still showed clearly at the bottom of the screen. "Jindigar," said Arlai, "I'm sure. The Squadron is still there—and I think they're changing course in this direction." Numbers appeared on the screen. "There's the data. You'll have to plot it. I can't."

Jindigar's head drooped as he leaned on stiffened arms, a very human posture of dejection. "They will search every asteroid in this system until they find us."

"Their instruments will find this ship," she agreed, "but I doubt if they have anything that can locate thirty-one protoplasmic beings on a planet this size."

Arlai interjected, "Eighteen living protoplasmic beings—that I can discern. So many sensories out. . . ."

"If it was a livable planet, we'd have a chance," she accused bitterly, grieving for the dead she'd hardly known.

Jindigar twisted his head to focus his midnight eyes on her. The Dushau face was so humanoid, despite its short nap of dark indigo, large midnight eyes, and nearly bridge-less nose, that she believed she could read his expression: excitement and a revivification her words had given him.

"Of course it's livable. I told you that!"

She pointed to the other screen that still held the faint impression of the Raichmat team's report. She knew how those reports were generated because that had been her job.

His eyes held hers from a bare handspan away, and his voice was penetratingly honest, as he said, "That record is in error. We will lose ourselves on this planet until the Squadron leaves, and then we'll be able to live here."

She knew how those records were made and how ships' Sentients accessed the master files. There was no way the record could be wrong—unless a Dushau had lied, just as the Emperor had accused them of doing. A chill shook her. She'd defended the Dushau, sure in her heart the Emperor had persecuted them unjustly. If she was wrong—

She was about to ask Jindigar how he *knew* the record was in error, when Arlai groaned and his screen went into a pyrotechnic whirl. Jindigar said compassionately, "Easy now, Arlai, it's all over. You've been the very best, and we'll never forget you." As he spoke he moved to the cables Krinata had been struggling with, cables exposed by the sprung seams of the cabinets. "Krinata, help me!"

She gripped, and together they terminated the computer's agony. His last intelligible words hung in the air. "I'm sorry, Jindigar. You were so good to me, and I failed you."

Tears sprang to Krinata's eyes as she remembered all the times she'd felt that she'd failed Jindigar's trust and had been driven to find unsuspected reserves within herself. She couldn't have been wrong about Jindigar.

She sighed as the last of the echoes died away. "Oh, Arlai, *I'm* so sorry."

"In a way it's for the best. Arlai would have gone mad left alone here while we hide in the hills. He couldn't just turn himself off, you know."

Dushau feared insanity almost more than death. Krinata wiped at a tear. "I know." She'd often wondered if Arlai had been Jindigar's only real friend for the last three thousand years of the Dushau's incredibly long life.

But there was no time to mourn. "Only eighteen survivors," muttered Jindigar, surveying the dead bridge.

She moved her left hand to cover his where he still gripped the cable, needing to comfort him. Jindigar caught her arm, examining the bleeding. "Here, let's tend that," he said, and noticed the blood on her face. He fumbled for a handlight. "Hold still." He shined it in her eyes, searching for signs of concussion.

She squinted against the ultrabright Dushauni light, protesting, "I'm all right."

"It seems so," he answered, setting the light aside as he fetched down the first aid kit.

In the hours that followed, Jindigar's pragmatic, one-step-at-a-time way of dealing with the emergency got them all over the shock and into motion. Injuries were bandaged, roll call and inventory taken, and the bodies respectfully gathered and laid out, as if it were all routine.

But Krinata saw his face in the unguarded moment after they found the seven dead Dushau in the nearly crushed cargo hold above the landers' docking bay. With a lifespan of well over ten thousand years, death by accident was different for Dushau than for ephemerals. The death of a friend close for thousands of years could be a paralyzing blow. She alone saw how shattered Jindigar was by the seven deaths, and knowing more of what he'd just been through, she alone marveled at his regained composure. He'd pay a price for that stoicism.

Soon after that they assembled outside the ship in the desert afternoon sun to plan their next moves.

Only eighteen survivors gathered in the shade of the half-buried hull of the *Ephemeral Truth*. The ship's nose was buried deep in a sand dune, the tail stretching out farther than Krinata would care to walk in the loose sand. The bottom of the hull had crumpled, but even so, the ship rose many times Krinata's height. Around them, white sand dunes showed ripples from the action of ferocious winds, and no hint of vegetation as far as the eye could scan. The sky was a vivid magenta behind the blinding copper sun. A pale rosy peach moon was rising near the horizon.

Krinata hugged her ankle-length desert cloak around her. She'd never been to such a place, yet it was oddly familiar. Seized with inexplicable anxiety, she found herself searching the horizon for she knew not what. *Lots of habitable planets have places like this,* she told herself, trying to be the professional ecologist she'd trained to be. *They're vital to the biosphere and shape the weather.* The sourceless anxiety receded, and she told herself it had been mere rational terror at being marooned, a quarry at bay who'd just found she'd been lied to by the only one she trusted.

Using all the discipline learned during the last few months' adventures, she refused to think about the dead and considered the survivors and their possible choices.

None of the eighteen were of desert species. There was the small family of Cassrians, two adults and three nearly grown children, as tall as Krinata but wasp-slender. They had their heat-repelling desert cloaks drawn tight around their dark exoskeletons. The male, Trassle, was a fair space pilot, a shrewd businessman, and quick in an emergency. The children were well controlled and responsible. The three of them had taken over the care of the ship's two mascots, a mated pair of piols. But the male piol, Imp, had not been seen since the crash. Now the children consoled Rita, the female, who was busily trying to shred the hems of the children's desert cloaks with her long fishing claws.

Next to the Cassrians, squatting on the soft sand, were the four Lehiroh men. So humanoid you could mistake them for a Terran race at first glance, they had vastly different organs, could eat substances humans could not, and could tolerate radiation exposures fatal to a human. They were professional explorers who worked with the Dushau Oliat teams, the ecology specialists like Jindigar. Their young bride, Bell, had been among the dead. Krinata wondered if they'd be too grief-stricken to function.

The two Holot—a mated pair—huddled beneath two of the silvery desert cloaks so you couldn't see their six-limbed forms at all. They were warm-blooded, densely furred, and miserable in the unrelenting heat.

The other four survivors were humans, from Terran colonies much younger than Krinata's home world. Two men and two women, though Krinata wasn't sure if they were paired. They had hardly spoken to her since they'd come aboard. Such uncivilized pioneers had a much better chance of surviving here than Krinata did. And they were the only humans she'd ever know now. She had to make friends with them.

So she chose her place near them, seating herself with a glancing smile at the older woman. Jindigar, and the only other surviving Dushau, a male named Frey, whose nap was a lighter indigo than Jindigar's, indicating he was centuries younger, came out of the ship last.

Jindigar was dressed in loose white shirt and baggy yellow trousers of standard desert wear. He wore his usual yellow turban, and on top of it perched a chittering piol, the male, Imp. Under one arm was a small, glittering square package, while in his other hand he carried a half-eaten ration bar. Frey followed, pulling his silvery desert cloak about himself, and together they negotiated the flimsy, improvised emergency ramp. Jindigar seemed to bounce deliberately, as if absently enjoying the swaying footing while munching his ration bar, though his overall manner was uncharacteristically somber. *Testing his thigh?*

The sun turned the Dushau a dark purple, the color of

dense shadow. Frey's head was bandaged, but he had no trouble balancing.

At the bottom of the ramp Jindigar set the snuffling, wriggling piol down, and the animal scampered through the gathering to his mate, greeting the Cassrian children effusively. The children shouted to Jindigar and gathered the ship's two mascots into a tumbling heap.

Jindigar unfolded the package he was carrying and, with a flourish, threw a desert cloak carelessly around himself as he approached the group. "Storm," he called to one of the Lehiroh, "is the burial finished?"

"Yes. We took all thirteen bodies into the drive chamber and laid them out respectfully." He glanced at the others, grief in his eyes. "We took care of Bell, but we had no idea what to do for the others, if anything."

Jindigar scanned the group, and as he spoke, he revealed light blue teeth. "I believe we've all said our good-byes privately. It seems fitting that *Ephemeral Truth* become their tomb and our monument to the Allegiancy Empire."

"Jindigar," said the older human woman, Viradel. "How can you set a monument to the Empire? The Empire's out to kill every Dushau loose in the galaxy, and every friend of a Dushau!" She looked around. They were all here because the Emperor had confiscated their homes and businesses and condemned them to death because they'd helped Jindigar or other Dushau.

Cutting off a rising mutter, the Cassrian male, Trassle, piped up in his reedy voice, trained to the single tones of standard speech, "The Empire's dead but doesn't know it yet. Dukes and Kings are still fighting each other for the throne, and I'll bet it's some Duke who's sent that Squadron after us to revenge the Emperor. They're not going to give up. Even if *Ephemeral Truth* could lift again, there's no place to go. This is no time to set monuments. Let's discuss how to lose ourselves on this planet before we're caught."

Jindigar knelt effortlessly, smoothing a spot of sand like an artist preparing a canvas. Then, as he spoke, he drew a map with deft strokes. "We're on the largest of the northern continents, but to the southwest quarter, with a formidable mountain range to the north. This is a desert valley, surrounded by wooded hills. The nearest edge of this desert is due east, which is the path the Allegiancy troops will search first once they locate *Truth.*"

The Cassrian female, Allel, said, in her untrained, multitoned voice, "If we'd left the bodies strewn about, maybe the Allegiancy would think we'd all died. After all, there were seven other Dushau, some pretty badly burned."

"That's disgusting!" spat Viradel, making the Cassrian recoil. But Krinata felt that the Cassrian's sense of decency had been overridden by desperation. After all, she was a Cassrian parent with young to protect, and Krinata had seen the ruthless savagery she was capable of in defense of her young. It had saved Krinata's and Jindigar's lives.

"Ugly," agreed the Lehiroh, Storm. "But it might have been worth a try if it had any chance of succeeding." He exchanged a silent glance with his co-husbands.

Jindigar cut in. "I doubt such a ruse would help now. When the Squadron locates *Truth,* they'll probably blast the ship because it was the instrument of our escape from the Emperor's flagship, and the home of a Sentient who could break Allegiancy law. They may assume Arlai left trap programs aboard and not even dare to search it."

Frey, the Dushau youth, shuddered, and Jindigar gave him a silent paternal look before continuing. When he tapped the map with one long finger, Krinata saw he'd embellished it with artistic curlicues to create a work of art while they argued. "We'll head northeast toward the foothills at the edge of the valley. Southeast of those foothills is a high plateau, and on the edge of the plateau should be a fertile area suitable for all our species. Distances? I don't know. Arlai—" He glanced toward the buckled and twisted hull of *Truth,* swallowed hard, and continued. "Arlai hadn't completed mapping, but I did see his scan of the area as we came down."

Charlie Gibson, who'd been elected second in command for the group's ground activities, asked, "Any idea how far to the edge of this?" The experienced colony manager who'd been elected leader had died in the crash.

"Oh," said Jindigar, turning from them. He gathered Frey's attention with a glance that prickled Krinata's skin, then bent to pick up a handful of sand and squint northeast as it sifted through his fingers. She watched avidly as the two Dushau made rapport with the place. For centuries Jindigar had worked in the Dushau explorer teams, the Oliat, honing that singular talent. And he was the best.

Recently she'd become Jindigar's debriefing officer, a Programming Ecologist responsible for certifying new worlds. She had dreamed of going into the field as an Oliat Liaison Officer, helping to plant a new colony. Now she was living that dream—but without the full seven members of the Oliat team. They had only Jindigar and his young student, Frey.

Jindigar turned back to them, momentarily shrouded in the distracted air of his Oliat skills, and she yearned to join him and Frey in the odd triune consciousness they had shared to escape from the Emperor's flagship. But his indigo eyes were fixed on the distance as he said, "If we start now, we could reach the edge of this sand-sea by dawn. It's another day's hard march to water. The only problem is the windstorm that's brewing. There'll be some shelter from that at the edge of the desert."

"Isn't there enough energy in that storm to bury the ship?" asked Frey of his elder.

"Good observation," granted Jindigar. "Here, the ship is our only shelter from the blowing sand. But if we stay, we may not be able to dig out and get clear before the Imperials find us. If we start, we must forcemarch to the edge of the valley and climb to shelter before the storm hits." He glanced once more at the sky, brushing the last of the sand from his skin. "Does anyone want to sit here and wait for the Imperials?"

There was a general murmur of negatives, and Gibson stood up to say, "Come, if we're going to outrun that storm, we've got to hurry."

Jindigar sat staring at his map as everyone rose, breaking into groups and heading for the ramp. He added a finishing touch, then wiped the area clean and, with a few deft strokes, sketched a frolicking piol. To an objective observer he might seem untouched by tragedy, but Krinata sensed an undertone of anguish, and recalled how Imp, as a piol pup, had rescued Jindigar's spirits by just being alive.

Finally he rose and turned to go back inside while Krinata stared at the horizon that had captivated Jindigar's attention. *Sandstorm?!* Why did that send preternatural terror through her nerves? Shuddering, she scrambled to catch Jindigar, drawing him aside at the foot of the ramp.

"If the storm is that close," said Krinata softly, "why don't we make our triad again and push the storm aside?"

"I've told you, Krinata, you can't. You don't dare join us ever again. I should never have allowed it, even once."

"But I could do it. I know I could."

He summoned patience to reiterate wearily, "Desdinda *died* while trying to make a tetrad out of our triad, and she was insane at that moment. You took the brunt of the shock because you'd had absolutely no training—Frey was hurt so he can barely tolerate the duad now, and I—didn't get away unscathed, either. A triad is out of the question."

"We won't know that until we try it," argued Krinata, part of her acknowledging his expertise, but another part frightened enough of the sandstorm to try anything. She knew the danger. She'd seen Oliat members die when others of their team died. "We've all had time to heal—"

Jindigar sighed. Frey had gone on into the ship, and the Cassrian children were chasing the piols up the ramp. He said, "This is no time to play games with your sanity. You're lucky your imagination isn't running wild during ordinary consciousness. Don't even think of experimenting with other states. I stand in awe of human mental pliability—but even humans have limits."

She pointed, a sense of outrage starting to build, as if her only chance at real life were being snatched away. "That sandstorm out there could scour the flesh from our bones. Isn't it worth a risk to save the group?"

"Krinata, I know you've never seen anything wrong with Inverting the Oliat function to affect the environment. But to us, it isn't to be done lightly. It's so dangerous, it's often better to accept death. Even if we could triad, I'd never consider influencing that storm's course. It's not the Oliat way to step onto a world and arbitrarily remake it to our convenience."

His words made complete sense. No decent ecologist would interfere with such large natural phenomena without the guidance of a complete Oliat. But, irrationally, her whole body yearned to battle that storm and subdue it. She put it down to her enchantment with the triad rapport. That one taste of the multicentered awareness told her how it could be to perceive the whole ecology of a world. That was what she'd been born to do. Any training, discipline, or purging she had to go through would be worth it.

Then an odd thought occurred to her. *They're afraid to attempt a triad with me again!*

Seeing her capitulate, Jindigar turned and climbed the ramp with the Holot, Storm, and the humans, leaving Krinata to follow.

TWO

Sandstorm

The interior of the ship had heated to baking oven temperatures, hotter than the open shade. They found the three Lehiroh and Frey using cutting torches to open the side of the ship to let them pull their anti-grav sleds out. Long ago they'd loaded the colonizing equipment onto the sleds. A mass of less portable items had been stowed in the crushed and inaccessible cargo holds with the two-seater skybirds *Truth* carried. The orbital landers and the atmosphere skybirds were all useless now. So the only way to take the bare essentials with them was to pull the anti-grav sleds.

Jindigar took up a cutting torch, only the set of his mouth betraying his distress at butchering his ship. Then, as they were guiding the sleds down the ramp, the Lehiroh instructing them in the use of the sled controls, Jindigar left to return minutes later with a long, flat box Krinata instantly recognized, a Sentient computer's core, which stored the essence of personality if not all peripheral memory. Lovingly he inserted the box into a compartment in one of the sleds and then claimed that sled for his own.

At first Krinata couldn't imagine why he'd done it. Arlai couldn't be revived without a higher technology than they'd be able to rebuild. Then she thought again. In perhaps a thousand years they'd have regained it, Jindigar would be here to use it, and Arlai would wake again.

Minutes later they walked out of *Ephemeral Truth* and into the ankle-deep sands. She saw Jindigar caress the ship's

17

skin as they passed through the opening. Then, out in the direct sun, Krinata pulled the hood of her cloak over her head. Though her hair was dark, her skin was fair. Despite months of exposure to high-actinic light, she could get the burn of her life in such a desert.

The padded sled harness fit her shoulders so she could lean into it, getting the massive but weightless sled into motion. The sled consisted of a thick platform housing its machinery, surrounded by a peg-and-rope fence set back from the edge to restrain the cargo, which was covered by tarpaulins of the heat-repellent fabric of the desert cloaks.

On each of the four sides of the sled was a covered control panel with one conspicuous lever, the brake. The ones on either side were down to keep the sled from drifting sideways. She'd have to be fast with the brake if she stopped, or the mountain would float inexorably over her and into the sleds and people in front of her.

Jindigar had placed Frey and Storm at the rear, towing the sled loaded with water and indispensable supplies, certain they could keep the pace. They had only one sled to tow between them, so if something happened ahead of them, one of them would be free to help. The two piols chose to ride atop this sled, and Frey made them a small lean-to for shade.

It was past noon when they started, the hottest part of the day yet ahead. She slogged through the sand, turning her mind off, setting her body to endure. Jindigar said they'd make it, and everyone, even the Lehiroh, who were seasoned explorers, Oliat Outriders, believed him. And she'd heard their leader, Storm, say that Jindigar hadn't survived thousands of years on strange planets by miscalling sandstorms.

As the afternoon wore on she grew accustomed to the thumping of her canteen against her thigh, the abrading sand in every crease of her skin, the desiccating heat. She had been strengthened by the hard life she'd lived since she'd defied the Emperor to break Jindigar out of prison.

Gradually, without intending to, she began to move faster than those ahead of her, and rather than waste the momentum in the sled, she stepped out of line and passed them one by one, exchanging cordial words with everyone but Viradel, who looked her up and down as if Krinata were trying to show her up. The sun was perceptibly lower, beginning to blur behind a dirty haze gathering at the horizon, when Jindigar led them to the eastern trough of a huge dune that could provide some shade for a rest stop.

She was tiring. It was getting harder to ignore the places where she hurt, but she was approaching Jindigar, who was towing his sled far in the lead, setting a cautious pace, working his eyes from side to side searching the ground. The moon, off to their right, was riding higher. Sunset would not stop them.

She shivered in sudden dread of the desert night and fought a growing sense of menace as if she were walking into a nightmare where however hard she ran, she could not escape.

Just then Jindigar turned his head, saw her coming, and gave what could only be a warmly welcoming smile. Suddenly the smile flicked through alarm to anger. He shrugged out of his towing harness, leaving it to trail in the sand as his sled kept going on momentum, and waded to her sled, nailless fingers working the controls adroitly. In seconds he had slowed and turned her sled, inserting it at the center of the line next to his own, dragging her with it.

As he slipped back into his own harness he roared, "Are you trying to get yourself eaten alive by sandswimmers? I thought you were an ecologist!"

"But—"

"Didn't you hear me state explicitly that no one should stray from the direct line of march?"

Jindigar never gave orders, he made statements. But she'd never seen him angered by someone who ignored one of his statements. "I got going so fast, I couldn't—"

"Trying to wear yourself out before the night's over?"

"Jindigar, nothing happened," she said reasonably.

"No? You miss walking yourself—and one sixteenth of our gear—into a traplair and you say nothing happened?"

Sandswimmer? Traplair? Tasting the words, she recognized them as generic terms for sorts of desert life she'd rather not meet on a dark night. She twisted to glance over her right shoulder at the strip of sand she would have walked on if Jindigar hadn't pulled her into the line. She saw no sign of any animal lurking beneath the sand surface, but if Jindigar said it was there, it was there.

She shuddered, but the sense of menace had evaporated. Had she picked up some awareness from the duad Jindigar and Frey maintained? "Thank you, Jindigar. I'm sorry."

He studied her as they paced side by side, his anger evaporating. "Not really your fault. I expect too much of you." A troubled look crossed his dark indigo features. "I don't know why." Then he smiled, the warmth of welcome back again as he asked, in a softer tone, "Is your arm hurting?"

"It just aches, but I think the heal-jelly is working."

"Good," he replied. Then, as if he needed to rationalize his interest in her, he added, "I hope the others are doing as well. Serious infection could jeopardize our survival."

"And what about your thigh? This is a hike, not a mountain climb. My thighs are killing me!"

"The Dushau body handles infection a little better than the human," he replied.

That was the biggest understatement Krinata had heard

in a long time. The Dushau were virtually immune to even the most virulent cross-species infections that had developed in the galaxy. "But you don't heal so very much faster, and you were bleeding even more than I was."

"I took a blood replacement accelerator, and the heal-jelly is working." He brought his ever-roving gaze to focus on her and said in a different tone, "Yes, it *does* hurt."

"I'm glad you admitted that. Maybe your thigh will tell you when us office workers could use a rest?"

"Soon. Right in the shadow of that big dune, there. The sand should be cool enough to sit on by now, and there are no lurkers waiting to eat us. Also, notice how the ridge of the dune runs right along our course? It will shelter the sleds from the wind so we won't have to chase them."

When they reached the dune and the entire marching column was in the shade, he glanced at her. "Ready?"

"Anytime!"

Before she knew what had happened, he had slipped out of his harness, ducked under his sled, and as it passed her by, he gave it a hefty shove. Only then did he notice she had not followed suit. "Need help? Here."

He paced with her, helping her worm her injured arm out of the harness. "I'll shove it for you," he offered. "Help me get the others unharnessed!"

He worked his way back along the line, shouting, "Get loose, let the sled pass over you, then give it a good push. It will come to rest about an hour straight on, and we'll pick them up after we rest!"

She helped others out of their harnesses, until they came to the trailing sled, pulled by Frey. "All right, Frey, let's get this thing stopped!" called Jindigar. It was the water sled, massive enough to pose a problem.

The young Dushau slipped out of the harness and turned to catch at the control panel on the leading edge, dancing back before the oncoming mass. He got his hand on the brake lever, but it would not move down. "It's stuck!" yelled Frey.

"Storm!" yelled Jindigar, throwing himself at one corner of the sled. "Drag it down!" And then to Frey, he called, "Take the other corner!"

Krinata took the middle of the front of the sled, held on, and let it drag her heels in the sand. The Lehiroh caught the rear corners, and as the mass dragged them toward the group of humans, the two men, Gibson and Fenwick, joined on the sides. The commotion excited the piols, who scampered from side to side and chittered happily, as if this were the grandest entertainment.

The sled stopped just short of the two exhausted Holot who'd slumped in their tracks without noticing the commotion.

"Our first equipment failure," said Jindigar, grimly eyeing the furred, six-limbed Holot while examining Krinata's arm. "Is it bleeding again?" With a medic's firm touch he pushed her sleeve back to poke at the bandage. "Looks all right. How does it feel?"

"Fine," she lied. She didn't think it would bleed.

Jindigar knelt beside the drooping Holot, who were blearily aware they'd almost been run over. Examining their eyes, one hand feeling each sweat-plastered pelt, he said, "You just need water. You'll be fine. You've done well so far, and it's going to be easier now that the sun's down."

For Jindigar, Krinata knew, the darkness would bring the greater hardship of near blindness. The intense desert light was dim to his perceptions, while the slightly higher gravity was his norm. She asked Frey, "Can you get at the water?"

"Yes." He attacked the shrouded cargo, the two piols peeping over the edge at him as he loosed tethers.

Gibson helped, saying, "My canteen went dry hours ago."

Krinata remembered her own canteen, which she'd barely

touched. She gave it to Jindigar, who held it for the Holot female, Terab, who'd been a spaceship captain until she'd lost her license for helping Jindigar's son, and Jindigar had financed her new start in life. She struggled to drink from the spout built for humanoid lips, then curbed her eagerness, shoving the canteen toward her mate. "He needs it more!"

Jindigar rose, pleased they'd revived enough to share the water. As he passed Krinata, heading for where Frey had the cargo exposed, he scolded, "You shouldn't have refrained. You could go down with heatstroke."

He's changed so since our escape! But she was too tired to be charitable. She followed him, complaining, "Why are you always thinking of the things that could happen to me? Haven't you learned I'm not so frail—"

He turned, desert cloak flying, indigo face unreadable. "I've worked on many worlds with human Outriders who competed with other species until they collapsed, endangering everyone. Experience is a harsh teacher. If I've wronged you—"

Abruptly it seemed to Krinata that he was using the group's welfare to rationalize his behavior, so he wouldn't have to admit how much he really cared for these ephemerals. It was unlike him. He'd defended his friendships with ephemerals before other Dushau. But after what he'd endured lately she couldn't blame him. "Forget it. I'll be more careful."

She bent to untangle the lashing cords, and Jindigar went to where the Cassrian family sat, cleaning sand out of the joints of their exoskeletons. He played with the piols, fed the smallest child, and cheered them by twittering in their own language. The father, Trassle, had once pulled Jindigar out of a fire, saving his life. Now he seemed to be concealing weakness and pain from his family—but not from Jindigar. *He respects Trassle.*

Later, she was leaning against the sled's cargo and drinking greedily when Jindigar paused to apologize. "I've been treating you as a patient because I perceive you as gravely injured. *I* failed to keep Desdinda out of our triad, so your injury is my responsibility. From your point of view, you took a risk to save us all—and succeeded, which is worth taking pride in. I suppose we're both right."

She stood up straight. "Does that mean you're going to give me another chance in the triad?"

"Krinata, that's impossible. For all the reasons—"

"Humans heal certain things more quickly than Dushau."

"Perhaps, but—" Storm called to Jindigar, and he shouted back, "Coming!" He left, muttering, "We'll talk!"

She slumped down to the sand, propping her back against the sled, hips and thighs aching. Jindigar had taken an awful risk letting the first human into a triad, an Oliat subform used to train Oliat officers. And in the end she had done what no Dushau could ever do: she'd deliberately killed another Dushau who was linked to them all, having invaded their triad and made it a tetrad—a different Oliat subform. Did Jindigar feel he'd created a monster? How could she prove to him that he hadn't?

Her eye drifted to the shaded side of the dune where Frey was sitting munching rations, staring into space. On impulse—the kind of instant action Jindigar had praised in her, calling it a trait cultivated by those who studied Aliom, the philosophy behind the Oliat practices—she grabbed another ration bar and went to join Frey.

He glanced up in welcome and made a place for her beside him. "I wanted to talk to you," he said. Silence stretched until she asked what about, and he offered hesitantly, "We're zunre, you know."

"I've wanted to think of the three of us that way." Zunre, those bound to the same Oliat, were considered closer than blood relatives. "Only Jindigar doesn't accept me."

"But he does, and that's the problem. Krinata, do you understand why he mustn't?—It isn't my place to say it, but I see you gravitating to Jindigar's company, and I see him fighting to protect himself and the Archive he carries, and—it's hard to watch your zunre hurting each other."

He's thinking of Desdinda too. She was zunre to us, if only for a moment. "I've never meant to hurt Jindigar—or any Dushau."

"You were there when Grisnilter promised Jindigar he could take the Archive from him and still work Oliat without the Archive interfering. Jindigar didn't believe it—Grisnilter knew nothing of Oliat dangers—but he took the Archive, anyway."

Krinata remembered the windowless bus in which they'd been prisoners. Grisnilter, the oldest Dushau she'd ever seen and a famous Historian, lay across the backseat of the bus, dying. Grisnilter was custodian of a historical record, the Archive, a living memory impressed into his mind, and it would perish with his death if he couldn't impress it on another Dushau with the talent to become Historian.

"It hasn't given Jindigar any trouble," offered Krinata.

"Not until Desdinda's death," answered Frey. "He tries, but he can't hide it from me. He's erratically accessing the Archive, and he's frightened. It's a . . . a sacred trust. He mustn't mar that record, he mustn't become lost in it, he mustn't lose it behind grieving scars, and he mustn't die before he can pass it on to a Historian. Do you understand?"

"Dushau memory works differently from human." Krinata nodded. "You re-experience emotional pain every time you access a memory of something that happened before it."

"Yes, and Jindigar was always very good at farfetching, despite his many scars and lack of Historian's training."

Farfetching was the eidetic recall of memories thousands

of years past. The danger was to go episodic, to become lost in memory, a fatal form of insanity for a Dushau. Grisnilter had thought Jindigar immune to that—but he wasn't.

"Now he's afraid that his lack of training," continued Frey, "may cause him to betray a trust. Everything seems to evoke the Archive for him—even just talking to you."

"So that's why he won't attempt the triad again—"

Frey shook his head. "Jindigar's been qualified to Center an Oliat longer than I've lived. I couldn't guess at all the factors he's considering when he says no. I'd never dare go against his judgment."

"Even when it may be impaired by his personal problems? Even when the survival of the whole group may depend on it? Frey, you're surely old enough to think for yourself!" She couldn't believe she'd just said that. "I didn't mean. . . ."

Frey laughed. "And you, zunre, are likewise old enough to think for yourself." He sobered. "Krinata, we may be zunre, but I don't wish to acquire ephemeral friends. I don't know on what grounds to appeal to you—professional, personal, or ethical. I can only beg—stay away from him."

"The group is too small to promise that, but I'll try not to hurt him." *He should have told me.* If Frey was right, that explained why none of her arguments affected Jindigar's decision. He didn't fear *her* infirmity, but his own, and his own was not aggravated by the Cassrians.

As the young Dushau gathered his canteen to rise, Jindigar mounted the dune to join them. "Storm's right," he called as he drew close, "there's no way to fix the brake on the water sled without tearing it apart. And there's no time for that." He surveyed the western horizon where the dirty pall was creeping higher into the magenta sky. "Frey?"

The youth's eyes flicked to Krinata, then fixed on the ground as he replied, "Yes, I've been studying the storm.

We're not going to make it at this rate. But now that we're this far, there's nothing to do but try."

He said we could make it. Is Jindigar's judgment slipping?

"With the sun down we'll be able to pick up the pace," argued Jindigar.

"Jindigar," Krinata said, "a triad could read the situation better. Perhaps if we change course, the storm would only graze us? Or maybe we can find a closer shelter?"

Below them the line of march was forming up under the Lehiroh's guidance. Frey offered, "It's your decision, of course, but if you judge the danger to the Archive from the storm greater than the danger from the triad, I'd be willing to attempt the triad with Krinata again. I think I might be able to hold it this time, and it would increase our range."

"What's changed your mind?" asked Jindigar.

"That storm frightens me more than Krinata does. I've never been in a sandstorm before."

"That's not it. That storm frightens me too." As Jindigar compared Krinata and Frey, then gazed into the sunset, she wondered what she'd said to win Frey's confidence. Then Jindigar muttered, "Perhaps we should attempt a triad, though it may incapacitate Krinata."

"Jindigar," she pled, "just try it for a second or two. We have to get a glimpse of what's really out there. And I'm not as fragile as you think!"

The Lehiroh were coaxing the water sled back into the air and turning it so the rear end would now lead. Jindigar glanced down, then fixed his back to the scene, agreeing reluctantly. "Just for a second or two." He issued technical instructions to Frey, then gathered Krinata's eyes.

Presently she felt a wall enclosing the two Dushau, shutting her out. It dissolved and re-formed behind her, and then she lost touch with the sand dune, and the people below.

Boiling, raging, churning storm, a billion particles seeth-ing skyward, organized as a living being; the helpless, aban-doned sliver of metal half swallowed by a dune; scattering of stick figures, glittering against the sand in artificial desert cloaks; line of massive lumps floating beside a long ridge; and beyond, slightly north of their course, the rising ground broken, scraggly bushes, a fan shape of dead bushes leading to the mouth of a dry wash whose sides were cave-riddled.

She was the sand, the wind, the struggling life, and it was all one, its oneness a painful beauty. She was also the storm, her anger rising at the escape of the sparkling parts of the sliver she needed to bury, to destroy. She looked out of the whirling chaos of storm, and she also watched herself looking out, undisturbed by four loci of perception. She saw her face, as if in a mirror, indigo against dirty magenta, bridgeless Dushau nose, hate-filled indigo eyes, sickly white teeth—Desdinda's face. She was herself and hated Des-dinda, and was Desdinda and hated the human intruder and Jindigar, the Aliom priest who had befouled an Archive with his Inversions. Destroy!

Krinata felt the ravening madness reaching out to shake the very sky, and everything in her defied it. Then, another presence was attracted by the turmoil, a sevenfold presence that stretched her brain and distorted her mind as if to rip her identity apart. She didn't hear herself scream.

A wide, meandering river approached a sheer cliff, and between its bend and the cliff, dirt roads cut across an area strewn with half-finished foundations and piles of logs. On one side a stockade was going up, on the other, orbital landers were parked.

A subaudible hum shimmered through the scene, a grow-ing vibration. She could feel everything in that settlement beginning to thrum to a complex rhythm, linking and af-fecting everything and everyone else. Her teeth, her bones, every nerve vibrated with increasing energy. She was being

*shaken apart from within as another Dushau woman's face
formed. She was lovely, about the same coloring as Jindigar.
As the vibration increased, her serene pleasure turned to
recognition, shock, and then alarm.*

Krinata, her heart stuttering as if she hadn't breathed in
minutes, her bones aching with inaudible hot sound, saw
through a screen of black dots Jindigar's face suffused with
a naked pleasure that was embarrassing. Then everything
went black. She never felt herself hit the sand.

When she came to, the sun had barely moved, and Storm
was bending over Jindigar, who was muttering, "Darllanyu,
darllanyu..." while Frey knelt over him arguing, "No, it's
sunset, not dawn. Jindigar!"

She sat up, holding her breath, remembering Frey had
been afraid that Jindigar could become lost in the Archive,
episodic, disoriented beyond cure. That settlement they'd
seen must have been from the Archive. If he thought it was
now dawn—

Storm saw her clutching her pounding head. "Krinata!"
He came to her. "What happened?"

"Not sure—some—ooohhh!" She hurt all over.

Jindigar, on his knees, shaking his head to clear it, saw
her. "You—" he started. "Desdinda!"

"She's dead," Krinata reminded him insistently.

He got to his feet, drawing Frey with him, reassuring
them both. "I know. Frey, don't you remember now?"

Bewildered, the younger Dushau said, "Remember what?"

"What Krinata did while we were unconscious after the
crash!" He looked to Krinata as if normal people always
remembered what they'd been doing while unconscious, and
at her denial, prompted, "You linked us in triad, and Desdinda Inverted us and brought the storm down on *Truth*."

"Jindigar," repeated Krinata through the buzzing ache in
her skull, "Desdinda is dead."

"Yes! I should have realized!" He gazed down at the

three Lehiroh who were testing the water sled brake, but he wasn't seeing them. He was abstracted as pieces of a puzzle fell into place. "It's a Loop, of course."

Frey exclaimed, "You mean Desdinda is looping in Krinata!" He turned to her. "Oh, Krinata, I'm sorry!"

"It's only apparent," continued Jindigar, "when we link triad. I *knew* we never should have tried it!"

"Now wait a minute," protested Krinata, getting up despite the explosion of pain. "I seem to recall an image of a dry wash—and caves—a bit off our course to the north. Wouldn't it be a shorter trek to head—"

"I remember!" said Frey. "Jindigar, we can make it!"

"Yes, but, Krinata, you must understand. This Loop is dangerous. A fragment of Desdinda's hatred resides in your mind like a flight of electrons trapped in a superconducting torus, or an endless-loop recording. Whenever we tap you in triad, it's activated, Inverts us, and uses us to destroy ourselves."

She felt soiled. "Well, it didn't win this time. And it won't—ever—I promise."

He put one hand on her shoulder. "No, it won't win, zunre. *I* promise."

Then, in a whirl, they were pulling out, racing the storm again. They found their sleds drifting lazily, and Jindigar swiftly made the assignments, giving one to Shorwh, the eldest of the Cassrian children, when he insisted he was strong enough to spell his father at the chore.

She trudged behind Jindigar's sled, contemplating this alien *thing* inside her, wondering what the cure would be. Revolted by the idea of being dominated by a malevolent spirit, she had to force herself to think about it, to formulate questions to ask Jindigar at the first chance. Knowing what it was, she could surely control it.

As the hours wore on she spent most of her energy ignoring the rough chafing of the straps of her harness where grit had sifted through her clothing. She'd bound her hair tightly on top of her head, but wisps escaped and plastered themselves to her sweating face. The explorer-issue hiking boots she wore were full of sand again and seemed to weigh more than she did. There was a blister on her right heel that screamed with every step.

Angling north, Jindigar set a faster pace now that the cruel sun was down. He walked with his desert cloak thrown back and his head high, as if sniffing the wind, no sign in his stride that he was nearly blind and using the duad perceptions to guide them.

It was a race now, she told herself, banishing the image of the storm swerving and chasing them across the desert. Desdinda's rage was not hers and would not dominate her.

The moon had passed zenith and begun its descent before Krinata stumbled for the first time. "I tripped on a rock!" she exclaimed as she regained her balance. "A rock!"

Jindigar glanced over at her and called, "Good. Watch your step now. We're coming to the edge of the valley." He had her pass that message back, and Krinata heard grumbling protests that it was too dark to watch anything.

Throughout the long night's march she battled the insidious voice of failure and helpless horror which she now identified as her awareness of an inward festering sore, Desdinda. Every triumph left her more confident, until finally the attacks on her will ceased. Jindigar didn't know everything about humans.

She was concentrating on keeping her numb legs going like pistons, telling her brain to ignore damage signals from her tortured feet, lungs, and chest, when a shadow covered the moon. She looked around to see it glowing dimly behind a haze about forty degrees above the horizon. They hadn't much time left. Shortly after that, Storm worked his way up the now-elongated column of marchers speaking encouragingly to each one. The Lehiroh reached the front, panting, and paced along to exchange a few words with Jindigar. "I took Shorwh off the sled and had him drop back to march with Frey until I get back. I gave his sled back to Terab."

Terab, the Holot female, had been hardest hit by the heat of the day. If she collapsed, what would Jindigar do? Strap her to one of the sleds like cargo? They'd lose one of the sleds then.

"How is Viradel holding up?" asked Jindigar.

The Lehiroh drew closer to Jindigar and said, "Swearing luridly in nine languages and determined not to be shamed by Krinata. But I think she may have sustained some injury she hasn't mentioned."

"Who do you think will be the first to collapse?"

"Well, *we're* all right, of course, and the human males aren't in bad shape. The Holot are in the most physiological distress, but they've got spirit. The Cassrians have perked up since sundown. But the male, Trassle, is in difficulty."

Jindigar clamped a hand on Storm's near shoulder. "Not a good situation, I know."

"If this was an Oliat expedition, there'd be no problem! It's trying to drag a bunch of cityworms out of their lairs that's making it hard. We've already got enough breeze to rig the sails and *ride* out of here! They couldn't sail a dinghy in a reservoir!"

Jindigar laughed. "Don't look down on them. The whole purpose of exploration is to build more cities, so we can breed more cityworms, so we can explore more territory. You and I are as awkward in their territory as they are in ours. And by the time they learn to cope with ours, they'll have built a city in which we'll be awkward."

"Well, if they do, exploring the rest of this planet will take the rest of my life—if not yours!"

"We've got to win that life first, my friend. When you drop back, tell Frey I'm extremely pleased with him, but he should pay attention now to the wind. If we have to cut losses, we must save the water sled at all costs."

"I told him that before I came up here. But I'm praying we can hang on to Sled Four as well."

As Storm stepped out of line to wait for the end, Krinata realized their conversation had carried to her because a definite wind had arisen. At first it blew toward her, then, as they passed the end of another dune, it swirled around to come at her from behind, adding a gentle push to her sled. She had to walk faster to keep ahead of it.

Gradually the rocks became more prevalent. She had thought the footing impossible already, but now her pant legs caught in snarls of dead vegetation, adding bruises and scratches to her miseries. Her throat was on fire, and she could barely swallow, let alone speak, when Jindigar called to her, "Pass the word back, everyone should take a stimtab now, and drink well. The climb is just ahead."

We made it? Her fingers were clumsy at the belt pouch as she got out the precious energy capsule, and she spilled some of the irreplaceable water as she gulped it. But then she was able to pass the word back to Gibson, and she heard him hollering to the other humans strung out far behind.

In moments they hit a gentle slope, and she had to pull the sled upward, at an awkward angle. Then Jindigar called, "Here we must set our sleds on tilt-climb!"

Fuzzily she remembered being shown how to do it, but not in the dark! Letting the harness go slack, she waited for the sled, then danced backward before it as she fumbled with the control cover. She ran numb fingers over the controls, and then, panicked, she called, "I can't do it!"

Jindigar dropped back, free of his sled, risking letting the wind take it away in order to help her. Two moves and he had the cover closed again, the sled now climbing obediently. "Gibson, can you set your sled on climb?" he called.

"I got it now. I passed the word back."

Then Jindigar was gone into the forward gloom, chasing his sled. Krinata squinted against the curtain of fine grit in the air. She had given up trying to keep it out of her mouth. Before long, her feet rolled on fist-size rocks, a dry riverbed that felt like a highway after the sand.

When it was so dark she couldn't make Jindigar's sled out ahead of her, his voice floated back on the whipping wind, "Time to break out the handlights!" A tiny point of light flared to mark his place. He swung it in an arc to mark the path, and Krinata passed the signal back. He led them from side to side, over a fallen log swept down from some distant hilltop. The wind tore at them, their desert cloaks no protection. The sand abraded Krinata's face right through her face screen. Her whole body was raw, and she was about to give up when she smashed full-tilt into Jindigar.

While she was still stunned, he stopped her sled next to his own, making it settle to the ground. "You can sit here!" he yelled over the roaring wind. Her light showed his face whitened by the sand powdering his indigo nap. His eyes were closed, the bulging eyeballs shrouded by opaque lids, but he moved as if he could see clearly as he helped Gibson stop his sled at an angle to hers, making a shelter. She rested as sleds accumulated and people huddled, exhausted. Then there was an ominous gap in the line of arrivals, and Jindigar took off into the murk, saying, "I'll be right back." His tone said he knew, through Frey, what had gone wrong.

Krinata forced her protesting legs to carry her after Jindigar. Walking into the wind was harder than pulling the sled with the wind. But it was downhill. Her feet slid out from under her, and she fetched up at the bottom of a slope. One of the Cassrians sprawled behind a sled which was dragging him while Frey wrestled it to a halt.

"It's Trassle," Frey announced to Jindigar.

Storm freed the Cassrian of the harness as Krinata joined them. Jindigar swept his light over her, then bent to examine the stiff sectioned body as Frey said, "Cassrians don't have a central circulatory system, but he could be suffering a kind of circulatory collapse."

"Maybe it's just exhaustion," suggested Storm. "If we get him onto the sled, I can pull—"

Jindigar interrupted. "I've got everyone stopped near a place where we can climb to a cave. It's not the best choice, but we've got to try it while we have the strength."

"And before the storm hits," agreed Frey.

"It hasn't?!" asked Krinata.

"Not yet," answered Jindigar. "Frey, can you climb onto the cargo and make a place to tie Trassle securely?"

Handlight swinging from his belt, the young Dushau swarmed up the cargo heap as if he hadn't been hiking all day. Jindigar fashioned a rope cradle for the exoskeletal body, and the three men easily hoisted the Cassrian to the top.

Surveying the situation, Jindigar said, "Krinata, would you be willing to ride on top with Trassle in case he comes to? It may be a dangerous ride."

"I can do it," she replied.

Frey jumped down as if it were no height at all, and Krinata took a grip to climb, wondering where she'd get the strength. Jindigar said, "Let's pamper that arm of yours a bit. Here, I'll give you a boost."

He made a cradle of his two hands. She placed her boot gingerly, and his strength seemed limitless as he raised her until she could scramble aboard and secure herself beside the Cassrian. The three men maneuvered the sled up the slope, keeping it almost level. Another sled followed, and then they were all gathered in one place.

Allel, Trassle's mate, scrambled up beside Krinata, calling piteously to her mate in the Cassrians' multitoned speech, and Krinata slid off the cargo and joined Jindigar, Frey, and the four Lehiroh beneath a forbidding cliff at the side of the river wash. "I think we can get the sleds up there," said Storm, and the three other Lehiroh agreed. "But you've got to get the cityworms out of our way."

"I think they can climb it by themselves," said Jindigar. "What do you think, Krinata?"

"None of us are mountaineers, but do we have a choice?"

"No. We don't have time to make it to the next possible climb. Good thing we came north." Krinata didn't exult in being proven right.

Gibson joined them, asking, "Strategy council?"

"Could you climb that without help?" asked Jindigar.

"In daylight, and without this wind," allowed Gibson.

"Frey?" prompted Jindigar.

"I did something like it once, in snow. Does anybody know where we put the climbing gear?"

"Sled Four," answered Storm.

"On the bottom," added Jindigar. "But we've got enough rope loose for a few traverses of this thing."

"I can't make the height," admitted Frey, flashing his light upward. It was swallowed by murk.

Jindigar pried a rock loose from the wall before them and tossed it to Frey. "Here, try this."

Frey caught it, then held it between both hands. "Five or six times my height. Not too bad. Hey! *Now* I've got the cave! But will it be big enough for all of us?"

"We'll leave some of the gear outside for a barricade. Notice the wind, though. Sand won't bury that cave."

"I thought Dushau needed bright light to see," said Gibson, squinting up the cliff.

"We can't see as well as you can in this," answered Jindigar. "But Frey is learning to balance."

Before Gibson could pursue that, Frey said, "I'll get the rope. Give me a hand, Gibson?"

"Sure," answered the man, and he followed Frey.

"When Frey has the rope rigged, we'll have them climb it," said Storm. "Then we'll take the sleds up—a twenty-minute job. Allow an hour. Will we make it?"

"Maybe," answered Jindigar. "Just barely."

Moments later Frey was back, a heavy loop of rope over one shoulder and a bundle of lights slung from his waist. He tackled the cliff without hesitation, and until he was well over Krinata's head, he didn't even pause to consider hand- and toeholds. Every so often he stopped to plant one of the lightsticks, or to use the butt of one to dig a hold. Then he was out of sight, and they waited, Jindigar narrating Frey's progress until the rope snaked down to dangle before them, and Jindigar said, "I think it's time to see if anyone has the ambition to go first."

Gibson replied, "I'll go see."

Krinata considered the increasing wobble in her legs. With every moment there was less chance she'd have the strength to make it. "I'll give it a try."

"I'm worried about that arm of yours," said Jindigar.

"I think it'll hold. Besides, I'm right-handed."

She grabbed the rope, a large, padded climbing rope with knots evenly spaced along it. Jindigar secured a loop around her waist and gave her a boost. She braced her feet against the cliff, finding toeholds Frey had made, and for a few moments it was just like an exercise class. But then her general fatigue caught up to her, and next to the fifth light, she was once again caught in the down-rushing suction of flagging will. She fought back as she'd learned to fight off Desdinda's attacks. She'd banish the ghost here and now.

Sweat ran into her eyes, stinging, and her hands became slippery. Once her feet swung free, and she clung to the rope listening to the sob of her breathing. If she let go, she'd be nearly cut in half by the safety rope around her waist. Then her foot found a crevice, and warm hands reached down to roll her onto a ledge.

"Good climb," said Frey. "Here comes Gibson."

Panting, she lay on the edge, looking down into occluded air. She could only see three lightsticks. The fourth was a mere blur, and there were nine or ten. "The storm's worse."

"It'll hit in less than an hour. I'm going back down as soon as Gibson gets here. Can you help him with the lines?"

"I'll do my best."

He sprawled prone at the edge of the cliff and pulled Gibson up. A quick exchange and the Dushau was over and down the rope as if it were a staircase. She used all her weight and all her remaining strength to help belay the rope as Viradel made the climb. The human woman lay panting, limp with exhaustion, until the male Holot joined them. Krinata couldn't imagine how the six-limbed Holot had climbed a rope, but he had. And he was strong enough to help others up and over the edge. So Krinata retreated to look for the cave. They were on a rocky slope dotted with scrub and small trees.

The bushes had stalks as thick around as her thigh, polished to a gleaming dark red surface. Picking her way beyond the bush, she confronted a solid wall of darkness. A few more strides and the dim lights and cries of the group were swallowed by the roaring dark. An irrational terror rose to a scream clogging her throat, and she turned and stumbled back through the wildly lashing branches to the edge of the cliff where the others worked.

Feeling like a silly child scared of the dark, she clung to the puddle of light where everyone leaned over the edge to watch the Lehiroh begin raising the sleds.

Krinata joined them. The four Lehiroh had stationed themselves along the rope at intervals, one foot braced against the cliff, the other wound into the rope, one hand free. With much shouting they got the first one into the air. Frey rode atop it, piloting it neatly.

He was on the edge of the sled nearest the cliff, so he could work the controls. A mooring line was looped around the taut vertical rope and passed from Lehiroh to Lehiroh as the sled rose. The ferocious wind pulled the sled this way and that, but Frey compensated while the Lehiroh played the sled like a large fish on a line. In minutes the sled landed a good distance from the edge, the only damage a loose tarp.

Fourteen times they repeated this performance, with much shouting, cheering, and congratulating, making it look easy. Frey and Jindigar took turns riding the sleds, Frey piloting the second-to-last sled with Trassle and Allel aboard. Jindigar, after some argument with Frey about risking his life and thus the Archive, had descended to bring up the sled with the malfunctioning controls, their water sled, insisting it was vital and that he was the best at this sort of maneuver.

Krinata couldn't tear herself from the cliff edge as the process began, even though her vantage point was downwind of the rope and she had to squint into the dense hail of sand just to make out the vague glow of the lightsticks.

The Lehiroh who had shouted confidently through the whole operation were now as calm and quiet as a medical team in the midst of the most delicate part of an operation.

The sled, with Jindigar clinging to the long side, turned to the cliff, finally rose from the murk like a marine creature surfacing into the light. It was moving much slower than the others had and had drifted to the end of its tether downwind. Clinging with one hand, Jindigar was working the controls with singular concentration. Krinata fought that battle with him, her whole will focused on bringing him and the sled safely to them. She could see it there already in her imagination. Her yearning made the vision so real, she couldn't quite believe what she was watching.

Storm, stationed near the top of the rope, called authoritative directions to the Dushau, but his words were suddenly torn away by a roar as a wall of wind hit the river channel. As darkness engulfed them Krinata glimpsed the sled capsizing, the cargo dangling by the restraining ropes, Jindigar hanging from the side by one arm, the whole sled straining upward, pulling the mooring rope, the climbing rope, the four Lehiroh, and the tree to which the lines were secured upward and toward Krinata.

Then she was left in utter darkness, wind pressuring her like a giant wave, devouring her. Without thinking she reached out in a way she'd never been taught, groping for wider awareness. The triune consciousness she'd learned to treasure as well as fear bloomed within her, and instantly it lit with the vividness of her imagined vision—just as Jindigar had taught her to do when they'd Inverted their triad to escape from the Emperor's flagship—and she saw Jindigar on top of the sled, and the sled right side up on the ground.

For long-drawn moments her image was the palest ghost of the reality she sensed, and time after time, a rush of despair weakened her. But each time, she caught herself up and redoubled the effort, her whole will behind it. They couldn't afford to lose Jindigar—they'd all die here. She was not going to let Desdinda's ghost rob her of Jindigar, or Jindigar of the good life he'd earned.

Suddenly resistance weakened, and she commanded the triad, forcing Frey to channel her vision and make it real. Her vision etched over reality and was solidifying when her guts churned with a gloating triumph, gratified by power at last. *Desdinda!*

In a fit of unthinking panic she flung all her strength

against the menace. To no avail. Frey, nerves afire, screaming pain, squirmed and fought the grip on him, reflexes
slamming against her invasion. Krinata, determined, reached
for Jindigar. Abruptly, something flipped inside out.

She tumbled into a black abyss, bright points streaming
past, out of control, terror vanishing into numbness, just
like the time she'd spun away from her tether in deep space.
Phobic paralysis gripped her.

THREE

Scars

There was a warm weight on her chest, and a rough tongue licked her face. She smelled the odor of piol fur and felt the sharp prick of claws kneading her chest.

She was in a cool enclosure, a cave, lit only by the dancing orange flame of a camp fire. The air was pungently moist with the aroma of soup. The roof was low. There was barely room for all the people curled, huddled, or sprawled on the sandy floor amid piles of cargo. Dim beige light filtered through cracks around the cargo piled at the entrance, but fingers of dry wind pried into the cave. Gusts produced an eerie, whining howl, above the constant dull roar.

Krinata's head hurt. The rest of her body seemed to have been chewed on by something with sharp teeth.

At last she gathered the strength to shove Imp aside. He promptly curled up by her left ear and began grooming her hair. She discovered she was lying on a sleeping bag. Then it all came back to her, and she levered herself up on one elbow, trying to sift reality from nightmare.

Jindigar was propped against the wall beside her right shoulder, a white bandage wrapped around his forehead like the turban he often wore, and his napped skin was mottled with darker indigo patches, bruises and abrasions. He assured her, "Yes, you're alive."

Relief was followed by awareness of a lonely, *single* feeling she'd suffered after the triad had been dissolved the first time, not the walled-away feeling that had come when Jindigar and Frey had joined to read this planet. So even the duad was gone. "Where's Frey? What happened?"

"He's finally asleep." He gestured to the other side of the fire. "I think he'll live."

His tone bespoke an ordeal she didn't dare ask about. Raising her head a bit, she could just see Frey's indigo head outlined against a bright sleeping-bag liner. He was curled in a near-fetal position, shuddering with each breath.

She looked back at Jindigar. "You're all right?"

"Banged my head when they finally fished the sled down."

"The triad—I shouldn't have—I nearly killed us. Or—Desdinda did. I only meant—"

"To help? I thought you understood that every time you balance triad, you evoke the Loop, and Desdinda died wanting nothing but to kill us all." He hugged his knees and looked over them. "What do you remember after Desdinda hurled you into the Archive?"

"Is that what happened?" *How could a ghost do that?* She remembered the sled capsizing, a surge of heightened awareness as the triad bonded them, and a chance to right the sled—pain, Frey's pain, then horror. "I dreamed I was out in space again, falling away from *Truth* into the galaxy." There was a stray image, a pond and a huge, improbable figure.

"The ephemeral mind is amazing." There was a thread of his normal delight in that, but a pall hung over his spirit.

She tried to raise herself, but her vision blurred and pain seized her. Against the noise of the storm, and in the semi-privacy of the heaps of goods, their voices had gone unnoticed. But when Krinata's head poked up, Shorwh, the oldest of the Cassrian children, whistled. "She's awake!"

There was a stirring on the other side of the fire, and

Storm came around, saying reproachfully, "Jindigar, you promised to call me when she woke."

"How's Terab?" asked Jindigar, starting to get up.

"She's fine. Sleeping," answered Storm, pushing him back down. "Sometimes I envy the Holot constitution more than the Dushau! Arlai would have you under sedation, you know." He turned to inspect Krinata's head.

She realized her skull was swathed in bandages and explored them with a finger. "What happened to my head?"

"You hit it when you fell."

Storm sported no bandages, and Krinata asked, "How did you get the sled down?"

"When Terab grabbed the tether rope and Jindigar got his weight shifted to the side, we flipped it back over easily enough, but it barely missed crushing Jindigar, hit the ground, and dragged all of us a good way before we could stop it. I'm afraid that sled is done for."

"I suggest," said Jindigar thoughtfully, "we leave it in the cave here. We might come back for spare parts one day."

Storm agreed, adding, "We won't be traveling today, and you should be better tomorrow. Now, we've got some soup over here that the humans said wasn't bad, and I've dug out some medication that should help you. Willing, Krinata?"

"Yeah, sure," she answered. As Storm rose to get it she asked, "What about Trassle?"

"Trassle . . . died," said Jindigar.

Her breath caught. *The children!* Trassle's spacemanship had saved their lives more than once. "Allel and her children?"

The Lehiroh wilted. "She seems to be in shock, and the rest of us are helping the children. They're trying to be brave, but . . . Trassle was a survivor. They'll make it."

When he'd gone, Jindigar said, "That's the highest compliment I've ever heard Storm pay to anyone not a licensed Outrider. And I agree. I'm going to miss Trassle, but— Allel—She married an officer with unlimited potential who was cashiered for an injury, then started a lucrative business, only to have it confiscated and their eldest son murdered by Imperials because they had a Dushau investor. She's been snatched from a safe life, dumped on a wild planet, and widowed. Cassrians mate for life, you know. They live for their children." He buried his face in his hands. They were bandaged. "I've got to convince her she's not alone here. She'll come out of it for the sake of her children." He rolled to his feet, one hand against the wall, and moved carefully around to the Cassrian family as Storm brought Krinata the soup.

The food was good, and the medicine put her to sleep before Jindigar returned, so she couldn't ask how such a small group could survive alone on a marginal world. Certainly Jindigar knew it took more than seventeen to form a colony. Had he ever really used that word? Or was that only her impression of what he'd meant? She'd have to ask.

She slept away a day, and the following morning, she woke to find bright sunlight spearing through the chinks in the wall of cargo at the mouth of the cave. They dug themselves out. The fresh air smelled marvelous, for the searing heat of the desert had not yet developed. In the long shadows of early morning the arroyo below them was decorated with clean new sand drifts and freshly sandblasted rocks, some of which gleamed as if they had precious gems embedded in them.

The higher ground on which they stood was dotted with reddish-brown bushes covered with tiny russet-and-gold leaves. Her eyes seemed to be adjusting to the odd-colored sunlight, making things seem normal.

The cliff that housed their cave meandered east, turning into slowly rising hills. The near ones seemed barren, but farther away, magenta, gold, and scarlet vegetation made an autumnal display that caught at the heart. "Jindigar, are you sure it's spring here?" she asked as he walked by.

He followed her gaze, staring wide-eyed into the rising sun as if it were the dimmest lightglobe, apparently calculating visual acuity ranges. "It must seem like fall to you. Will it bother you if the vegetation turns green in late summer? But I assure you, it is livable."

"I'm almost convinced of that, but—" He was called away before she could finish.

She helped prepare food for everyone and coaxed the children to eat. But nothing could hold Allel's attention long enough to convince her to eat.

It took all morning to repack the sleds. As Jindigar and the Lehiroh decided which items to leave behind, they all pitched in to hide the broken sled and a few crates that could not fit onto the other sleds.

Trassle was buried in a cairn at the front of the cave, disguised to look natural, and Allel had to be dragged away while Shorwh watched, clutching Imp to his chest. He had seen his older brother murdered, and now he'd buried his father.

As the Lehiroh were settling Allel and the younger children atop one of the sleds, Krinata took the piol from Shorwh and sat him down on a boulder. She talked to him about his siblings and his mother, until she got him to admit that he was afraid. Then she explained, "I don't know how it is with Cassrians, but human adults have to live with many fears. Sometimes it takes awhile and all our physical strength to overcome a new fear. It's especially bad when someone who's been part of our lives for many years is suddenly gone."

"You're talking about my mother."

"Yes, I guess so. It's terrible for you. It's even worse for her right now. We've got to take care of her. And we've got to take care of the children, to keep her from worrying about them too. We're all going to help you."

He looked up at her. She was sure he'd grown even in the short time since they'd first met. *"We've* got to take care of the children," he concurred, accepting her judgment that he wasn't a child anymore. "But I don't know what to do for Mama. My father didn't tell me that." His voice went reedy and uncontrolled.

"Give her time," said Krinata. She handed Imp to him. "Or maybe Imp can help. Do you ever tell him your troubles?"

He gave her a sidelong glance, the sun sparkling off his dark exoskeleton. Then he looked down at the piol, seemingly embarrassed. "I didn't think humans knew about things like that. I guess I have a lot to learn?"

"Imp's very understanding. I've told him a lot of my problems that I couldn't talk to anyone about."

"Even Jindigar?"

Oh, especially Jindigar! She sidestepped the issue. "Do you suppose your mama might be able to talk to Imp where she just can't talk to you?"

He held the piol up to look him in the eye. The long furred limbs dangled down ridiculously, and the piol's tail flicked around for balance, but he wrinkled up his black nose, showing sharp teeth in a lopsided grin. "I will try."

When he'd gone, Krinata looked around for Jindigar and Frey, who'd recovered slowly but had not spoken to Krinata. Now there was no sign of either Dushau. The Lehiroh had formed them into a double line, for there would be no danger of being blown sideways today, and a more compact line was easier to defend. She found her sled near the middle of the line, next to Viradel's.

Krinata was checking the harness when a cold feeling came over her, as if a cloud had blocked the sun. But she was standing in warm sunlight. Probing inward, she found the feeling familiar, though more acute than ever. Frey and Jindigar had retempered their duad. Jindigar had warned her that they had to try it, but she must not attempt the triad or it might kill Frey.

"What's the matter?" asked Viradel sarcastically as she checked her sled. "They pack your sled too heavy?"

Krinata bristled. "I presume it's the same as it was."

"Oh. Too light, then," she muttered, and walked off.

Krinata straightened and stared after her, unbelieving. But there was nothing she could say. So, while the column was waiting for the two Holot to finish filling in the refuse pit, Krinata wandered to the front where the Lehiroh were hunkered down over a map scratched in the loose sand.

". . . we get in under those trees, it'll be cooler and we'll consume less water—" Storm looked up. "Krinata! Did Arlai set your watch for this planet, too?"

She looked at the field timepiece, strapped to her right wrist, and noticed that it stood at about noon, which was indeed local time. "It seems so." She blinked back a tear. She missed the Sentient computer. "Where's Jindigar?"

"They'll be back in a little, and—"

Just then the two Dushau came around an outcropping. "Krinata!" called Jindigar. "Would you gather everyone? I think we've found a good camping area."

Frey wouldn't meet her eyes. She nodded and went to gather everyone. Jindigar made it brief, giving them an idea of the route they'd follow. The duad had been able to discern a confluence of waterways ahead of them, tucked into a sheltered valley that teemed with enough life to mask the refugees from orbital sensors. But they had to cross two ridges to get there, and that would take a couple of days.

"One thing you must absorb now," finished Jindigar. "The life on this planet is organized into hives. The hive tends to be paranoid and territorial but not aggressive. If we stay clear of marked territories, we won't be attacked. So each of you must stay in line, follow the path we cut, and keep the pace. Straying could bring disaster. Don't experiment with fruits from the bushes we pass—let Frey and I do the foraging. There's a great deal we can eat, but we mustn't compete with native creatures for the food."

With that, they got under way. The first few steps were an agony on Krinata's shoulders, but after the sled was moving and the kinks worked out of her stiffened muscles, she was able to unclench her teeth and ease her breathing.

As the day passed the land rose steadily and began to show signs of abundant, if sporadic, water supply: dry washes with the scum of flood wrack plastered high on their sides, foliage that stored moisture, dormant plants, and insect and small animal life. But the breath of the desert followed them until near sundown, when a freshening breeze stirred the brittle bushes that had needlelike green leaves.

Viradel had refused all of Krinata's conversational gambits, taking her rest breaks with Gibson, Fenwick, and the other human woman, Adina. Krinata had sat alone, trying to come to terms with being a loner, but had only hatched a stronger determination to make at least some friends.

When they re-formed, Jindigar placed the sled carrying Allel, the younger Cassrian children, and the piols right behind Viradel, where Krinata could see it, and assigned Shorwh to pull it. "Keep an eye on him, Krinata, and let us know when he tires," said Jindigar with apparent effort. Though a wall shut her away from the duad, she felt Jindigar struggling with Frey's inability to hold to the duad.

Viradel said, "I'll take the youngster's sled, Jindigar. With riders like that—a child. . . ."

Jindigar's eyes closed as he summoned the strength to deal with the objection. Krinata said, "Jindigar knows Cassrians. The responsibility is probably good for Shorwh right now, and when he tires—"

"I didn't ask you!" spat Viradel.

Gibson had come to see what the fuss was and jumped into the argument. "You can trust Viradel, Jindigar—"

"I know," assured the Dushau. "Later—we'll shift again." Even those few words cost him a tremendous effort Viradel seemed not to notice. He went to murmur a few words to Frey and then take up his place at the head of the line beside Storm. Gibson calmed Viradel and left. Krinata spent the next several hours trying to find words to explain to Viradel that Jindigar was a proficient Emulator, capable of manifesting within himself the imperatives of many species.

When they finally entered the cover of taller, riotously colored trees, loaded with fruits and inhabited by busy flying creatures, Krinata commented to Viradel, "Jindigar said the green plants, like those over there, produce edible fruits." She pointed to a stand of trees with long, needlelike leaves and luscious yellow fruits.

Viradel looked around and muttered, "He did?"

The woods was relatively clear of underbrush, dead needles heaped in places as if a gardening team had been interrupted. "If we can camp here, Frey and Jindigar will pick our spot very carefully and maybe forage some fruit."

Viradel looked at her sharply and offered a woman-to-woman comment. "You toady to them too much. What you think it'll get you? Dushau make good business partners, but lousy friends, and worse bosses 'cause they can't care how we feel. Those two ain't an Oliat. They was wrong on the sandstorm, could be wrong on anything."

Viradel and her friends had transferred to *Truth* from

another refugee ship and had not known Jindigar before. "I've never heard Jindigar issue an order," she protested.

"But he's controllin' what we do that oughta be decided by vote. Otherwise, you got a boss. If that's what them two wanna be, they ain't gonna share it with you. You oughta join the right side o' this, afore it's too late."

Side!? She knew Jindigar had no personal interest in how ephemerals governed themselves. "With the Squadron after us we can't discuss every decision. The Dushau and the Lehiroh are professionals weighing hundreds of factors—"

"We don't think as good as them? Where I come from, a person don't let nobody do their thinkin' for 'em."

Krinata gestured at the shade all around them now, as if it made her argument self-evident. "They found this for us."

"Yeh," Viradel agreed, surveying a stand of saplings surrounding a taller tree drooping under the weight of a crop of globular yellow fruit buried in gorgeous sprays of green needles. "And then he forbids us to touch anything! As if we had no wilderness sense. Now, where I was raised, fruit like that was fer pickin'! There's so much—we wouldn't be competin' with no animal—"

As Krinata took a routine glance at Shorwh she said, "But Jindigar knows what he's talking about!" Turning back to Viradel, she found her shrugging out of her harness, eyes fixed on the ripe fruit. "Viradel, no! Don't be a fool!" It came out as a command of Lady Zavaronne.

Viradel flashed her a defiant grin, and before Krinata could move, she darted to the saplings where she picked two of the fruits. She was back in line with her treasure, shrugging into her harness when a liquid, wailing ululation filled the peaceful woods. *Oonnoolloolloolloollllloooo!*

Krinata heard a thud and whirled to see a creature on top of Shorwh's sled. It was a bipedal, brown hairy ape with an extra joint in each arm and leg. Its most splendid feature was a pair of gleaming black horns growing from its forehead over its skull. Its tail was curled up over its back and hooked around the horns as it stood on top of the sled and issued a splashing stream of yellow urine toward Allel and the children who huddled, clutching the piols.

Krinata yelled, "Shorwh, get out of your harness!" She smacked the brake on her own sled. Turning to comply, Shorwh saw the creature and froze. The sled plowed straight over him, and at the last second Shorwh had to dive under it. It bobbed with the weight of the creature, almost flattening Shorwh. The beast emitted another *Onnoolloo!* and bent to rip at the cargo tarp with its horns.

Krinata threw herself flat to fish Shorwh out from under the dangerously low sled while Viradel went for the sled's controls. She got Shorwh clear just in time to see the creature, frustrated by the tough fabric, stomping and hopping about chasing after the two Cassrian children. Both piols leapt at the creature's back and, clinging to its horns, began savaging its eyes with their long fishing claws.

Simultaneously Allel came out of her stupor. Her children were threatened. She gave a piercing cry and leapt at the animal, almost knocking it and herself over the side of the sled. But the thing recovered, cried out again, and swatted Allel so hard, she was pitched through the air to land hard on the flat ground.

Shorwh screeched and ran to his mother. Krinata watched in horror as the creature captured both the smaller children, who were screaming piteously. Without even knowing what she was doing, she *reached*, as she had during the sandstorm, and found the triad accommodating around her.

For an instant she saw the battle through Jindigar's eyes: a hive-ripper, challenged by a hive-swarm passing through his territory, was simply demonstrating his authority, while incidentally picking up a meal.

Jindigar's hand came down firmly on her shoulder. "No!" She felt Frey, nerves screaming, struggling to be free of her. Stricken, she tried to tell Jindigar, *I don't know how to get out!*

"Let me!" His bulging, swirling indigo eyes loomed, and she felt the wall intruding between them again. She curled in on herself and tried to shut off the horrible sounds, the seductive awareness.

As Frey and the Lehiroh gathered, Jindigar wound his fingers into the sled's guy ropes and shook mightily, his voice going up in a perfect rendition of the creature's howl. The thing hugged the two children to its chest, shook off the piols, and leapt down directly between Jindigar and the still form of Allel. Shorwh flung himself over his mother.

The animal kicked Shorwh aside, shifted the two small children to one arm, and grabbed up the unconscious Allel. Her stiff-jointed exoskeleton made her an awkward burden.

Jindigar retreated, drawing the animal away from Shorwh and toward Frey, emitting low *llooollooo* sounds. The thing followed Jindigar as if hypnotized, though showing no signs of letting his prizes go. Viradel tackled the creature, as if to pull its feet out from under it.

Surprised, the hive-ripper swiveled in midair and thumped to the ground in a sitting position, still almost as tall as Krinata, and maddened. Viradel rained blows about the creature's head, screaming, "Let 'em loose!"

The hive-ripper leaned back on his tail, kicked Viradel, and used Allel as a ram to knock Viradel backward. Then he was on his feet and heading for the largest tree in sight.

Only then did he realize he couldn't climb with both

hands full. Casually he tossed the two children aside and flung Allel over his shoulder. In a flash of brown and green he disappeared.

Jindigar attacked Krinata's sled cargo with both hands, loosing the guy ropes and the tarp to flip open the sides of a crate, revealing slender stunner rods, which he seized and tossed to the Lehiroh. Without a word, the four Lehiroh and Frey took off after the creature.

Dusk was gathering swiftly now, and Jindigar announced, "We can't camp here. It would only invite another attack. We can find a flat spot behind that ridge over there, and it should be safe for the night. But there must be no foraging, and no fire to disturb the animals."

"We need fire for safety," protested Gibson, and there was a murmur of agreement.

"We need darkness for safety," corrected Jindigar. "Anything that glows will be savagely attacked in this part of the wood, and we can't make it beyond in the remaining light. I think you've all seen how important it is for us to humor the locals. Viradel's mistake in picking that fruit may have cost us dearly." He never referred to the incident again, but later Krinata overheard Viradel confessing to Gibson that she did feel guilty, though she blamed Jindigar for not explaining his reasons for proscribing foraging.

Krinata jumped into the overheard conversation, to defend Jindigar: "Because he didn't know why we shouldn't forage! He's only got Frey to help him, not an Oliat. He didn't know about the hive-ripper until he actually saw it."

"And how do you know?" challenged Adina, the woman Krinata had never exchanged a word with.

"She's just making that up," claimed Gibson. "Jindigar was practically talking its own language to it. He's been on this planet before!"

"Jindigar was just imitating the creature's call. He's expert at that—it's an Oliat skill, Emulator!"

"If Viradel hadn't o' hit it," said Fenwick, "maybe—"

"Viradel was very courageous," Krinata interrupted him. "She did her best to save the children."

"If anyone, blame Jindigar," suggested Fenwick. "If I had my way, we wouldn't even be in this woods."

She turned and left them to their wrangling. The exchange had left a bad taste in her mouth and a guilt in the pit of her stomach. Perhaps if she hadn't gotten Viradel all upset over Jindigar's leadership, she wouldn't have taken the fruit from the hive-ripper's tree and challenged it.

When she brought the last sled up to the circle of sleds, Jindigar guided it into place, leaving a slender gap for a door. Then he stepped out to stare in the direction the hive-ripper had taken. Krinata leashed back an impulse to seek for that ineffable contact again. Then she squelched an impulse to ask if he could sense Frey. The duad locked her out as firmly as ever, and it was better to leave it that way. But the temptation welled up.

Strangling a sob, she slid down the wall of cargo and huddled with her forehead on her knees, willing herself to be strong until Jindigar went about his business. But he didn't leave. He hunkered down beside her and let the tip of one velvety finger stroke the back of one of her fingers. It was the tiniest gesture, but it undid her. The suppressed tears came. "I'm sorry," she gasped, ashamed.

"We're all very tired—and frightened. Can I help?"

"No." After a time he rose to go. "Jindigar—"

He knelt beside her. "Let me help, as you've helped me so many times."

They don't make good friends, huh? "Jindigar, I—I'm not sure I can make myself stay out. I'm so afraid—of

Desdinda, of hurting Frey, but—I could hardly help it!"

He hugged her to his chest as if he could shelter and protect her. "Oh, Krinata, what have I done to you!"

Before she had herself well in hand again, the Lehiroh arrived with Frey—and Allel's body.

FOUR

Imperial Wrath

The funeral was held in the last light, then the Dushau guided everyone back to the circle of sleds. After the children were sedated and put to sleep, the adults talked bleakly about this world and their future on it.

Jindigar admitted, "I've been here before, yes, as Outreach to Raichmat's Oliat, nearly two thousand years ago. I can't farfetch those memories now. Most of what I know, I'm learning in duad with Frey."

Everyone accepted that excuse for not warning them of the onnoolloo, but Krinata thought, *If he can't farfetch two thousand years, he's in worse shape than he lets on.* She rolled up in her sleeping bag, dwelling on how he'd shut her out of the triad by shaking her rather than imposing his stone wall between them. She catalogued the signs of fatigue he tried to hide, the worried glances, the increasingly distracted air as he struggled with Frey's skittishness.

She woke in the dark, slim shafts of moonlight lacing the camp. Jindigar was sitting guard duty beside the "door," drawing on the ground in total absorption. It was long before dawn, but she was wide-awake. She opened her bag into a cloak and picked her way through sleepers to him. He'd been sketching weary and bedraggled piols. She touched his arm. "Jindigar, you're not solely responsible for our situation. We all chose to come with you. And now I'm convinced this world is 'marginally livable,' as you said."

"Maybe too marginally. We've lost two people and a sled and are functioning on a crippled duad. We're almost out of water, and the Squadron can't be far behind us now."

"The losses can't be replaced," said Krinata, sitting beside him. "But if we all knew more of this world, perhaps we wouldn't lean on the duad so much."

"I doubt it would be helpful for everyone to know more."

"Keep us in ignorance and Viradel will have good reason for her attitude." And she told him what Viradel had said before picking the fruit. "I wonder what she'd make of that official record I found for this world, which you claimed never existed." She had meant to cheer him up, but suddenly all the unanswered questions swarmed into her mind. The Emperor had accused the Dushau of withholding information on planets to control Allegiancy expansion and prosperity.

He sighed. "It started nearly two thousand years ago, just after humans came onto the galactic scene, and the Allegiancy was founded...." He rubbed out his drawing. "I told you *Phanphihy* had not been reported—and that was true. The Lehiroh and Treptian Outriders with Raichmat's on that expedition perceived a very different environment than we did. That report was based on their perceptions, not ours, and the planet was labeled with their name, not ours."

"Why?"

"If we'd reported our perceptions, the others would have thought we were lying. Raichmat saw the way the Allegiancy was headed. Dushau needed another home besides Dushaun. But the idea of planting a multispecies colony here governed by a King was not popular on Dushaun, so Phanphihy has been forgotten except among Raichmat's zunre."

The zunre of an Oliat—all who've been members, and

their relatives—formed a more tight-knit group than most families. "You could have applied for it. Surely the Emperor would have granted Raichmat's a world."

"If the idea had been more popular, we might have," agreed Jindigar. "But this world is far from ideal for Dushau—and—we tend to be rather conservative."

"But why did other species see it as unlivable?"

"Raichmat's was one of the first Oliats to work for the Allegiancy. We didn't choose our Outriders with such wisdom then. They worked by the book and antagonized the hives, which defend themselves by casting a veil of perceptual distortion—to make enemies see menace where there isn't much. Our Outriders saw hideous menace everywhere—three quit the profession, one had a nervous breakdown."

She raked her eyes over the black forest around them. "Then this is a very dangerous world! You didn't tell—"

He shook her shoulders. "No! Respect the hives, and they'll be good neighbors. I didn't mention the hives' defense before because we mustn't cripple ourselves with imagined horrors, and your imagination can be very powerful."

She drew a deep breath. "I'm sorry. I should know better." He was right, it wouldn't help if everyone knew that. "Well, if we must rely on the duad, then we've got to heal the damage I've done you and Frey."

"Frey is—mending."

"He's still sleeping under sedation."

"You are observant."

"Frustrated," she corrected. "Jindigar, what is wrong with Frey?" When Jindigar was silent, she added, "You don't want to talk about it to me?"

"Krinata, his fear of Desdinda is nearly a phobia. Your touch on us when we're working seems like her touch. It happened again this afternoon with the onnoolloo, which is why I ordered the sedative."

"But not for yourself?"

"I'm more experienced—"

"Nonsense! You're suffering as much as he is, but you're afraid if you're both unconscious, I'll take over—like I did with the sandstorm! I'm a walking menace! Why didn't you tell me?"

"You're human. The Loop is functioning in you very much as it would in a Dushau, but there's been no time for tests. A human could react unexpectedly—I can't risk hurting you."

They'd endured Desdinda's death agony, and it had nearly killed them. Frey was right: Jindigar accepted her as zunre and therefore couldn't tolerate hurting her. "Tell me what has to be done. I'll decide what risks I take."

"Of course," he agreed. "And I'll decide which ones I take. My decisions limit your options; yours limit mine. That's what Grisnilter wanted me to avoid with ephemerals."

Grisnilter, the elderly Dushau Historian whose Archive Jindigar carried, had objected to Jindigar's policy of befriending ephemerals, just as Frey did. "Jindigar, how would a group of Dushau deal with a Loop? What is the cure?"

"To convene an Aliom grieving-with to grieve Desdinda," he answered as if it were obvious. "But, it's not my area of expertise. I'd have to farfetch for what else I might know, and I don't dare attempt that."

"For fear of being caught in the Archive?"

"Or worse."

The Aliom science behind the Oliat practices was a mystery to her, but—"I'd be willing to try it, but I can't find it in myself to be sorry Desdinda died. I do feel a personal sense of horror that my hand killed her. I still have nightmares about it."

"We all do, but we dare not attempt anything involving you and Desdinda until we've a stable base camp and the duad can be spared. Also, there's the problem of the Archive to solve first, or we all might be lost in it before the Desdinda Loop could be integrated into your personality."

"Integrated into—oh, no, she's not part of me—"

He said, as if grasping why they weren't communicating, "Desdinda had dedicated her life to murdering me because I, an Aliom Priest turned Invert, had custody of Grisnilter's Archive. She'd been taught how Inversion distorts an Archive—altering the recorded history of our species. When she saw she was to die, she already felt so soiled, she had no use for life except to kill me. Her outrage became the core of her insanity, and I believe it grounded into a part of your personality that harbored similar feelings."

"You mean—like a—a ghost? Possessing me?"

"No. There's never been a Dushau ghost—can't be. Desdinda is gone to dissolution/death. She's left us a legacy of compressed anger and hatred lodged in you because I had no time to train you to protect yourself or to prove the Archive had come through our triad Inversion unscathed."

Three times since their escape she'd Inverted the triad. "Have—have I damaged the Archive?"

"I don't think so. But I hardly dare touch the duad now, and Frey knows it. With his limited training he knows he might accidentally damage the Archive, and now that he carries the Invert stigma, too, delivering the Archive unaltered means as much to him as to me."

"It should have meant as much to Desdinda too."

"She wasn't rational. Yet we're bound by her pain—and won't be free until we can grieve it. We must each feel how she felt, and why she felt so, finding the resonances of those feelings within ourselves and integrating them. But we can't try it now because we've no idea what complications your humanity might cause. The Squadron will find *Truth* soon, and we're still too close for safety."

Krinata had to accept that. Jindigar could do nothing to help her expunge Desdinda, yet it had to be done. So, she'd have to do it herself, in her human way. She probed him mercilessly on the characteristics of a Loop, learning that it took very little resonance to provide a rooting point—as it took very little to attract lightning. She didn't hate Jindigar, not even unconsciously. But there had to be something Desdinda's hatred had touched. If she could rid herself of it, the Loop would dissipate—or so theory said. In practice, Dushau never attempted such things alone. But then, humans didn't practice group telepathy, either!

At dawn they were up and in harness, Jindigar moving among them as his normal self, twittering to the children and the piols, summoning joy in a piece of fruit, or casually hanging by his toes to inspect the underside of a sled. But she saw the weary depression he masked from the others. *He hasn't grieved for his friends yet. I must see that he does soon or he'll collapse. It could be centuries until a Historian arrives to take the Archive from him.* There was nothing she could do about that, but Desdinda—

As they marched she mulled over the problem and became ever more determined to vanquish Desdinda herself.

They skirted dense thickets and plowed through sparser ones, tromping up and down the ever-rising hills. Krinata was paired with Shorwh, his two brothers riding atop her sled, clutching the piols in an unnatural silence. Shorwh was now the only one, except Jindigar, who could speak to the children. While they seemed to be in shock, Shorwh was withdrawn the way an adult might be. But he ate, fed his brothers, and pulled his load without slacking.

During the first rest break she tried to take her mind off her troubles by tending the children. Terab, huge, six-limbed, warm and furry, also tried to mother them. But neither soft-skinned human nor furred Holot could begin to replace a mother's smooth chitin for the Cassrian children. When Shorwh said, fretting, "Why don't you both just leave us alone?" Terab withdrew, but Krinata went after her.

"I don't think he really means that," she said to Terab.

"Neither do I. A Holot wouldn't. But I thought perhaps Irnils might try to get through to him, male to male."

"It's worth a try," agreed Krinata.

Irnils, Terab's mate, had lost his parents early in life, and when he sat down among the orphaned Cassrians, somehow, gradually, the atmosphere lightened. The four Lehiroh, as usual, spent the rest break sitting in a close circle, talking softly about their lost bride. Krinata left them to their grieving. The four humans provoked heated political conversations among the Holot and Cassrians, seeming innocent enough until one time Terab came on them cornering Shorwh with a diatribe against Jindigar.

Seeing her, they turned to go, but she commanded, "Hold orbit there!" Even weaponless, she intimidated them. "You never knew Jindigar before you boarded *Truth*, but surely you've measured him by now. He got us across that desert, which could have been a challenge to a full Oliat. Riding the water sled, he damn near got killed, but he saved our water. He's told us how to keep out of trouble, and even when one of your women stupidly ignored him, he didn't hold a trial—so the children wouldn't blame her.

"Jindigar never shirks a risk or stints on compassion for Dushau or ephemeral. He's loyal beyond reason, generous in soul and goods, a Prince of his people—"

"Terab," said Gibson, shoulders hunched more than usual. "Aristocrats ruined the Allegiancy—" He looked at Krinata, who was almost as highborn as Jindigar, spat, and left.

They fell in for the afternoon haul, and she returned to

ruminating on her feelings for Jindigar. He'd won her respect as he had Terab's. She'd never seen him do a mean or dishonest deed. But she didn't understand his motives, so every once in a while, he failed to do what she expected of him. That hardly seemed cause for a repressed hatred.

Jindigar, knowing they were all getting into condition, lengthened the time between breaks, so Krinata had no more energy for her thoughts until they emerged from an open wood into magenta sunlight at the lip of a valley.

Erect dead trees, truncated limbs jutting in every direction, filled the valley, surrounded by glittering black-and-gray soil. But it was not a bleak sight, for from every limb hung bright translucent globes of rainbow hues.

Flying creatures with handsome wings covered with transparent shell-like flakes the same colors as the suspended hives flocked around their homes. Wings folded, they resembled beetles—flat, multilegged. Alone or in swarms, they darted into the woods that bordered the valley.

Jindigar called a break, climbing up to bring the two younger children down, twittering to them as he pointed at the valley. It elicited the first response since their mother had died. As the Lehiroh spread a canopy over the circled sleds, Jindigar warned everyone to stay under cover, explaining, "Those creatures made a forest like this into that. Their body waste kills trees and animals. If we do nothing to anger them when they fly over us, they may provide us our dinner." When he'd translated for the children, they both climbed into his lap and fell asleep with their heads on his shoulders. Shorwh embraced Jindigar around the neck. "Now they know they're not alone and don't have to die too."

Squirming self-consciously, Jindigar returned Shorwh's hug. Krinata watched, remembering how in moments of extreme distress Jindigar would turn to the young. Dushau cared for the young only during Renewal, the period of a century every thousand years when they took a mate and regained youth. Jindigar had insisted it would be another fifty years until he entered Renewal, but he admitted that he could allow it to happen anytime. He'd passed up an offer of a mating to bring them here, for in Renewal, the Oliat functions could not be practiced. Who could hate such a person?

Krinata's thoughts were interrupted as a flock of the colorful flyers crackled and rustled overhead, raining deadly excrement on their tarp. Moments later Jindigar said, "Come on, Frey, let's see if we can collect some dinner."

By the time they'd re-formed their caravan, Frey and Jindigar had returned from the forest with several dead animals strung on a stout branch. She shuddered and wondered if she could eat from the animals killed by bird excrement, a thought that never occurred to the Dushau, for they were evolved scavengers. But, roasted, the birds were quite good.

Krinata went to bed dwelling on the Loop, searching for its root inside her mind. She slept badly, waking with nothing to show for her effort but a fuzzy headache.

The next day, the Dushau and Storm went foraging and returned with a basketful of eggs. "We found a hive destroyed by an onnoolloo," explained Jindigar happily. "These eggs would've rotted before they could hatch."

Terab, the Holot female who'd been a space captain and shopkeeper but never a colonist asked, "Where did you get the fine basketwork? I could make a profit on those!"

"Made them," answered Storm. "Jindigar found the reeds in the top of a tree." That discovery alone, reflected Krinata, might save the group from extinction. Civilization couldn't be constructed without cheap, light containers. The next morning, Jindigar admonished them, "Your canteens hold the last of our water. We haven't made such good time as

I'd anticipated, so we'll make a dry camp tonight if we don't push today."

Jindigar's initial pace didn't slacken until noon, when they tackled a ridge of bare rock that almost forced the Lehiroh to break out their rigging equipment again. But they made it, and at the top of the ridge, they found themselves facing a cleft in a blank wall of rock. They rested, the sleds gathered in a double line on the strip of flat ground.

As Jindigar and the Lehiroh strode tirelessly back and forth, checking everything, Krinata snuggled into a puddle of sunlight nestled among boulders. Imp and Rita scampered headfirst down the side of her sled and licked Krinata's hands, snuffling in her pockets for crumbs. She tilted her face to the sun, almost falling asleep right there. Sleepless or nightmare-haunted nights were wearing on her, but that could be a good sign. If she stirred up her nonconscious mind enough, perhaps it would reveal where the Loop was rooted.

As she relaxed she noticed a roughness to the stone she was leaning against. Overcoming lethargy, she sat up to look. There, carved deep into the living rock, was a regular pattern of lines—rustlebird hives, onnoolloo, and small game they'd roasted. "Jindigar! Jindigar!"

Jindigar came on the run, followed by the four Lehiroh and Frey. She pointed, croaking. Jindigar climbed up to examine her find as people dragged themselves from their rest to see what had happened. Jindigar touched the carving and frowned at Frey. Krinata felt the duad coalescing, their unsteady, tenuous contact making a flutter in the pit of her stomach. She held her breath against it until Jindigar nodded. "We won't be bothered by rustlebirds and onnoolloo in the valley. But there's quicksand downstream, and prey and predators come here for water. Their life readings will mask ours if the Squadron—"

"Jindigar!" complained Krinata. "That—that was carved! You're *reading* it!"

"Yes." He frowned at Frey, whose eyes were closed.

"Who—or what—carved it?", demanded Krinata.

"The natives," he admitted gravely.

A murmur went up all around. Gibson spoke for everyone. "There are laws against colonizing a planet with intelligent natives, and with good reason."

"Of course," agreed Jindigar. He looked about at the weary, trail-stained band. Then, hunkering down, he gathered them around a thin patch of soil and drew with a stick.

"When I was here with Raichmat's Oliat, the highest evolved natives were proto-sentients at about the level of a Rashion. They were beginning to use chipped stone tools and to trade among hives. They had no agriculture and lived at the mercy of the elements, protected only by their hives."

He'd drawn a large domed structure, crosshatched with circles, entered by a tunnel. "They build their hives out of fieldstone mortared with a body-excrement that dissolves on exposure to onnoolloo urine. They're very thinly scattered, so we can avoid them. Their population was receding under attack of natural enemies and a changing climate. Either they'll rely more on intelligence or they'll become extinct.

"Raichmat's predicted they'd become victims of the Allegiancy's galactic expansion. This world has no exportables and isn't well located for trade. The ecology will fight offworld invasion ferociously." He looked to Krinata. "The Allegiancy would have grabbed this world for living space, destroyed the ecology, and created a world-city that depended on imports. You all know many such places."

They assented, and he continued, "The natives would have been either exterminated by the shifting ecology or exploited mercilessly by the local Duke."

Through the murmur of assent Terab asked, "An Oliat can foresee two millennia of politics?"

"Not an Oliat," corrected Jindigar. "A Historian. It was as clear to her as the sound of that waterfall is to us."

Only then did she notice the distant roar. "That must be a terrible talent, foreknowledge."

Jindigar nodded, contemplating his drawing. "Raichmat's wanted to protect the natives by founding a Dushau-dominant multicolony here under the laws of our King, not the local Duke. When we presented the plan to Dushaun, it was rejected. And there the matter has rested until now, when we need refuge." He looked up at them. "We must, of course, avoid all contact with the natives. If we find any more of these"—he indicated the carving—"we may have to alter our course to settle where there are no natives."

Krinata shivered in the shadow that had crept over her while Jindigar spoke. He'd told her the same story, only he'd left out the natives. What else wasn't he bothering to mention? And why?

Jindigar announced, rising, "We must make camp before dark. The moon won't rise until very late."

They broke up, arguing among themselves, but going about the business of starting the caravan moving. The two piols could not, however, be coaxed back onto the sled with the children. They frisked about, running ahead and dashing back to nip at heels, and then run ahead again, made eager by the smell of water. But, as thirsty as she was, all Krinata could think of as she trudged through the long, narrow gap, the sides of her sled scraping the walls, was whether she'd have come with Jindigar if she'd known of the natives.

She'd decided before she saw how Emperor Zinzik exploited the Rashions, helpless telepathic proto-sentients. She probably would not have come with Jindigar. He'd have put her off on some planet, and later she'd have been hunted down by the Emperor's Rashions and would have known in the moment of her death that she'd made a mistake. *But was Jindigar manipulating me? Or is it that he only answers exactly the question asked? Is he like that among Dushau, or is that how he deals with ephemerals?*

She felt her old distrust of Jindigar aroused. She'd agreed with Terab's description of Jindigar, yet how easy it was for her to look at him as a monster in disguise. Was this the rooting place the Loop had found in her psyche? Her ruminations were interrupted when they came out into a slanting sunset light, at the head of a moraine. It took until dark to negotiate the sleds down the loose rock and shale, though the piols scampered ahead without difficulty. But then they were on a beautiful valley floor.

To their left a high waterfall plunged into a series of three cascades, which widened into a network of ponds draining into a wide river that bisected the valley. Tall trees laden with fruits clustered around the river. The valley walls were sheer and deeply undercut, providing shelter for their sleds from orbital snoops. A herd of four-legged grazers were watering on the other side of the river.

They shied away when people went to bathe, wash clothes, and fill canteens. By the time camp was set, fires were going, and fish the piols had caught were grilling, Krinata was too exhausted to think. They had come twice the usual distance that day, surmounting two hard climbs and a treacherous descent. Even Jindigar and Frey sat unmoving at their fire, waiting for their clothes to dry. The firelight glistened on their bare chests, highlighting their lack of vestigial breasts. They hardly talked to each other.

Revived by the good meal, people began to stir. The discontented tone Jindigar had cut off at the carving was back, though Frey and Jindigar seemed oblivious. Frey's eyes were closed, though he sat upright, tremors shaking him, a symptom she'd seen in Jindigar only when he was frightened. Compelled, she went to their fire, wanting to reach Frey.

Jindigar motioned her to sit beside him but whispered, "I shouldn't have asked Frey to read the plaque."

"Did he know about the natives?" He nodded, and she said, "Then it's Desdinda. If we have to risk trying to deal with that—I might be able to now. I don't know—"

"No!" said Frey hoarsely. "I'll be all right. Really."

"You will," assured Jindigar, saying to Krinata, "This is no worse than normal subform expansion throes. Quietude and sleep will heal. I've already given him a sedative. Have you discovered the contact point of the Loop?"

"Maybe. It seems embarrassingly trivial—ridiculous—but—" And she told him how she'd felt about the natives.

When she stopped, he let out a breath that could have been a smothered cry of despair and put an arm around her shoulders to hug her as he often did the Cassrian children. "I didn't mention the natives because there weren't any in this area before. There are other hopes I've not mentioned because as an Oliat officer I've learned to speak only clear certainties to ephemerals. But, Krinata, I do believe you have every hope for a good life here."

"You're asking me to take you on faith."

"No. I don't know how things will work out. I get clues that a singleton, or duad, can't interpret." His arm about her shoulder felt warm, trustworthy. "But there's cause for hope, and when I know—I'll say."

At that moment the Lehiroh called Ruff, the least talkative but strongest of them, came into the firelight and squatted before Jindigar, who kept his arm unself-consciously around Krinata. "Jindigar, it was my fault. I should never have opened my mouth—but—when they accused you of lying, it just came out."

Jindigar put his other hand on the Lehiroh's shoulder and looked up at Storm, who was behind Ruff. Storm said, "About Krinata working the triad with you—the whole story from the escape from the Emperor—Desdinda—Inversion, the whole thing. Ruff broke confidence, Jindigar—but we all accept the guilt—it was unprofessional—"

Jindigar started, "It's all right, Ruff—"

But Gibson and the other humans pushed into the circle, Gibson saying, "So we're finally getting to the bottom of things." He turned to the Holot, who were crowding up too. "Did you know *Prince* Jindigar and *Lady Zavaronne* were over here deciding—without consulting any of us peasants—what to do about the natives?" He turned on the Lehiroh. "They don't consult you, either. Did you ever think about that? Isn't it time we found out if we have a trained duad to rely on, or some crazy, unnatural triad?"

For the first time Terab seemed less than friendly to Krinata. "You could have told us what the problem was. Withholding vital information—"

At first Krinata was offended, and then she suddenly saw that she'd done just what she distrusted Jindigar for—not mentioning uncertainties to people with a lot on their minds. "I never saw any point—"

"Of course, she wouldn't see any point in telling you!" Gibson declared sarcastically. "She and Jindigar are the natural leaders here. Why should they consult us? Aren't you sick of this? Don't you all think it's time to demand an accounting? The Allegiancy is dead—we've got to build something new, and it's got to start here. Are you with me?"

There was a silence. He'd landed a telling blow. Jindigar withdrew his arm from Krinata's shoulders and rose. Frey tried to get up, too, but Jindigar motioned him down, throwing a thermal cloak to him as he gathered up his shirt. "Go to sleep." He led the group toward the main watch fire.

Gibson paced Jindigar, saying, "And what about Frey? Is he sick or something?"

"He's recovering from injuries sustained in the crash," said Jindigar truthfully.

Krinata stepped out to confront Gibson. "If you must fix blame, blame me. Jindigar knew from the moment the Emperor's ship blew up that I'd never again be able to work in triad. Since you'd never known I'd done it, you didn't have to know I'd been invalided. But I was too stubborn to admit defeat. I invaded the duad, accidentally hurting Frey and Jindigar. I'll make up for that, even if it costs my life!"

"Spoken like a true aristocrat," mocked Gibson.

"I'm sorry," said Krinata sincerely. Ever since Emperor Zinzik had reinstituted aristocratic privilege, she'd loathed the system that had titled her at birth. She couldn't fight Gibson's attitude. Shaking, she gathered her thermal cloak and went off into the darkness.

She came to the latrine pit they'd dug at the very edge of the firelight—a hole with two branches across it to squat against. It stank of the mixed excrement of several species plus the degradant they poured over the mess. Upwind of it, she leaned against a rough boulder, trying to sort her emotions out. Behind her, voices mixed in urgent argument, shreds of Jindigar's tones cutting through the rush of the waterfall. ". . . was not born a Prince . . . father appointed King when we joined the Allegiancy . . . not interested in status . . . our situation . . . vote and let us know what we'll do tomorrow . . ."

All she could think about was how she'd edited the problem with the triad to avoid explaining the Desdinda Loop. Could it be shame at being possessed? Or contempt for their intelligence? Or a desire to keep secrets from enemies? She couldn't relate to any of those ideas.

A bulging shadow whispered through the perimeter of the camp, disappearing into the dark. *Jindigar!* She'd almost lost sight of him before she knew she had to follow. She hurried around the circle of sleds to the point where he'd left, then struck out along the line he'd taken. She could barely make out the bushes, knee-high grass, and occasional tree. But as her eyes adjusted she caught flickers of movement ahead of her. Then they disappeared.

"Jindigar!" she called. "Jindigar?"

"Over here!" echoed a voice. "Krinata? What—?" He appeared again and she saw he'd gone into a side canyon. Seeing her, he came back to meet her, taking her hand. "Careful, lot of rocks here. What's happened?"

"Nothing, I just—" He was carrying something. "What's that?"

"Lelwatha's whule." He held up a long-necked, bulbous instrument gleaming even in the barely moonlit dark. Lelwatha had been zunre to Jindigar. She'd heard Jindigar play only once, while grieving over Lelwatha's death. "I shouldn't have come," she said, knowing how he occasionally craved seclusion, and not wanting to invade a private moment.

"It's all right. They don't want you back there, either. Come, look what I've found!"

There was a trickle of waterfall at the end of the small canyon. Jindigar built a fire in a rocky space just before its catch basin. The firelight danced in the ethereal spray. "Won't the dampness ruin the whule?"

He laughed. "Krinata, this instrument hasn't survived all these millennia by being sensitive to the weather!"

Here the roar of the falls was muted. They piled soft foliage into seats around their fire, and he played.

The whule was a simple stringed, resonating chambered instrument, not amplified. Yet he drew such shapes of sound out of it, weaving them with silences flooded with waterfall and the echoes of the small canyon, that the darkness had texture and the firelight danced in eternal rhythms.

Spellbound, she dismissed the nagging thought that Frey had warned her to keep away from Jindigar. She forgot being a Zavaronne, forgot her short, ephemeral life, and became one with Dushau eternity as if it were native to her identity.

Gradually his music changed, not to a dirge but to a paean to life, acknowledging pain of loss as an essential part of what made things real. He poured his deferred grieving for Rinperee and the other Dushau who'd died in the crash, for Arlai, and *Truth*, and all they'd known together into his music, and she cried with him, opening depths of herself she'd never suspected, finding pain she'd never known she harbored, hearing within his music the chattering voices of all those lost to them.

The music, familiar yet strange, cathartic, intimate, personal, took her on a journey through soul to confront her God at the gates of death-and-life, to confess weakness and secret failures, and to be accepted, anyway. Hours passed as she sat huddled in her cloak, oblivious to the dying fire, experiencing and wanting only to experience.

As the sun was rising she became aware of a lightness, an inner healing. The grayness of predawn revealed the small waterfall of their alcove filling her vision. The music described every plume, every eddy, every lacy spume tracing rainbows that hadn't been born yet.

To her the waterfall was the power of life, of all creation. Tingling currents of power swept down through her own body. She could not stop it. She dared not try, for it was eternal and infinite. She was caught within it, and was of it, for all time—as if she'd achieved Dushau Completion.

Once before she'd glimpsed this infinitude where all was lashing energies—once before when Jindigar, summoning his role as Aliom Priest, had shown her the symbol of Aliom—a branched lighting flash, power whipping up and down along carved channels faster than the mind could comprehend—she had known but had been unable to encompass. Now she saw the lightning and the waterfall, and knew them for the same power. It was the power that carried her to a decision-action so fast that she didn't think or feel. It was what Aliom called a "strike" and Jindigar admired in her.

She could feel his admiration, as if she were Center of an Oliat and he merely an Outreach trainee impressed with her feats of Aliom art. She gathered him in close, and with the illogic of dream, they became a duad, sharing deep resonances of the peace of Completion at the brink of death.

Into the placid euphoria billowed black clouds of fear. Suddenly she was falling, out of control, bewildered by the forces acting on her. *No!* she screamed out with every shred of her being. But it had no effect. Cruelly battered and buffeted, she careened into emptiness.

No. Jindigar was there—within her and without. His arms circled her, his eyes filled her vision, his perception echoed in her: the granite cliffs, the hives of native life, the networks of plants like protohives, and in the distance, the intruders' camp like a sore on the land, but over all, the smooth human warmth; tangy odor; silky strands of hair; inefficient ears; hidden, secret eyes.

"No!"

The familiar brick wall shimmered between them. She could almost count the stones that formed it. "No," she gasped. "Not the stones, not a wall. No, don't . . ."

He pushed away, large hands swallowing her shoulders as he shook her, and the wall solidified. His voice echoed off it, but it was a groan ripped from him: "Stop!"

The penetrating awareness faded. She fought double vi-

sion and disorientation as he pulled his hands away. Just as
his fingers trailed over the back of her hand, his soft nap
sending shivers through her, she glimpsed the ecstasy evaporating from his expression, as if he'd firmly closed a sensory door. As she caught her breath, he sat back on his
heels, chest heaving. His voice made her throat ache as he
said, "Such a precious gift—how could a human—no, of
course, you're closer than I, and I—I'm sorry, Krinata, but
sometimes it happens. It doesn't mean anything."

She had no idea what he meant, merely *felt* his gratitude
for something she'd given him, and shame he hadn't responded properly. The duad resonance faded even as he
spoke, the wall becoming so huge, she couldn't even sense
it. "I could live with anything you do except that wall!"

"Wall?" He cocked his head aside, Emulating human
body language like a cloaking disguise.

"When you cut me off," she explained, recounting how
her whole being had clutched at the euphoria his music
brought, "I'd have done anything to get back there, because
I thought for a minute I'd begun to understand what you
are. But I guess I overstepped somehow and touched your
duad, evoking Desdinda—the wall is better than Desdinda,
Jindigar. For a moment, I felt—clean—of her. But I guess
I'm not."

He listened intently, then commented, "Frey was not
involved. I doubt he could have survived that. But he and
I perceive our duad barrier as a gulf, not a wall. I don't
understand. The Loop is stronger than ever, yet I'm sure
you grieved with me. Didn't you?"

"I thought that's what it might have been." If so, perhaps
she now knew how to rid herself of the Loop, though the
experience was already fading to a memory of a memory.
"You grieved Desdinda?"

"I began when we slipped into duad. It was a strike,

Krinata. I wasn't thinking. If I had, I'd have known better, for all I managed was to evoke Desdinda while I was too—" There was that flicker of ecstasy. "That's not a good state to approach a tricky plexus like this Loop, though I don't usually strike wild. I don't understand. Tell me again about this wall."

She described how it built, sounded, looked, felt.

"And when Desdinda threw us into the Archive?"

She described the void, panic, falling, and he was amazed at the processes of the human mind. "When I see a walled structure, you see a void, when I see void, you see a wall. You fear void and Desdinda, and equate them? But Desdinda isn't the Archive, and she's not the void."

She shuddered, awareness of the dead woman heightened. "Jindigar, what did you mean, there are no Dushau ghosts?" *If ever anyone was haunted*—

"Ephemerals reincarnate, but we do not. If we die before completing a life, we simply dissolve. But if we succeed before death, we exist eternally without need to reincarnate. Madness such as Desdinda suffered can only end in dissolution, as she did. That is a true void."

She'd read that theory in Arlai's library but had passed over it without interest. Now it suddenly seemed like the fallacy underlying Aliom philosophy. "But, if she's really gone, why is she still here?" *Not that I really believe in ghosts.*

"I don't know, but the clue must lie in your void. Perhaps if I'd ever served as Center in Oliat, I'd see it."

"Frey said you'd been qualified to be Center since he was born, and I know even Dushau consider that unusual." It was a personal question she'd never dared ask before, but she needed to get away from talk of Desdinda.

"One can be Center only once. For the many who've not chosen priesthood, it's the end of Oliat training, and they then seek other paths to Completion. For a vowed priest, dedicated to achieving Completion only via the Aliom path, it's a supreme test. Those who succeed become Observing Priests; those who fail go to dissolution/death. Success often means remaining Center for centuries, so a Priest takes an Oliat only just after Renewal, for Renewal terminates Oliat. Twice now I've avoided taking Center because events during Renewal rendered me unstable. Now I'm facing Renewal again. Perhaps that's Desdinda's hold on me, for her death could so easily be mine." He looked at her bleakly. "I feel panic when she clutches at you."

For a moment it seemed obvious that Jindigar's fear of dissolution/death would be triggered by Desdinda's attack on her. But the insight faded, leaving her puzzled but deeply touched, vowing silently to rid herself of the demon for his sake, if not her own. *Even if there's no such thing as dissolution/death*. Yet, to her, all death had always been dissolution. Now, amid the echoing residue of the night's experience, she couldn't think of it that way anymore.

Life—pervades.

The rising sun had crowned the waterfall with morning rainbows, and the camp fire was dead. Suddenly there was a splash in the pond, and Imp scrambled out of the water with a fish in his mouth. He swarmed up Jindigar's pant leg, presenting the wriggling creature. Jindigar rose with the dripping piol under one arm, the whule in his other hand. "He says it's time for breakfast!"

"I'm starved!" she agreed, unsurprised and unfooled by his swift change of mood.

When they arrived back at the camp, they found everyone gathered around the main camp fire inside the ring of sleds. The moment he saw them, Shorwh leapt up from where he was helping Frey gut fish and ran to Krinata. "They let me cast three votes, one for me and one for each of my brothers. And I voted to do what Jindigar wants, and we won!"

Everyone looked to Jindigar. "In that case, we'll forage, gathering supplies, so you can all learn what's good to eat and what's dangerous. Day after tomorrow—"

At that moment the sky lit with a flash that eclipsed the rising sun, and Jindigar yelled, "Down! Take cover!"

The piols screamed, and everyone dived under the cliff. Long moments later, the thunderous roar reached them. Pebbles rattled loose and showered down on them, but their cliff held while something ominous blotted out the sunshine.

When it was over, Jindigar stood and dusted himself off. *"Ephemeral Truth* has been destroyed—"

FIVE

Hive Massacre

Two days they foraged and learned the idiosyncrasies of the ecology while casting anxious glances at the sky. But it was time well invested, for during the next seven days of hard marching to the end of the river canyon, they barely disturbed the ecology as they passed. Once, Jindigar remarked wistfully that an Oliat might have convinced the local hives to eradicate all trace of their passage.

Jindigar and Frey quested for signs of the Squadron during rest breaks, sure that searchers expected the blowing of their ship to flush them out. As Jindigar explained, "I think they're searching the trail we would have taken *logically*. But we're cutting a circle, treading respectfully among the interlaced network of hives. If we move swiftly, we'll stay ahead of them until they conclude we've all died."

"But if they pick up our trail—" started Irnils.

"Once they're on the ground, the hives will probably convince them we could not have survived," answered Jindigar.

Despite the time he spent isolated with Frey within the duad, Jindigar found time to begin language lessons for the young Cassrians, encouraging Shorwh to help train their voices and leaving Krinata to referee the inevitable squabbles. She didn't mind. The children refreshed Jindigar so much, and they kept her mind off the ominous nightmares.

Nightly, now, she was having repeating dreams. Usually it started with Jindigar playing the whule near the little waterfall, then, lulled, she'd drift into becoming Desdinda, believing she was the only sane one left able to protect all Dushau by destroying Jindigar and the Archive he'd sullied. But she'd fail and fall into a ruined Archive with scenes of bombed and burned-out cities, cindered worlds, drifting hulks of dead spaceships, scenes from their flight across the galaxy reeling before her eyes as if the pristine beauty recorded in the Archive had been blasted to rubble. If she fought out of that horror, she'd fall back in a terrifying swoop until she was Center of an Oliat, with Jindigar as an Officer, and treacherously he'd turn on her, ripping away her power of decision, rendering her helpless.

Sometimes she woke, fist to her mouth, stifling a scream, then lay awake dredging the evaporating dream for any clue of how it symbolized Desdinda's hold on her.

They emerged from the valley over a series of rolling hills. Where the river turned west to cut deep canyons with foaming rapids, they filled every container with water, then angled to the southeast.

The duad identified many medicinal herbs, but all too often Jindigar would shake his head, admitting the limits of a mere duad. Once, Terab became ill on a root-and-leaf soup she'd improvised, and Jindigar halted the column for the day, saying, "This is my fault. I should have noticed that combination would prove to be a strong laxative."

They used the day to forage. Eggs were plentiful, but Jindigar instructed, "Take only unfertilized or abandoned eggs, or a few from large clutches."

Gibson scoffed, "Dushau may be evolved scavengers, but humans ain't. There's nothing wrong with taking what we can find. It's not like we're overpopulating this world!"

That afternoon he returned to camp limping, one hand bound up in his shirt. He was swearing luridly. "Frissin snakethings near killed me!" While they were bandaging his wounds he complained to Jindigar, "Why didn't you tell me them blue wormthings were dangerous?"

"They aren't," answered the Dushau mildly, "if you don't steal their last egg of the season." *Gibson had assumed Jindigar's motives were human,* thought Krinata. A human might impose his morals on others, but Jindigar wouldn't. He just seemed human because he was a good Emulator.

The next day they emerged from a crease between two hills onto a russet-and-gold grassland dotted with stands of the dark green trees, liberally sprinkled with purple and white flowers. *Breathtaking! I could live here!* She romped up the hillside with the children and piols, gathering the purple wild flowers with exultation until Terab, climbing to the summit of the hill ahead of Krinata, found another native plaque and called Jindigar.

He summoned Frey, and together they pored over the inscriptions. Just when it seemed they couldn't decipher it, Jindigar saw the bouquet in Krinata's hands. "May I?" He took the flowers, savoring their fragrance with a blissful smile. Then, analytically, he held the flowers next to the crude carving declaring that they were of the species drawn there. "This tablet describes the surface water availability by seasons, and gives the water table depths, too. I don't know the animals, but I'll recognize them when I see them."

"It means," said Frey, "there're natives on the plain."

Jindigar scrambled down the hillside. "Yes, their habitat has spread. It would probably be most efficient if the group camps here tomorrow while Frey and I explore."

"I'd be happier," said Terab, the ex-Captain, casting an eye upward, "if we had a less exposed position."

"Deactivated, the sleds shouldn't register on orbital sensors. Cast an irregular pattern, and I doubt even atmosphere observation would notice us," answered Jindigar.

Late the next night, in a driving downpour, Frey and

Jindigar returned with a sketch of the terrain. Gathered around a lightstick under a tarp, they all heard the bad news.

"The natives' hives are clustered near the hills, in the section just ahead of us and to our left. That's the area of the most abundant surface and ground water." Jindigar smoothed the paper and pointed with a damp finger. "Our first idea was to bear south, away from all habitation." He looked up at them. "But we found an old camp of a Squadron's ground unit. They were headed east. We could circle west and go around behind them—if there aren't any more sweeping in from the west."

Mentally Krinata added, *Which a mere duad can't tell.* Storm asked, "Which is worse, to invade the natives' territory or risk being spotted by the Squadron?"

"There might be no avoiding both," said Jindigar. "The unit was heading toward a concentration of natives' hives."

Viradel challenged, "What danger can a bunch of primitive naties be? We got stunners—"

Krinata answered, "It's not what danger they are to us, it's what danger we, and our stunners, are to them and their culture. We shouldn't be on this world."

"But we're here," said Terab heavily. "Unless we decide to commit suicide, we can't help harming the natives. We just have to do as little damage as possible, because—well, I'm glad we're here, not dead."

Viradel agreed. "We were run off Plinshet 'cause we run a open hostelry—even let in Dushau. We'd be dead now if Jindigar hadn'ta taken us into *Truth*." Krinata would never forget the harrowing rescue in deep space when one of the two refugee ships they'd rescued from Imperial pursuit had blown up. She'd never known she had agoraphobia until she'd lost her moorings and drifted away from the scooter, helpless.

Jindigar drew a dry blanket around himself and sat back

on his haunches. "This is what we know about the natives. They live in multispecies hives in symbiosis with other hives. One of the species binds all the species in the hive into a single group mind, quick, adaptable, intelligent, sometimes centrally controlled, sometimes not.

"Outsiders attacking a native hive are made to perceive hideous distortions of reality, sufficient to scare off any local predator. But offworlders are harder hit, often experiencing a genuine, personal hell.

"Raichmat's Oliat was not so affected, we believe, because we were a group mind. Our civilian staff was severely affected, and so this world is judged uncolonizable, though a hive is not aggressive and won't bother us if we don't attack them. Frey and I believe the Imperials have attacked some hives, and the others in this region are already gathering forces against the intruders. It's only a matter of time, and they'll be forced off Phanphihy."

"Empty-handed?" asked Krinata. "No, our dead bodies are their ticket into the aristocracy of the new Emperor— or at least to the favor of a powerful Duke."

"That's a point," Terab conceded. "Perhaps we can retreat back up the valley, at least until they're convinced we're not *here* and move on."

"That could be a long time," objected Frey, "and to survive the winter, we must be settled—"

"So," said Krinata, "we must convince the Squadron we're not among the hives, then go hide among the hives without getting near any of them." They could do it with a triad, if only she'd whipped Desdinda, but she'd made no progress. "Can the duad lay a false trail for the Imperials?"

"We could do that," offered Storm excitedly. "Lay a cold trail so they'd think we passed this way days ago, heading due south?"

"But it'd tell them we're alive," warned Terab.

"They'll search this plain," said Gibson, hunched over.

"We can't settle with them looking for us," warned Terab. "We must destroy them or send them home appeased. We can't destroy them. So it's got to be trickery."

Krinata spoke, tapping the map. "Suppose we cut due east from here, follow the foot of these hills, skirting the inhabited region, then, if necessary, we can cut through hive territory way beyond where the Imperials turn back." With one finger she described a lazy, swaybacked *Z* on the map. "Then we can come back to our course, southeast. Meanwhile Storm can backtrack up this valley and lay a cold trail leading north. Look," she pled with them, "inevitably their scouts will find trace of us. Letting them think we went the other way will gain us *days*."

Frey agreed but added, "It would be very slow going. The forest is thickest along this edge of the plain, and Jindigar spotted some interesting predators—"

"Yes," said Jindigar, "changing weather patterns have shifted habitats. We'd have to move with extreme care."

Ruff nudged Storm, and the Lehiroh conferred. Then Storm announced, "We support Krinata's plan."

"Now wait a minute," said Gibson, and that started a debate. Jindigar and Frey left, as always uninterested in ephemeral politics. Krinata, impatient with the wrangling she knew would consume most of the night, followed the Dushau out into the rain.

They were pointing their lights at the lashings holding the sleds under a webbing of tarps, to form dry sleeping areas. She watched as they adjusted lines. Jindigar had been more at ease since the waterfall, though Frey had seemed withdrawn. Now, as he worked, Frey spoke in Dushauni, which Krinata had learned on sleep tapes. "I don't see what they're arguing about. Krinata's plan is what we'd suggest."

"They'll adopt it by morning," assured Jindigar. "But

Gibson believes himself the leader and so must convince himself it's his plan, not an aristocrat's decree."

Frey shook his head, puzzled. "You've spent so much time studying ephemerals. You really understand them?"

"No. They're more complex than Dushau because you can't tell the children from the adults. I once met one who seemed near Completion."

Frey seemed amazed but asked, "What got you interested in them? Surely you knew the dangers before you—"

"Before I met Ontarrah? No, I didn't know they could be true friends. When I was Protector of Takora's Oliat, I felt as you do. But after I'd Inverted Takora's and found how people thought of me for it, I became Raichmat's Outreach, so I had to deal with ephemerals again. They didn't know or care what an Invert was. *Then* I met Ontarrah." He tightened a line, grunting, "If people can be wrong about Inverts, maybe they're wrong about ephemerals too?"

"I don't see how. They don't live long enough to become friends. When they die, they just leave you a scar to impede farfetching. They may be good people but not worth that."

"Dushau die too. 'To dam love behind a barrier of fear is to prevent Completion,' or so Shoshunri used to say."

"Love?" Frey looked at his mentor.

Jindigar leaned on a sled's cargo. "Would it shock you if I said I loved Ontarrah?"

"Yes. I'd always thought they maligned you with that."

"Well, I did. But I learned from it. I'll never let that happen again, any more than I'd ever again snatch an Oliat from its Center and Invert it. Neither act Completes."

"Then Krinata doesn't really mean anything to—"

"You said she came up with the best plan. Are you going to throw it away because she's bound to die soon?"

"No, but it's nothing personal."

"Exactly."

Satisfied, Frey ducked into the dry area, and for a moment, as the flap opened, firelight danced over Jindigar's features. He stared after his protégé, his jaunty confidence fading swiftly. *Frey was right, he's fighting a losing battle against liking me, and it terrifies him.*

Long after Jindigar went inside, Krinata stood in the rain, huddled in her cloak, emotions crystallizing with understanding. She should never have followed him to the waterfall. He needed those private moments. Her job was to uproot Desdinda and free Jindigar to go his own way. As she cast herself emotionally into that future, to test it, she found a renewed joy and satisfaction. She remembered the time, as a child, when she'd found a wild bird with a broken wing. She'd mended it, and she'd loved that bird so much, she cried when it was time to loose it. But later, the keen joy of its elation in freedom had been enough.

Later, her mind replayed the overheard conversation, leaving her chasing elusive fragments of memory. *Ontarrah.* Jindigar had often called her that in delirium as if *she* were Ontarrah. Takora—another name he'd mumbled.

Sometime toward dawn she twisted and turned and fought her way free of nightmare, hands clamped over her mouth to stifle sobs as she realized she was fighting Jindigar, and she wanted to kill him. The feeling evaporated as she caught her breath, but it left behind one phrase: "Takora's Oliat."

In the morning she found that the night's debate had yielded the decision to go with her plan, as Jindigar had predicted.

While everyone worked to free the sleds, Storm and Ruff hiked back to plant the false trail. They caught up with the group again while Frey and the two other Lehiroh eradicated every trace of their passage. Jindigar had them walk on leaves in one direction, then turn into a game trail leading east along the trough where the hill joined the forest.

The next day the trail narrowed, and they strung out single file, Frey or Jindigar always off scouting with two of the Lehiroh, leaving three sleds to be tied onto the back of other sleds. It was dangerous, but they had to keep moving.

Krinata had suffered another bad night, this time with nightmares of helplessness. As they settled for their second stop of the afternoon, she saw Jindigar, Storm, and Ruff about to leave the group, saying they'd be back before the rest break was over. On impulse she walked up to them, saying, "I'd like to go with you." *Maybe if I drive myself hard enough, I'll get some real sleep tonight.*

Frey objected, but Jindigar said, "She could carry the tripod, leaving Storm and Ruff both hands for the stunners."

"Tripod?" asked Krinata.

Storm produced a backpack. "To the snooper. Hand-held, it'll only tell us *if* there's energized equipment out there. But on the tripod it can read location too." He held up a hand to Jindigar. "And don't say it! I know the Oliat could do it even better without instruments."

Ruff had the snooper pack on his back, and Storm carried energy cells for the stunners. Jindigar carried the medical supplies. She hefted the tripod. "This is nothing after hauling that double sled." And she slid into the harness, letting Storm adjust the shoulder straps.

As they were about to leave, Gibson came up, looked them over, and asked, "Mind if I come along?"

"This may be dangerous," said Jindigar. "We've had indications of Squadron activity—"

"So it's my job to take a look." Gibson took a stunner.

They followed a game trail through dense undergrowth, using all they'd learned of woodcraft, though it still seemed she and Gibson made all the noise.

Finally Jindigar signaled a halt at the bottom of a rise.

"You can set the snooper up there," he whispered, pointing to the bald top of the hillock. "I expect you'll get a strong reading—but all residual."

Krinata whispered back, "What's out there? Troopers?"

"A hive, maybe. But—I don't like this—" He stared off to the left of the hillock, shook himself, and got Krinata out of her backpack to help the Lehiroh rig the snooper.

Feeling useless as they all climbed the hill, Krinata let her attention wander. Off to one side she saw a smaller game trail that seemed to lead around the hill—perhaps to a view of the plain beyond. Bent over double, she followed the trail. Vicious thorns pulled at her tough clothes, but after a bit she won through to clearer going. Just as she heard Gibson notice she was gone, she came to a wall of vertical stalks.

Parting the stalks, she saw a grassland crossed by a stream that had cut itself a ditch. The ditch was choked with young trees. Not far beyond the trees a column of greasy smoke rose straight into the air.

Twisting to look behind her, she caught a flash of indigo against the rust-and-green forest. She peered out at the plain, looking for the dangers she'd learned about. It seemed peaceful enough, except for the smoke. *If I let Jindigar talk me out of this, I'll feel helpless all day as well as all night!*

As Jindigar, followed by Storm, Ruff, and Gibson, arrived, she wormed through the stalks and headed for the source of the smoke. The others emerged cautiously, Jindigar kneeling to sift pebbles through his hand. Then they came after her. Jindigar caught her by the elbow as she was looking for a place to ford the stream. "It's a hive—destroyed by energy weapons." Intense anguish in his eyes, he warned, "It's ugly, Krinata—"

"I've got to see. We might learn something." Needing to defy his attempt to make decisions for her, she plunged into the gully, waded across, and scrambled up the other side. "Come on!" She pushed through the young trees and, intent only on confronting her fears, saw the hive.

It was smoking rubble, reeking of burning meat. The dome-shaped fieldstone building had been flattened as if by a blow from a giant fist. Smaller stones scattered in a splash pattern across the meadow to her feet. Some of those stones were covered with charred blood. In places the organic mortar had burned. Jindigar arrived and, hand trembling, picked up one of the bloodiest stones and stared at the ruin. Behind them, Gibson gagged, and the Lehiroh spat.

The tunnel entrance was still standing, bodies splashed about it as if they'd been trying to escape—or sally forth to attack. Few of the bodies were intact, and so it was difficult to sort them into species, but by the time Jindigar moved, Krinata had identified three main types. The smallest seemed exoskeletal like the Cassrians. Larger ones were mammalian and furred like the Holot but four-limbed. The tallest and slenderest were very humanoid but white-skinned with dark saucer eyes and tall ears on top of a bald skull.

There were many armored Imperial troopers sprawled about, their armor showing gray or charred where their force-film combat protection had failed. Some had died locked in combat with the furred defenders who wielded only wooden spears and bone or flint knives and hatchets. Had the Imperials set an explosion that killed their own men?

Jindigar rose and croaked hoarsely, "There's someone still alive. . . ."

Storm unlimbered his stunner, knees bent, eyes roving.

Krinata scanned the armored bodies, counting four species of soldier. Which type would they have to care for? "Where?" she asked. Jindigar led them into the tunnel, careful not to step on any of the body parts.

Taking a good hold on her stomach, Krinata followed. Beyond the end of the armored bodies they came to a white form propped against the side of the tunnel, red blood trickling in a branched tree shape across his—definitely his—skull. His chest rose and fell, and another wound in his side bled. He wore only a few ornamented leather straps around his body, with loops perhaps for tools.

Jindigar slid out of his pack and knelt before the native. As he pulled out water and cleansers he said, "I don't think he can hurt us, but be careful."

The native started, murmured, and his dark eyes widened. He shrank back against the wall, trembling weakly. Jindigar put his hands on the native's face and stroked downward. He did it again, then raised the native's hands to his own face. The whimpering lessened.

He permitted Jindigar to wash and bandage his wounds. Then Jindigar said, "This happened early this morning. His internal bleeding has almost stopped. We may be able to save him, but only if we take him with us."

"He'll die of fright," predicted Gibson sourly.

"He'll starve here," countered Krinata. "Imagine what this last day must have been like for him! If we weren't on this planet—this never would have happened to him!"

Jindigar nodded. "The troopers panicked under the hive's defenses. I'm amazed they held together long enough to do this much damage. They must have been drugged."

"Which means," said Gibson, "this has happened before. We've got to move fast—the Squadron will be back for its dead any minute now." He hefted the stunner and went toward the entry. "Come on, we've got to tell the others."

Krinata said, "Jindigar, we can't just leave him! I won't allow it!"

He studied her. "Did you think I intended to?"

Resignedly Ruff announced, "I'll rig a litter." As he

passed Gibson, Krinata heard him mutter, "There's no arguing about it." For once, Gibson seemed to take their advice. He followed Ruff, slinging his gun to give the Lehiroh a hand.

Storm asked, "Jindigar, what can we do with him?"

"When he's recovered, he'll take off into the woods. I just hope he can find a home. I really don't understand the hives well, you know. It might be kindest to kill him."

Storm nodded. "I know, 'If we had an Oliat—'"

"I don't say it that often, do I?" asked Jindigar.

"No," answered Krinata, "but it's in your eyes." She watched the two of them prepare the native to be transported, Jindigar calming the terrified primitive with soothing noises, delicate touches, unjudgmental compassion.

When Ruff brought his litter, rigged from the bamboolike stalks with lashings of supple vine, Krinata and Jindigar carried it. The native was lighter than he looked, but though her shoulders were now strong enough for such burdens, her feet felt painfully squashed, and her hips complained. At thirty-three she was rather old to adjust to one-third more gravity than her home world.

Outside, Gibson had taken a position behind a pile of bodies, scanning the sky to the west. As they emerged, Storm and Ruff with stunners at ready, he rose, beckoning them to hurry. They were no sooner out of the tunnel, however, when Jindigar turned, staring into the sky. Then Krinata heard it—a flyer, coming fast. She was set to run for it, but it was too late. The machine screamed to a hover overhead, the armored shield that protected the pilots drawn back, showing a Lehiroh head and the snout of a blaster. The bay door was also open, a row of armored troopers poised to leap, weapons already blazing.

Jindigar cried, "Down!" and, lowering the stretcher, he threw himself on top of the native, motioning Krinata to do likewise. As she hesitated Gibson went down with a strangled cry, his stunner discharging into the air.

Storm and Ruff loosed stunbolts at the pilots. The stunbolts traced rivers of bright blue through the air with the high-pitched, sizzling crackle of full power. The pair of Outriders fired again, despite Jindigar's sudden shout: "No!"

Krinata wasn't sure what happened next, it was so fast. But later Jindigar explained. The pilot had her hands on the landing controls. When the double beam hit her, her full weight came down on it, and the machine went into a power dive—barely three body lengths from the ground.

It hit and exploded in bright, leaping hot flames that seared Krinata's skin. "Run!" yelled Storm. And he took one side of the litter from Krinata as Ruff hefted Gibson over one shoulder. With Storm yelling "Left! Right!" to keep in step with Jindigar, they plunged across the meadow toward the brook. When the second explosion hit, they were all prone in the water at the bottom of the ditch.

Debris rained down, young trees whipping and splintering above them. Jindigar threw his body over the native's and was pinned by a crashing branch. When Krinata's hearing cleared, the native was whimpering pathetically, eyes squeezed shut, arms and legs wrapped around Jindigar.

Mercifully he soon lost consciousness. When they pried the branch off Jindigar, he was able to stand. But Gibson was dead, chest burned away by the blaster. With only a brief but heartfelt groan of regret, Jindigar turned from the dead human to the living native. "He has central nervous and circulatory systems. Shock could kill him." They hadn't brought blankets. Picking up their packs, they doubled the pace on the way back, Jindigar and Krinata carrying the litter, the Lehiroh taking turns with Gibson's body.

Exhausted, mud-caked clothes chafing everywhere, they threw themselves into the arms of the party Frey brought to meet them. Krinata blessed the duad that allowed Frey to apprehend what had happened and accepted cool water and cold meat while Irnils and the other two Lehiroh hoisted the native to the top of one of the sleds.

"They all died," reported Jindigar to the gathering. "But the Squadron will send another unit after them, so we've got to make good time now. We did learn something. Those troopers were drugged to offset the effects of the hive's mental broadcast. They were extremely fatigued, reaction times down. And it's taken an unconscionable time to get their hospital corps out here. That implies they've taken heavy casualties—and—that flyer's fail-safes didn't work. They are beyond the ends of their supply lines here—no replacement parts. Soon equipment failures and personnel shortages will defeat them if the hives don't."

"Precious little to learn at cost of a man's life," said Viradel bitterly.

"Yes," replied Jindigar. "But if he hadn't drawn their fire, we might all be dead. He was a hero."

That wasn't the way Krinata had seen it, but it was the right thing to say—and it might have been so.

"How can they be having such a hard time," asked Terab, "with all their tech backup, when we've been living off the land and have only been hurt by accidents?"

Frey answered, "We know enough not to steal the last eggs of the bluesnake hive or not to sit on leathergrass because it grows over stingbug hives. We're learning the manners of this world; they don't believe they need manners. The world is teaching them, anyway."

"Very well put," agreed Jindigar. His pride in Frey's brilliance had grown with each day. "But it only leaves us with a moral dilemma. How much damage can we allow the Squadron to do to this world in our name?"

"You sayin' we gotta surrender?" asked Viradel.

"No," said Jindigar, and rose to get the caravan moving.

After the burial that night, while they were all sitting around the cook fire and Jindigar was off tending the native, Adina tried to drag Krinata into the controversy. "Compassion is all very fine, but why didn't you stop Jindigar from picking up that native? You wouldn't have been caught by the Imperials then!"

Krinata retorted, "I suppose you could have just left him there?" But something about the whole thing bothered her. Even though she'd have bullied Jindigar and Gibson to take the native back with them, she seethed at Jindigar for not even thinking to consult her or anyone before deciding.

"I don't know what else you could have done," Terab put in, "but I wish you'd thought of it. It's too late now, though. Anyone want to vote to abandon the waif?" She glanced around, listening to the mumbled negatives.

Shorwh said, "No, but he scares me."

"You probably scare him too," said Irnils.

"Actually," said Jindigar, joining them, "Shorwh would seem more familiar to him than I do. Could I convince you to take a turn nursing him?"

Shorwh looked at Jindigar, stunned. Then, in perfect imitation of Terab's manner, he said, "I'll think about it."

Jindigar took a bowl of stew and sat beside Krinata. Before he ate, though, he surveyed them all. Silence grew as they realized he'd heard Terab's question about voting to abandon the native. "I want you all to realize that if you vote to abandon Chinchee, you'll go on without me."

Into sudden, strained silence Krinata said, "And without me." Storm and his co-husbands added themselves, then Shorwh, Irnils, and Terab joined in.

Viradel bowed her head, but Krinata saw the sullen fire in her eyes. To change the subject, she asked, "Chinchee? You've given him a name?"

"No. He told me his name."

"Might have known Jindigar would start to talk to him!" said Storm. "Jindigar can talk to a babbling brook and understand the answer!"

They all chuckled, and that broke the tension, so when Fenwick said, "We oughta elect a new leader. Charlie would want it that way," it didn't seem like an attack on Jindigar.

Immediately Shorwh piped up, "I nominate Krinata!"

"I decline," said Krinata quickly, but already there was a murmur of agreement among the Holot and the Lehiroh.

"You'd make a good leader!" protested Terab.

"So would you!" retorted Krinata. "I nominate Terab."

The usual furious debate erupted, and before long, Krinata noticed that the Dushau had left. When it was all over, Terab was elected and issued her first order. "Remind me every once in a while, I'm not the Captain here."

Later, Krinata went to volunteer to sit up with the patient and found Jindigar giving a language lesson to the children. Shorwh immediately stood up and volunteered for the same job. Jindigar accepted, asking, "Shorwh, why don't you take the first watch, and then Krinata can relieve you?"

"Agreed," said Shorwh, and climbed onto the sled where Frey was with the native.

Krinata watched him going to confront his fears, wondering what it was about Jindigar that triggered her fears. It wasn't just how he acted without asking, it was the way his "striking" made her feel helpless. That night the nightmares were worse, and she relieved Shorwh early.

The next morning, they were off with the sunrise. Jindigar led the group forward while Frey and the other two Lehiroh explored. Then Jindigar took off with Storm and Ruff while Frey led. During the rests Krinata tended their patient together with whichever Dushau was present. They had a time getting him down to let him eliminate—he wouldn't use a bedpan—and then he fainted and had to be raised by the two Lehiroh and Frey using the litter and a rope.

The next day, the piols befriended the native, bringing him small fish from a nearby brook. At that, the two young Cassrians overcame their fear of Chinchee to ride with him, for he was awake more now, though still weak. He took to the Cassrians as Jindigar had predicted, seeming to understand that they were children and as frightened as he, though he had a harder time grasping that the piols were pets. Soon, however, he was sleeping amid the pile of four small bodies.

Two more days they headed east along the ridge, spotting no energy usage. They almost believed themselves clear of the Imperial penetration zone when Jindigar returned from one foray with the news. "The Squadron is on our trail."

Alarm rippled up and down the line, the mood alternating between panic and despair. "How sure are you?" asked Terab when they'd gathered everyone.

"There's a slight chance we could be mistaken," Jindigar allowed, looking at Frey.

"We have nothing to lose," said Krinata. "Let's turn southeast, across the hive territory, as planned."

They stirred and objected, but in the end the motion carried. Jindigar went scouting as Frey turned them along a streambed. They hiked in the dim shallows, avoiding the water creatures with stingers and poisonous bites, taking care not to disturb the hives of the creatures that were all teeth and stomach. But Krinata, depressed, wondered why they bothered to run. All the harrowing chances, miraculous escapes, and satisfying triumphs that had begun when she rescued Jindigar were about to come to nothing.

At nightfall they broke out of the edge of the woods and made camp. Frey and Jindigar, conferring, added to their map. "We saw troopers here, here, and here," Jindigar said, marking the paper. "We've got to go this way, but there's a large hive here. We don't *think* they have any nocturnal hunters, like some of the other hives, but the duad can't be certain." He looked around grimly. "Do we try to pass them at night? We can't use lightsticks—but there's a moon tonight."

As they discussed it Krinata saw Chinchee peering over the edge of the sled where he rode with the children. He moved more freely now. Krinata was amazed at his swift recovery, for they'd had no real medication for him. She watched his saucer eyes scan them as they argued and finally voted to press on that night.

Jindigar set their course wide of the hive's position, and he and Frey stayed with the caravan to pull the sleds faster. The pace picked up until Krinata's legs ached miserably, and she was sipping from her canteen too often because her throat was dry from panting. Their lives might depend on being well clear of the hive's ground by dawn.

The moon set way off to their right over the grassland. The plain here was composed of long, lazy swells. The rises and the hip-high grass hid all but the top of the hive and a curl of rising smoke. She was falling into the stupor of long-haul endurance when Jindigar called, "Down!"

Out of nowhere a low-flying skimmer screamed by over the distant hive and disappeared over the horizon. There was no place to hide. "It was a remote," called Jindigar, "but they'll send troops if the telemetry reported us."

They moved on, hoping to keep their fight clear of the hive. But they were about even with the bulbous crown of the huge structure when Chinchee scrambled down from the sled and, despite his injuries, ran to Jindigar at the lead sled.

At first Krinata thought the native was offering to help pull the sled faster, scared out of his wits by the flyer. But then she saw him talking to Jindigar, pulling the harness ropes aside toward the hive. Jindigar resisted, straining for a few phrases in the new language.

Finally he called to Terab, "He's offering us refuge in that hive, though I don't know on what authority. I don't think he understands that we've been spotted—but he does connect the flyer with the troopers who destroyed his hive."

"Maybe he thinks the bigger hive is stronger!"

"Maybe," said Jindigar. "Well, do we go?"

"What if the hive attacks us?" asked Viradel.

Krinata answered, "Chinchee understands that the troopers are our enemies. Maybe he can make this hive understand that too. Terab, it's got to be your decision."

Viradel craned her neck to look around her sled at Krinata. Terab said, "Try it."

Krinata curved her course to follow where Chinchee had pulled Jindigar's sled. Success depended on two things: the hive's friendliness and the flyer's either missing them entirely or blaming the recording of sleds on equipment failure when their search of the plain turned up no sleds. With the Inverted triad they could have messed up that recording, and that wouldn't have been attacking the world's biosphere, making it lash back at them.

Resolutely she focused her mind on the hive ahead of them. Chinchee had run confidently up to the tunnel entrance, and Jindigar was only a few paces behind him.

SIX

Hive Refuge

As each of the refugees arrived they struggled to halt the sleds in a semicircle behind Chinchee, who was half swallowed by the dark shadow of the tunnel entry. Moonlight glanced off something within—a door?—and the pale skin of a native. Chinchee was dancing about, gesticulating with both arms and legs, howling and clicking at the dark entry.

Jindigar hunkered down, motioning the others to join him. "To sit is less threatening," he advised, adding, "I think I understand now. Chinchee is an interhive herald, a news bringer, an itinerant diplomat. He doesn't belong to this hive—or any hive—but to the community of hives." Delighted, he added, "This is a very sophisticated society!"

Frey observed, "Perhaps it was fortunate you found him."

"If they turn us away," grumbled Viradel, "you won't say so. We'll a'lost our chance to get away."

"They're closing the door!" exclaimed Krinata, jumping up, one arm raised, poised to dash ahead and plead.

But Chinchee danced back toward them, unmistakable joy in his steps, though one hand held his wounded side, and as he got closer, she could see that he was panting heavily. He dropped down beside Jindigar and began petting the Dushau, crooning much as Jindigar had reassured him when they'd first met.

Krinata suppressed a semihysterical laugh and watched as Jindigar embraced the scrawny native, then pushed him away and hesitantly made sounds. Frey leaned closer, attentive. The three seemed to recede from the presence of the group, enclosed in a bubble of intense privacy.

In a few moments Jindigar stood and announced, "I think he says they're considering the problem. Chinchee told them we're enemies of their enemy. They heard the overflight and know the threat. Chinchee is optimistic, even confident."

Krinata settled to wait and was immediately buried under two furry piols and two young Cassrians who didn't know how hard their shells felt. She endured, trying to comfort them, as she watched Jindigar concentrating on the hive, frequently shaking his head as if to dismiss a phantasm.

"What is it?" asked Frey eventually.

"Nothing," replied Jindigar as Krinata felt the solid stone wall image intensify, protecting the duad, "but did you notice that?"

Frey followed his elder's gesture to the top of the hive. In the glancing rays of the moon, smoke was visible rising from short chimneys—so the natives used fire. Then Krinata saw the rustlebird hive hung from a frame at the top of the dome. Jindigar pulled Frey to his feet, muttering as he pointed out the arc of bare ground surrounding the hive. Frey scooped up a handful of dirt. "I don't believe it! Domesticated rustlebirds?"

"Not domesticated—interhive symbiosis. They use the birds for hunting! This is certainly new!" They studied the situation for a while, then questioned Chinchee, who seemed proud to be a host returning an obligation. Despite his demonstrative body language, Chinchee had a mature dignity. On reflection Krinata decided the natives were nothing like the Rashions Jindigar had compared them to. They were far more intelligent. But what would they be like, kidnapped and forced to live as individuals?

She knew the debilitating effects loss of culture had on social beings. Such individuals could be easily brainwashed, easily enslaved. Raichmat's Oliat had probably been right about this world—any Duke who got his hands on it would have used these natives or exterminated them.

Her sour cynicism was interrupted by the opening of the door to the tunnel. A delegation emerged, and she got her first look at the other hive species. Alive, the small, cara-paced ones did resemble miniature Cassrians. They walked on two limbs, using the other two as arms, though their hands weren't as dextrous as a Cassrian's. They moved in quick bursts and then froze to observe.

The medium-size furred ones went on all fours, but as they straightened, she saw each forearm branched into a hand, carried curled under the body, and a paw with re-tractable claws. As these swarmed from the mouth of the hive she detected a well-drilled order among them and was unsurprised to see that they all held spears and hatchets in their hands.

Among a complement of the white-skins like Chinchee she saw a new species. Broad but not as tall as the whites, these seemed to be clothed in thin plates, glittering like fish scales but loose like feathers, yet rustling as they moved. Perhaps they were evolved from the rustlebirds?

They seemed to be approaching in full ceremony, so she climbed to her feet as Chinchee rushed out to do push-ups on the ground before the rustlebirdmen.

Jindigar promptly took two running steps and fell down to do push-ups beside Chinchee. Frey motioned everyone else to do the same in place. *You're kidding!* thought Krin-ata, but she followed suit as the others did. Her form was rotten and did not improve when the children, intimidated by the aliens, climbed onto her back. When the ceremony was over, Shorwh offered to take one of his brothers, but the child clung to Krinata. So she hefted him onto her shoulder and hoped this wouldn't take long.

It didn't. After a brief exchange the tallest rustlebirdman

surveyed their trail-weary group and then came right to Krinata. Her breath caught in her throat until she realized that he was after the children. Then her fatigue vanished in a burst of protectiveness.

Her body must have shown it, for the rustleman stopped at a distance and said something. Chinchee came forward and called to the children in Cassrian whistleclicks. The older of the two children held out his arms to the native herald, and Shorwh said, "No!" and whistled piercingly.

Frey came over and hunkered down beside Shorwh. "Don't be afraid. They're friendly—and curious."

With Shorwh calmed down, Krinata let the youngster go to Chinchee, who presented him to the rustleman. After holding him and petting him, the rustleman seemed puzzled—as if an expectation were not fulfilled. He was showing a tinge of hostility when Jindigar made broad semaphoring motions and danced about, humming. Chinchee repeated that with more grace and style, adding polychromatic tones to the song.

After some negotiation the rustleman handed Jindigar the child and turned to lead them inside. Chinchee hooted and danced around proudly, then sat down suddenly, one hand on his side. Jindigar stooped to examine him and then had the Lehiroh help the native back onto the top of a sled.

Krinata didn't think the sleds would fit through the door without unloading the top course of crates. But the Lehiroh examined the door and approved it while the furred ones spread out behind them to herd them into the hive.

One at a time, Frey pulling the lead sled, they squeezed into the tunnel, which was much larger inside where the floor dropped a step. A few sled lengths into darkness Frey called sharply, "Halt!"

Krinata, adept with the controls now, came to a stop at the lip of a ramp leading steeply down into a hole. The planking that normally covered the hole was drawn aside.

Light, possibly from an open fire below, silhouetted Frey's sled, which was stuck.

Jindigar came up from the rear to survey the problem while natives chittered and danced about. As they pondered, a team of furred warriors attacked the sled, pushing it down the ramp, ignoring the loud scraping of the top against an overhead beam and the shower of dirt that resulted.

Krinata squelched all thought of being buried alive and hauled her sled onto the ramp. Its cargo, being more dense, wasn't quite as high and didn't scrape.

The tunnel led down into a dimly lit chamber from which other tunnels opened, but they were too small for the sleds. They grouped the sleds on the beaten earth floor covered with rushes. The air was fetid, hot enough to make Krinata sweat, and ripe enough to choke on.

A few rustlemen examined the visitors and the sleds with the bright-eyed air of university scholars presented with confirmation of a hypothesis. Only a few furred and chitined ones stayed with them, while the white-skins played host, though their manners weren't exactly interstellar standard. Their first priority seemed to be to undress their visitors.

Jindigar and Frey complied unhesitatingly. The scholars examined their unmarred chests and lack of visible genitalia with approval, or perhaps recognition. Jindigar reciprocated, running his hands through the rustleman's scale-feathers, then petting them back into place. The rustleman petted Jindigar in return, then eyed Krinata.

"Oh, no!"

"Calmly," admonished Jindigar. "They see us as a hive-swarm made of different creatures than theirs. As long as they understand us as a variant on the familiar, they won't hurt us. Only—" He looked at the Cassrian children. "They're disappointed our group mind didn't embrace theirs in ceremony. And—there's something odd—"

Viradel cut him off with a contemptuous comment on Krinata's modesty and disrobed, urging the others to comply. Krinata stripped, then gritted her teeth, closed her eyes, suppressed the memory of nearly being gang-raped before the Emperor's court—and the image of Desdinda being led off to be raped by the Emperor in private—and waited for the rustleman's touch. It came only as a whisper of air against her breast and again at her crotch hairs. She shuddered.

"He understands this discomforts you and apologizes," said Jindigar. "You can get dressed now."

But at that moment the attack began.

Alarm ripped through the hive, furred warriors scrambling through the central chamber. Then there was a low hum and a whump that shook the air. Chinchee crumpled, screaming in shock. He'd seen one hive destroyed starting just this way and had barely overcome the horror. She moved to comfort him—then the fire went out.

Jindigar's voice cut over the general racket. "They've closed the ventilation channels and extinguished all fires. The furred ones are preparing a sortie, and the shelled ones— yes, that's it, the shelled ones control the mind grouping! They're calling the hive to defend—"

That was the last Krinata heard, for everyone began screaming. The children, who had gravitated to her when darkness fell, now squirmed and kicked with their sharp chitin-edged hands, forcing Krinata to let them go. She stood, sweeping her arms about, calling, "Shorwh! Find your brothers! Shorwh!" She nudged a piol with her foot, and it bit her shoe, howled, and scratched at her bare leg.

A sudden image flashed across her eyes—a wild beast eating her leg while she still lived. Revolted, she kicked free and ran, smashed into a sled's cargo, slid around it, and ran into the dark, smashing at whatever touched her.

It was one of her worst nightmares come true. Images screamed into her mind, seared her inner vision, and she couldn't elude them by running. It became harder to move. Panting, retching, she dragged herself along. Somewhere aside from the chaos in her mind, she felt cold air on her face, laced with the stench of burning machinery.

Scrubbing at her eyes, she peered through the mental images, as if fighting off a drug, seeing double, swallowing panic, and finding reality more horrible than nightmare. She lay prone at the head of the down ramp. Beyond, the door closing the entry tunnel had been smashed, and from outside came a dazzling blue-white light. Against this, Imperial troops advanced into the hive, their armor protected by thin-film energy fields, clothing them in shimmering rainbows, brighter than the light.

But these marvels of technology were not winning. Rustlebirds swooped in the tunnel, dropping their corrosive excrement on the intruders. After several direct hits the armor field shorted out in a plume of sparks, leaving the gray surface exposed to the corrosive, which quickly ate through to flesh beneath.

Such victims were writhing and screaming on the floor when Krinata first saw them. As she watched, their comrades broke ranks and turned their weapons on each other. The tunnel became an inferno from which she began to retreat.

A trooper fell close to her, wrenching off his helmet, which had been eaten through. She was riveted in place.

Before her lay Desdinda, face twisted in madness—unmistakable in her hatred. *No. It's a hallucination.*

The knowledge didn't help, even when another tortured, dead trooper turned into Desdinda before her eyes and seemed to rise, an animated corpse closing on her. *No!*

In panic, she lost control, and the images roiling at the bottom of her mind swamped her reason. She was surrounded by Desdinda, chased by Desdinda, possessed by Desdinda, and worse yet, Desdinda was perfectly correct.

How could she have missed this obvious truth? She ran, blinded by the searing light, into blackest dark, pursued by grotesque horror, and became the very horror that pursued her. *No!* part of her screamed, but was swamped by the power of focused nightmare made real.

Then, before her loomed the huge indigo shadow-form she knew so well. He thought he was such a righteous priest of Aliom, but he was just a dirty Invert. That hadn't mattered until he tricked Grisnilter into surrendering his Archive to him. Now she knew he was out to destroy the Dushau species.

Jindigar! Madman! Predator! Fiend!

For all that was good and clean in life, for her children and their children, she attacked, willing to expend her life, her very existence, to remove this ultimate threat. Enraged, she fought with all her strength.

But all of her strength was as nothing before his might. He held her at bay easily, toying with her. She was no threat to him. She was helpless in his grasp.

Helpless. Falling helpless into void. Desdinda's snarling face spun before her eyes, an ethereal mask depicting the gutted ruin of a soul, a reflection of her own visage. She clawed at her face. *It's not me! Not me!* The helplessness! The helplessness! *I hate it!*

Krinata squirmed and turned to beat at the Desdinda image, bent on destroying it, but feeling every blow on her own face and body—as if she were both of them.

"Krinata!" Jindigar's voice.

A spear of bright sanity lanced through her. Her eyes saw Jindigar standing before her, clutching her arms in his big hands, holding her bloody fingernails away from herself. His bulging eyes were glistening in the white floodlights from behind her. His lips were moving, but it was a while until she heard his words, as if his voice came from light-years away. "Form in triad with us! It's the hive doing this to you. Form with us! They won't touch another group-mind!"

She fought that seductive lure, knowing he meant only to destroy. Then she thrust aside that absurdity and reached for the fulfillment of triad. *Oh, yes, it's been so long!*

The familiar triune consciousness blossomed, and for a moment, the multiple images of Desdinda, whirling about her head and chattering in madness, faded away.

Peripherally she felt Frey shivering under multiple stresses, Jindigar calming him, while the war was fought in the tunnel, the troopers still pouring in from the carriers landing outside, the ferocious attack on the rustlebird hive, the birds in the tunnel being slaughtered. She felt other hives mobilizing around them, large carnivores, small insects, marching in the unnaturally lit darkness to an ally's aid. "Jindigar, we've got to help the hive!"

"We can't—"

"Traitor!" Desdinda rose. "We can too!" Sick to death of helplessness, ignoring Frey's keening wail of pain, she possessed the triad and Inverted.

Frey screamed, voice and mind echoing hollowly as she used him to channel the power of her imagination against the Imperials, visualizing their armor losing power, becoming ashen gray, useless against their own weapons' energy splashing wantonly about the tunnel.

Krinata, no! Jindigar shattered her focus. Again he'd rendered her helpless. How could you strike back at some-one who gutted you of all power over your own life? You could only hate—and deny. *This isn't me. It's Desdinda!*

Frey's ragged, tortured scream seared through her mind and body, flowers of his pain blossoming within like sonic bombs. *I can't, I can't! Let me go! I can't!* But she couldn't let him go. His scream lasted forever, and when it was over, there was only blackness. Void. Falling. Out of control. Beyond help. Hopeless. Dissolution/death.

Down and down, world spinning into blurring nightmare, she tumbled out of control, clinging to Jindigar, pursued by a tall black scouring funnel of a tornado vortex, Desdinda's face formed out of its angry whorls and knots. Flinging her arms and legs out, grabbing at the insubstantial blackness, at Jindigar, she was unable to slow or deflect them.

The whirlwind took them. It stretched their bodies to a transparent blur, wrapping them around and around its own core, smearing them until their substance mixed and became Desdinda. They'd been triad, one had died, and still they were triad. Mad, warped, dying amid Jindigar's terrified screams. "No! Oh, no! I can't. No! I won't!"

She came to, snug and warm, cozy, happy, safe in the infirmary bed Arlai always allotted to her aboard *Truth*. So many times now she'd succeeded in saving Jindigar's life but nearly killed herself, and Arlai healed her. Those were always the best times, and she looked forward to it now.

Lazing back into dream, she found herself in a hive nursery snoozing amid a pile of other infants—a hard carapace digging into her back, powderpuff fur against her cheek, soft rustleplates tickling her toes. Her skin was stark white against the nest pebbles. Young as she was, she was already roaming through the hive, peeping through the eyes of her fellow crafters, watching the rustlemen trying to teach mind-gatherers to coordinate warriors in battle lust.

The freedom to wander the hive, be a rustleman producing mortar to repair a wall, or be a warrior training hard to defeat onnoolloo, or hunt bloodmeat for the young, be a mind-gatherer learning to sing mindtunes, or spur the mothers to procreation, was such luxury. She'd become a herald and share this with every hive. One wasn't enough for her. So she'd have to endure the long, lonely treks between hives. But it would be worth it.

Her attention was grabbed by her trainer, a rustlemother who held the Whole Memory. If she was to herald, she must absorb the Whole Memory of her hive first. It would be hard. What came naturally to rustles was agony to whites—but rustles couldn't herald. It was her bred-for duty.

Steeling herself, she reached for the Whole Memory.

Her mind stretched like a flexible ship-to-ship access tube inflated in space and about to burst. She looked down that long tunnel to infinity. Terrified, she searched through the walls and found only infinity massed with stars that swirled as if a tornado wind had scooped them up. And she was falling—into infinity.

Twice in space she'd felt this; the first time in a perfectly safe access tunnel, the second in a malfunctioning spacesuit cut loose from its safety cable. The terror had become a phobia, and now it paralyzed her mind and body.

And there was Jindigar. She grabbed, and they slammed into one another. Suddenly there was the hive, and there was herself, and they weren't the same thing anymore. This was the hive's tunnel, its history painted on its sides in morality plays, murals, and craft diagrams. It lanced Jindigar with terror, and she could not see why, except that the hive memory stretched back eons—perhaps as long as Jindigar had lived.

Images flew by, history blurring, incomprehensible as seen through an eternal mind that wasn't an individual. They passed juncture after juncture where new hives had swarmed off older ones. They spun around the walls, marveling at the images of Dushau and others exploring their world. Jindigar rode this corkscrew toboggan chute, perceptions

squeezed tight against it all, muscles locked, mind paralyzed
in the hard clutch of denial.

Now we're all helpless! How do you like it, Invert!

The Desdinda voice, mixed sonorously with Krinata's,
brought Jindigar's eyes open. She shouted into their paralyzed minds, *You'll never win! I'll never let you win!*

With a thrust Desdinda propelled them head over heels
into a cavernous void. Infinitely deep. But where the tunnel
had been walled with shallow murals, or chained concepts
of a linear group memory, here an *n*-dimensional space
archived events, Dushau ideas, Dushau problems, incomprehensible Dushau solutions. Events jammed on top of
ideas, within problems, overlapping solutions, integrating
other events, associated, interpenetrating, twisting, crazed
with reference lines, broken into shapes, transforming,
churning, tilting, compacted into a tesseract, then folded
around yet another dimension, wrapped around with walls
to contain and shape it, isolated from personal memory by
a great, gaping void.

In panic she flailed about for something familiar—

—and she landed on *Ephemeral Truth,* Arlai's Dushau
simulacrum bowing graciously before her Outreach. "Takora's Oliat is most welcome and will be properly served."

Jindigar was standing behind her, in the Office of Protector of her Oliat, but Arlai knew better than to speak to
him while the Oliat was balanced. In fact, his ship was so
beautifully designed, she was going to order a copy made
for herself. Perhaps she'd name it *Eternal Truth*. Yes, that
was a good name. She could travel now that her Oliat career
was ended by successfully Centering.

When they arrived at Dushaun, Arlai obligingly tendered
a copy of *Truth*'s plans, but by then she knew she was
terminally ill. It began with weakness in the limbs and

spread to a weakness of the mind—blurring memory, inability to reason without being caught by reminiscences, and a loosening grip on the Oliat. She'd experienced four Renewals and knew that, though she was in pre-Renewal instability, this was not normal.

It hadn't been until Dushaun was in their scopes that Arlai's tests isolated the problem—senile dementia. An organism she'd fought off on their last planetfall had altered her metabolism beyond repair.

Her last memory was the hospital bed, her Oliat about her, Grisnilter hovering in the background to retrieve her memories for his Archive. All her Officers were in Renewal, even young Jindigar, so earnest in his priesthood, so inquisitive and easy to delight, a point of bright, burning enthusiasm that could light her days through Renewal, if only she could make him understand that's what she wanted. But, though she knew she'd fascinated him, it often seemed everyone else did too. He was so undiscriminating. But she could live with that for one Renewal—it'd be his fourth. He should mature quite a bit.

A bright new thought occurred to her, and she couldn't understand why it hadn't come before. *It's time to Dissolve this Oliat.* If any of them were actually in Renewal, Dissolving now could kill someone. *Why have I waited so long?*

Yet, as the thought formed, it drifted away into the blurring daze of no-time that gripped her. With a little puff of despair she knew she was drawing them all with her into premature death—helpless to Dissolve. *Grisnilter was right. I shouldn't have tried the Oliat.*

She had no strength to impart this insight before it drifted away. Darkness encroached. She stopped breathing. Her chest ached, but it was too hard to draw air. They couldn't prevent themselves dying with her. *Dissolution/death, a bottomless void.*

She felt Jindigar's panicked sense of helplessness as on-rushing darkness swallowed them all. Without warning his strength flooded upward, wrenching, ripping the Oliat from her grasp, relegating her to Protector. A twist, and he Inverted the entire Oliat. Spinning, bruised, stunned, personally violated, she watched as he shifted to another Office and Dissolved. It was a desperate scramble for life that left them all pummeled, bruised, mindblood oozing from every thought, cutting her loose to drift alone into nothing.

Krinata/Takora felt his hands on her face, wet with her tears, cold as death. He was lying half on top of her, a gray armored body pinning his legs as he'd protected her. She felt no stir of breath in him. Her hair stank, blaster-singed where her scalp hurt. Behind her eyes, occluding the shadowed scene around her, Desdinda's features shimmered, a grotesque mask of hate.

Jindigar's panic in the moment of Takora-death saturated her nerves, the same feeling as when she/Krinata had stolen the triad from Jindigar's control and Inverted to help the hive fight the Troopers. She'd meant only to save innocent lives as he had saved her Oliat, helpless through no fault of their own.

Jindigar had said it. *My decisions limit your options; your decisions limit mine.* Grisnilter had wanted him—*and Takora*—to avoid that. Each renders the other helpless.

A hard knotted ball of emotions inside her melted away, leaving relaxation where she hadn't known there was tension. She was consumed with a vast sorrow that she hadn't had the fortitude to Dissolve her Oliat properly so they wouldn't die with her. Knowing her guilt and her weakness, she forgave him and became him, the walls of identity blurred beyond repair. Tears flowed softly from her eyes, and her breath came in little spurts halfway between laughter and sobs. Before Krinata's eyes the visage of Desdinda evaporated to mist, swirling away into limbo. Gladly Krinata followed Takora into dissolution/death, sure her life was over.

There was cool air on her naked skin. The pink dawn tinged the grayness. The beaten earth was tufted with grass under her bare back. Her legs lay across cold, dew-damp, napped skin. Ignoring the searing throb in her head, she pulled herself up to look. In the gray dimness of predawn she saw Jindigar's slack face, felt his toneless muscles, frigid skin, utter stillness where there should be breath, and remembered accepting his death—and her own—but was that a memory of a dream or a memory of reality?

Mind swimming, she was mildly surprised to find her skin to be pale white and almost hairless, her hands too small, her vision too limited. But she was also Krinata Zavaronne, sitting naked on a ravaged battlefield amid a hostile plain, staring at the body of the one she valued most in life.

Her future rang with emptiness, the present hollow and black. A sharp cleaver had divided her life into before and after Jindigar, and from the cut end flowed all the warmth, spirit, laughter, and tears that gave life true meaning.

She knew now why she'd rescued him, throwing away career and even life itself, to keep him from the Emperor's hands. And she'd do it again, in a second. But it was too late.

Her heart opened up, ruptured with the pressure of emotions that choked her. *Oh, Jindigar, I forgive you for everything you never told me. Raichmat's did right, protecting this world. I'd have done the same. I'd never have understood before—*

Paralyzed with flooding memory of the horrors the hive had evoked, she sat over Jindigar, transfixed by images, unable to blame the natives for what they'd done. It was a while before she realized it was only memory—devoid of emotional impact. Desdinda's face was just as horrible as ever, but not horrifying. She felt only a great sorrow for a valiant woman who'd died for what she believed in, which only added to the intolerable grief at loss of Jindigar.

Her diaphragm unknotted and heaved, squeezing a great sob out of her wide-open throat. She didn't recognize the groaning voice as her own, even when it came again and again. She knew only that *this* was Dushau grief for that which will never be again. She had been riven in two by loss of a part of herself. There could be no healing, for no scar could fill the rift. She needed the mercy of death.

His eyelids fluttered.

Shock throttled a sob half spent in her throat. She grabbed his shoulders, shaking him. "Jindigar!"

There was no further response, and she could find no pulse. She put her ear over his nose and thought she felt the slightest movement, the barest warmth. *He could be dying in shock!* It was the first time she'd noticed the predawn chill that had turned her own flesh to cold putty.

She swallowed panic and looked around. *A sleeping bag! Where?* Her impulse was to start tearing at the tarps that covered the sleds scattered about. She hadn't stowed the gear, had no idea what was where. *Storm!*

She staggered to her feet, shaking from suppressing frantic haste. The sleds were scattered amid broken flyers and dead troopers, the refugees slumped here and there like discarded toys. *How'd the natives get the sleds out of there?*

She dragged herself to her feet, touching the two naked Holot, Irnils and Terab. She noted they were alive with the detachment of the Dushau for an ephemeral. Something inside her would always see as a Dushau now. She didn't know who she was, or what was real, what mere phantasm or nightmare. But Jindigar's life depended on her.

She found Frey's body. *Not all a dream!* Had she killed him, seizing the triad? Had that really happened? She was too drained to grieve again. Beyond him were two amorphous lumps, odd amid the armored bodies, discarded energy weapons, and debris of crashed flyers. *Must be Lehiroh.*

Weaving and lurching, she made it to them and found the piols curled up between the bodies—a strange human male and an emaciated Dushau female. She knew the Dushau—she'd glimpsed her in the triad, when Jindigar had tried to read the sandstorm, and had found them the dry wash and the cave. Her image had set Jindigar's face glowing.

An irrational pang of jealousy seized her, and she turned to search for Storm. Suddenly Rita and Imp raced past her, chittering and squealing. Following, she saw Storm picking himself up near a sled. Weakness banished by adrenalin, she ran to him, shouting, "Storm—where are the sleeping bags? Jindigar's in shock!"

By the time she reached the Lehiroh, he had focused on her, and trained reflex had taken over. He surveyed the field, picked a sled, and attacked the lashings, saying, "Give a hand!" Then he climbed up and began heaving down piles of warm bedding and clothing.

Krinata dragged two fleecy bags to Jindigar, rolled him onto one and covered him with the other, folded double, and was about to climb in to warm him with what little body heat she had when a strange voice behind her asked, in awed wonderment, "That's Jindigar?"

She gasped, whirled, and blurted, "Who're you?"

"Cyrus Benwilliam-Kulain, Senior Outrider to Avelor's. Are you Jindigar's Outrider? Do you have any inidran?"

She shook her head. "What's inidran?" The stranger had a mop of sandy curls standing out in spikes around his head and was clad, as the rest of them, only in smudges and grime. Her head was barely shoulder-high on him. She looked up into a craggy, weathered face with a high forehead, aquiline nose, and an engaging smile that now mixed disappointment with a kind of stunned admiration that embarrassed her. She dared not let her gaze fall below his chest for fear of discovering the physical evidence confirming the meaning of that look.

"Did you say, 'inidran'?" asked Storm behind her, coming up to examine her scalp burn and to spray it with salve.

She gestured, holding her head still. "There's a Dushau woman over there. We need an extra sleeping—" Her flailing hand hit chill Dushau nap. She jerked her head around and discovered she'd hit the emaciated Dushau woman in the face as, body shaking with weakness, she crept up to bend over Jindigar, eyes wide in pure astonishment.

"Jindigar? It *was* you! Jindigar!" The look of sensuous rapture on her starved features turned to bottomless terror as she felt his cold flesh.

Cyrus bent to take her hand away, saying, "Darllanyu, you shouldn't be up!"

SEVEN

Darllanyu

"He's not dead!" exclaimed Darllanyu, and then looked beyond the hive to where the sun rose, a slice of new moon barely visible against the mauve sky. "Darllanyu!"

"Yes, I said 'inidran,'" repeated Cyrus to Storm.

"I don't need inidran, Cy," she insisted. "Look, the sun's rising darllanyu."

They all inspected the east, as she added, with equal parts hope and determination, "I was born at darllanyu—" At their incomprehension she elaborated. "—when the sun rises coupled to a new moon. Dushaun has two moons, like Phanphihy, but even so, such moments are rare enough to be regarded as omens—which even an Oliat can't interpret."

Cyrus muttered to Storm, "Inidran."

Storm nodded and turned to go. "Probably do Jindigar some good too. Krinata, did you know Frey's dead?"

She nodded, swallowing back a little choking cough at the reminder, trying not to feel the stinging pain of that death echoing out of the confused depths of memory.

"No, not inidran," muttered Darllanyu, pulling aside a fold to put an ear to Jindigar's chest. "This isn't just Oliat Dissolution shock. What happened to him?"

Krinata recited the pertinent facts with a clinical detachment she didn't feel. Cyrus listened with growing amazement but kept silent. When she'd finished, Darllanyu shook her head, the fear back on her face. "Then I'd say he's lost

121

in the Archive. Inidran won't do any good." She sent Storm in search of other medications that might help.

Cyrus glanced at the Dushau woman doubtfully, then went with Storm. Krinata asked her, "You're an Oliat Officer?"

Darllanyu settled weakly on the edge of the sleeping bag. "I was Outreach to Avelor's, but we lost three, and now Avelor, so we're just a triad." Imp came and curled up on her knees. She cuddled him. "You're a warm creature."

"I'll get us some clothes," said Krinata.

She found Terab soothing the children, and two Lehiroh helping Irnils with the medical supplies. Viradel, Adina, and Fenwick were breaking out rations. As she scrounged an outfit for Darllanyu, she heard Cyrus asking Storm, "You mean you brought all this across that desert with only a duad?"

"Jindigar's the best," bragged Storm. "And Frey, his protégé, was brilliant."

"Must have been," agreed Cyrus, taking the medication for Darllanyu. Krinata gave him the outfit for her, saying, "Go ahead, I'll bring some food."

He nodded. "The natives fed us, but their diet—" He shook his head, added a smile of gratitude, and left.

With increasing anxiety as day advanced, they dressed and ate, expecting the Squadron to return for their dead any moment now. Then they reassembled the caravan, Cy pitching right in. The Lehiroh—who never mixed with any of the others—accepted him instantly. He worked without a spoken direction, tossing and catching things like a member of their team. He even helped dig Frey's grave.

Krinata's tears flowed freely. Frey had never let her get close, but he'd have made a good friend. *Did I kill him? His death had probably trapped Jindigar. *Frey never did anything to deserve this! And neither did Jindigar!*

She didn't remember everything and didn't understand much of what she thought had happened. On the way back to the sleds after the scant moments of the burial, she told Darllanyu, "This may have been my fault," and recited Jindigar's warnings about Frey's condition.

"I'm sure Jindigar wouldn't allow you to accept all the responsibility. You responded as anyone might have." Dark Dushau eyes came to focus on Krinata. "I've felt the hive's attack too. I couldn't have done better than you did." They parted, but Krinata found Darllanyu directing a puzzled stare at her at odd moments as they formed up to march.

The Lehiroh set the course along the line Jindigar had held, but Darllanyu came to the lead sled and corrected the heading. "Our settlement is that way, ten days' march— maybe fifteen or twenty with this caravan."

"There're more people on this world?" asked Storm.

"Friends and associates of Raichmat's zunre," answered Cy. "Didn't Jindigar—"

"He never said others were already here!"

Krinata suddenly knew what had given Jindigar hope but left him doubting his own senses. "He must have contacted Avelor's Oliat from back in the desert!" Frey had thought he was trapped in the Archive, babbling about the dawn.

Darllanyu added, "Yes, we saw him—that's why we came out here, looking for you."

Storm said, "We'll be trailed by the Squadron. We can't lead them to the settlement!"

"Everyone there is waiting for us," argued Darllanyu. "Cy and I must bring Jindigar there, even if you choose another course."

Terab had arrived to hear part of the discussion. "We can't stand here arguing," she decreed. "For now, we head for this settlement. What's between here and there?"

"A river gorge and a grassland. Large herbivores," said Cy, "and predators to match. Dozens of kinds of hives, some scavengers." He ran a hand through his hair. "It's going to be fun getting the sleds across the gorge."

"Storm's a good rigger," said Ruff. "You any good?"

"The best. You got semis and half-blocks?"

"Yes," said Storm. "Maybe Jindigar will be able to help by then." They had him secured atop the sled that carried the children and piols, for none of the medications had done any good. Darllanyu had concocted a syrupy mixture from ration bars, which they'd managed to get him to swallow a spoonful at a time. It'd keep him alive—maybe.

Darllanyu answered, "Jindigar can't help himself. But there's a Historian at the settlement who might retrieve him—and save the Archive—if we get there quickly enough."

Krinata went back to her sled, which had the extra sled tied on behind, determined not to be the one to slow them up. If there was help for Jindigar anywhere, she'd get him there if she had to carry him on her back. But no sooner had Storm called, "for'd" than someone in the rear yelled, "No! Halt!"

One of the sleds had risen to travel height with one corner dragging. The Lehiroh adjusted it so the corner came clear of the ground and awarded it to Cy, in the position next to Krinata's tandem rig. Though he limped, Cy didn't complain about the hard pace the Lehiroh set. They were racing from the Squadron as well as to save Jindigar.

As the sun arced up into a cloud-studded sky, Krinata caught Cy's barely repressed grimace of pain and said, "Talking takes my mind off my aching feet." And she told him her theory of why Jindigar hadn't mentioned contacting them. "I'm sure he didn't expect anyone to come out after us."

"We've done it before. Avelor's knew there was a group here, but from that distance they couldn't figure who or how many. And they didn't know about the Squadron when they decided to send us out. Why are they chasing you?"

She confessed she'd fired the shot that had destroyed the Imperial yacht and Emperor Zinzik too.

After he got over that he commented, as if she'd confessed to petty larceny, "I guess the Squadron's not going to give up, then."

"Are you still sure you want to bring us to your camp?"

"You're not going to survive on this world without an Oliat—" He broke off. "Which we don't have anymore, but a tetrad will have to do—that is, if they can save Jindigar and he can mesh in with them."

She didn't dare think about that now. "How did the others die?"

"Ambush. We had a detachment from the Oliat—the Outreach, Emulator, Protector, Formulator, and five Outriders. Should have been enough, but native warriors, the furry ones, found us by the river gorge. Our Emulator had found a contact method Darllanyu was trying, but more of their warriors arrived, and they took us prisoner."

"I don't think you can communicate with the furry warriors. Jindigar called the white-skin we found a 'herald,' and I think they're the only ones who talk outside the hive," said Krinata, and then had to relate that story.

"You're probably right. But we didn't know that, and when the warriors got rough with our Emulator and Formulator, of course my crew moved in to do our job. They took it wrong and speared one of my women and—well, to be fair, I don't think they realized the Dushau were noncombatants, and they killed the Emulator, which paralyzed the others, so we couldn't get away. They had us trussed up and carried off before we knew what was happening. Two of my guards were killed at the river. They were the lucky ones.

"When they got us to their hive, before the Dushau could recover from Dissolution shock, the little shelled ones stung us. Powerful drug. I don't remember much but—I think my men killed each other. I never saw the Formulator or the Protector again. At least Darllanyu survived." He glanced at her sideways, his feeling for Darllanyu clear. "I guess I can't refer to her as Outreach anymore." He shook his head. "I've never lost a charge before."

The pain of that confession brought silence between them. At the first rest stop he joined the Lehiroh in their incessant checking of the equipment.

They were out of sight of the hive now, but they'd left a trail through the grass. Terab called them together for a conference, introducing Darllanyu as part of a triad.

The Dushau said, "Sometime tonight—tomorrow morning at the latest—there'll be a strong storm crossing through here. It should obliterate our trail from orbital reconnaissance. The farther we can go before the storm hits, the better chance we have of eluding the Squadron."

The rest of the day became one of those blurs of sheer endurance that had punctuated their lives since they'd left *Truth*. Only a few incidents stood out clearly.

Darllanyu, during their next break, tended Jindigar, murmuring in Dushauni, probably expecting that no one else here understood. "You'll be all right. I'll see to it." But Krinata heard the desperation in her voice. "You'll balance us, and when the work is done, there'll be time— together."

She means in Renewal, thought Krinata, feelings mixed.

Cy and Darllanyu munched extra ration bars as they went, trying to make up for their long starvation while promising good foraging ahead. But despite their weakened condition, they pushed the pace uncomfortably. When rotation of loads put Krinata beside Adina, she answered everything Krinata said with a complaint about the pace or Jindigar's bad judgment in getting involved with Chinchee. "He deserved what he got!" Krinata held her tongue, refusing to defend Jindigar where no defense was needed, and she passed the time probing into her own mind as one might tongue a sore spot in the mouth.

There was an aching hole where she'd become accustomed to Desdinda's rage. Her whole body felt relaxed and at peace, despite scrapes, bruises, and the scalp burn. But there was also something else. Every thought, every perception seemed tinged with a thought pattern she recognized as Takora—as if she halfway shared those memories. When she thought of Jindigar, it was as a tall, gangling youth of surprising energy and innocence, restlessly seeking, constantly testing his convictions.

Krinata had never been awed by Jindigar's nearly seven thousand years' seniority on her, but neither had she felt affectionately amused by him. Reluctantly she decided she'd traded Desdinda's ghost for Takora's. Exorcising Desdinda had been such a disaster, she couldn't think of throwing Takora out. Besides, she seemed benevolent. Ignored, perhaps she'd eventually fade away.

It was well after full dark when they camped. While hauling water to bathe Jindigar, she overheard a comment Adina made to Cy. "Our Lady Zavaronne never spoke a word to me all afternoon. Because she's in with Jindigar, she thinks she's too good to associate with common humans!"

"*Lady* Zavaronne!" But he swept that aside, asking, "What do you mean, 'in with Jindigar'?"

Adina and Viradel related their highly colored version of Krinata's adventures with the triad. Krinata had few compunctions about eavesdropping on shameless gossips, but listening to herself being painted as an interspecies whore hurt. She'd have no friends if they spread such things around the settlement. But she couldn't worry about that now. Jindigar was still catatonic and had to be carefully tended if he was going to survive.

It started to rain exactly when Darllanyu had predicted, but by then they had rigged tarps over the sleds and set a shielded smoke hole for a cook fire because they all needed hot food and a warm place to sleep. Krinata bedded the children down, with sedatives to ease the nightmares, then she signed up for the third watch, her favorite, because nightmares usually struck just at dawn.

She was asleep before she'd completely sealed her sleeping bag. She woke with two piols struggling to get inside to share her warmth. The fire had burned low.

Darllanyu was sitting next to it, feeding it twigs, while beside her, Cy roasted a chunk of meat on a stick, trying to argue her into going back to sleep. Krinata turned over, trying to block out the low voices.

As Cy ate his snack they fell to discussing the multicolony. It seemed Cy knew all about the conspiracy and approved of it. "So you say there's a chance Ambassador Trinarvil may still turn up to balance the Oliat?"

"She intended to but had to return to Dushaun first. If she can get away, she'll bring as many as she can—but Zinzik had Dushaun blockaded when we left. Trinarvil may be dead by now."

After a silence Cy asked, "Am I being too intrusive? I mean, it seemed like you wanted to talk—"

"I do. Jindigar—I never told you we were first mates. We had no children. That's typical of a first Renewal, you know. I last saw him at the birth of his first daughter. We agreed—to try again someday." She threw a stick into the fire. "But I don't know if he can work with Trinarvil now, or she with him. Or with me, for that matter. It's tricky—with both of us so close to Renewal."

She's close to Renewal too? This was completely different from overhearing Adina maligning her. This was private. Krinata extracted herself from bedroll and piols, pulled on jacket and boots, and went to check on Jindigar before joining them at the fire. Cy offered her a chunk of meat, and Darllanyu moved aside to make a place for her on the soft pile of grass. Even thus welcomed, Krinata couldn't meet Cy's gaze for thinking of Adina's words.

She knew he believed the worst when he offered to take a turn around the perimeter—out in the rain. When he'd gone, Darllanyu prompted, "Tell me more of what Jindigar had you doing in triad. He's known as a thorough trainer—"

"Oh, he never intended—" She cut off, assembled her thoughts in defense of Jindigar, and related how he'd used her talent to escape the Emperor's brig. "So, you see, we figured we'd all be killed in the attempt, but we couldn't just sit there and let the Emperor use us to force Jindigar to confess that all Dushau were conspirators in treason!"

"He used you in an *Inverted* triad!" She shook her head, astonishment turning to acceptance. "I admit I'm dismayed, but one learns to expect that where Jindigar's involved. Tell me, how did you feel when you discovered that the Emperor's accusation against Dushau was partly true?"

"Betrayed," she said truthfully, then explained about the Desdinda Loop. "It was mostly *her* attitude and seems to be gone now. You'd only withheld one planet, not dozens, and I think the report was correct—the natives make this place uncolonizable. Better the Dukes never get their hands on these natives!" She looked at the Dushau woman in a new light. Frey had not wanted to know anything about how an ephemeral felt. "May I ask a personal question?"

"Certainly, though I might not answer."

"Are you Invert too?"

She chuckled. "I see why Jindigar likes you!" Sobering, she added, "Jindigar's *survival* indicates he hasn't abused Inversion—though if he dies now, it'd seem otherwise. I respect him for that, but I'd rather have nothing to do with Inversion or, no offense, ephemerals."

"No offense. I'm beginning to see it's not healthy for Dushau to associate too closely with ephemerals." *Or perhaps vice versa!* But she noted Darllanyu's phrase, "with Inversion," not "Inverts." Was she being tolerant because she wanted Jindigar as a mate this Renewal? Krinata turned as Cy, cloak dripping, reaming water off his face, came back to the fire, and Darllanyu asked, "All secure?"

"Every line's tight. No sign of prowling animals."

"Nor likely to be," said Darllanyu. Thunder growled in the distance. "But there could be tornadoes," she added.

"Should I wake everyone?" asked Cy.

Darllanyu seemed to consider, eyes unfocused, communing in triad with her zunre at the settlement. Then, rising, she shook her head. "Not yet. The worst of the disturbance is over the Squadron's base camp. We should be in the clear, at least for a while. I'm going to sleep." She went to where Jindigar lay cocooned among extra bedrolls and, after checking on him, slid into her own sleeping bag, fending off the two restless piols, and seemed to be instantly asleep.

"It's almost my watch," said Krinata, intently feeding the fire. "Why don't you go get some sleep too?"

"What's the matter? Have I offended you?"

"I only offered to take part of your watch. Is that unfriendly?"

He settled at the fire, countering, "It's noble."

"What's that supposed to mean?" she asked defensively.

He stood again and gave a courtly bow. "May I introduce myself again, more correctly. Cyrus Benwilliam Lord Kulain." He sat again. "I inherited the title when my two older brothers died mysteriously after refusing to institute some of the Emperor's harsher edicts, but I don't use it because it puts people off. I prefer being just Senior Outrider."

"I'm just a Programming Ecologist. But Zinzik ruined everything, resurrecting the old titles."

He glanced toward the Dushau. "Jindigar's a Prince, isn't he? That's what they have against you two."

"They?" she asked, automatically pretending not to know who he meant. Then she had to confess what she'd heard Adina telling him. "But they know Jindigar's only—a friend."

"He sounds like the kind of friend I'd like to have."

They talked on for a while, Krinata relieved at his attitude, then checked on the lashings as the wind picked up, and on Jindigar, whose condition remained unchanged. Then Cyrus went to sleep, telling her, "Watch that west guyline."

She tended the fire and made rounds, pausing at intervals to stare out at the dark sky etched with the branched trees of lightning that grew, hung for a moment, and flickered to darkness again. She saw it with Takora's eyes, a symbol of life's energies flowing into manifestation driven by such power that it could scorch and burn if not guided to ground by the trained will.

As she repeatedly lashed down flaps of tarp loosened by the wind, she peeked out again and again, ever more drawn by Takora's view of the lightning. It was as vital as being caught up in the triad, offering insights for which her whole being hungered. An Oliat was a group bound by the agreement to *observe* reality, to discover how everything connected to everything else. But they knew, however penetrating their perception, that they could not possibly grasp it all.

To Invert an Oliat, or a subform, and use that imperfect understanding to act directly on the fabric of reality was to risk doing more damage than the group could possibly repair. That was why Inversion so terrified Dushau; it was like reaching out to grasp a lightning flash with bare hands.

If, however, that imperfect understanding was used to guide hand tools to affect environment, it was possible to correct accidental imbalances with other hand tools, to survive and learn from mistakes.

Either hand or mind was controlled by the trained will. Part of that training was to select goals and find where and how to apply the will to achieve those ends.

Peeking between tarps, face drenched in cold rain, she consumed each lightning flash, hypnotized, seduced by promise of further understanding. Mind blanked, worded thoughts silenced, she understood why an Oliat didn't have to Invert to deflect tornadoes or any disaster. The tight, knotted storms that were striking all around them were as much a part of the fabric of nature as they, themselves, were. They had only to perceive their correct place, and be there, and the storms would miss them.

A phrase floated into her consciousness and hung, as if written in advertiser's glowgas: Efficacious Helplessness. That was an Oliat goal: to observe the proper place to be, and be there. But if you were wrong and disaster rolled over you, you couldn't mend things, as Desdinda had tried, by striking back in fury at that which was in its correct place when you were not.

All the Aliom disciplines were aimed at perceiving what was connected to what, what caused what, so one could know one's niche in the scheme. Knowing, one could "strike"—act, as Jindigar said, without thinking—and be right. She'd done it, so some deep part of her knew, but only inadvertently, in fragmented moments of unthinking reaction. What would it be like to know constantly?

An indeterminate time later she noticed that the lightning had stopped, and she was staring into opaque blackness. Even the rain and wind had stopped, leaving the night freakishly silent. Exalted vision fading, she felt silly. Mopping her face dry, she built up the fire to reheat some soup. Every sound she made echoed against the quiet blanketing the land.

She'd only finished half her soup when a sudden gust hit the tarps like a solid blow. Startled, she dropped the cup in the fire and yelped as the scalding liquid burned her hand. But before she could even be sorry for waking people, the wind redoubled its efforts to demolish their shelter. There was an increasing roar, like fate approaching on the winds of eternity, accompanied by lightning sizzle-crack strikes ever nearer them. In moments the children were yelling, the piols running around, and everyone was fighting to hold the shelter together.

Darllanyu announced calmly, "There's a tornado touching down west of us—we think it will miss us."

Cyrus kicked dirt over the fire while Storm broke out the lightsticks. They couldn't risk anyone being blown into the fire and hurt.

A fist-size hailstone fell through the smoke hole and sputtered in the embers. The tarps bounced, and one mooring broke, the two Holot using their weight to tie down the loose flap. Frightened, all trace of her transcendent insights gone, Krinata went to tuck another sleeping bag around Jindigar, against the suddenly frigid wind. His body was still flaccid, his breathing barely perceptible.

Darllanyu called from where she was coaxing the children to huddle under a pile of bedding, "It's going to be close!"

At any moment the tornado could lift the sleds and smash the camp, dispersing their pitiful physical selves to a thin film over the plain. *Did the triad call this one correctly?*

Then she couldn't think at all. The tornado roared down on them. The world turned into a shuddering, moaning monster, pelting them with debris, ripping one of the tarps. She thought they were all doomed as she ran to help Fenwick hold a sled that was sliding toward the fire.

Suddenly, over the low-pitched roar, there was a loud crack, like an explosion. *What? Not lightning...* Turning, she saw the pile of cargo that formed the wall behind Jindigar sliding inward, tilting toward the ground where he lay, no longer restrained by the guyline. She tore across the camp, but Darllanyu was there first, her emaciated body not having the strength to budge Jindigar.

Krinata grabbed a hunk of bedding and put her whole weight into it, and he began to slide—but not fast enough. She scrambled around to dislodge his shoulders and push while Darllanyu pulled, knowing the crates were going to hit before they were clear. "Faster!"

With one supreme lunge she shoved Jindigar's head clear and fell prone. And Cyrus was there, astride her hips as he belayed the collapsing wall of crates. "Crawl!" he commanded, wet clothes plastered to bulging muscles.

She wormed forward, and Darllanyu grabbed her hands and pulled, scraping her chest raw against the ground. "Clear!"

She never saw how he did it, but Cy jumped free, letting the crates smash down behind him.

And then there was total silence. An odd smell permeated the air—turned earth, pulverized vegetation, dead animals splattered against their shelter, and the fear odors of their several species. Krinata lay where she was, panting, her heart pounding, sobbing her relief shamelessly. The funnel had missed them, and they'd all survived.

EIGHT

Multicolony

Nine days later they arrived at the river gorge. The tall, rusty grass of the plain gave way near the river to a shorter dark green grass, dotted with scrub and tall trees. Backpacks and equipment were scattered where the settlement's expedition had been ambushed. A few broken native spears lay among the well-scoured bones of the offworlders. An insect hive rose in a hump off to their right, and Krinata could not suppress the image of ants carrying away lumps of flesh.

Darllanyu's grief was reignited at the gruesome scene, so it was Cyrus who gathered the Dushau bones and organized a hasty grave-digging detail, saying, "The hive's hunters found us here once. We don't dare camp on this side tonight."

By the time the graves had been spoken over and well disguised from snoopers, the Lehiroh had rigged two parallel cables across the gorge, with a third cable strung above them. The river below was swollen to a raging torrent at this, the narrowest spot.

Everyone pitched in to unload one of the sleds, and then Cyrus rode it out onto the cables, which fit like rails under each side of the sled, the third cable being used to pull the rig across. First they used the empty sled to transport half the people, including Jindigar, then they unloaded the malfunctioning sled and placed it atop the other one. With Cy handling the controls of the bad sled and Darllanyu sprawled where she could reach those on the good sled, Storm pulled them across.

He brought the good sled back, and they began tediously ferrying cargo across, cautious in the erratic springtime winds scouring the gorge. They finished just before sunset, and Cy brought one sled back to get Krinata while the others made camp. She admitted to herself that she'd volunteered to stay behind because the crossing frightened her.

"Hop on," called Cy to Krinata as he steadied the sled. At her hesitation he jumped back to solid ground and took her hand. There was no solicitousness in the gesture, nor even courtesy. He was just professional and might have done the same for one of the Lehiroh who could have walked across on the bare cable in a high wind.

His attitude toward her had changed markedly since the tornado. He seemed to consider her an Outrider of rank equal to his own. There was no hint of sexual innuendo, either, for that was strictly forbidden to Outriders on duty. She took his hand and tried to seem as courageous and skilled as he expected her to be.

Numbed by hours of hard labor, she was too tired to battle the agoraphobia that struck the moment her foot was over open air. In her mind, being suspended like this was no different from falling into the limitless void of space. Cy rigged the safety line around her waist to a line fixed to the sled. There was no way she could fall off, and if the sled should capsize, she could jettison the safety line with a flick of a finger over the grommet and let the sled tumble into the water or sail off into the air, while she clung to the cable by her hands.

But if all three cables should break? The picture leapt to her mind, intense, vivid with the power of fear, which she fought down only by remembering that Jindigar was on the other side and there was no time to waste getting him to the settlement. Fear clutched at her throat, and terror mounted as Cy and Storm moved the sled out over the abyss. It rocked and swayed under them, the cables giving with each move.

I've got to look down. This can't go on.

She forced her eyes to look ahead, then off to the side. The white cables, the gleaming sled, the white, churning rapids beneath them, the brown, russet, gold, and dark green grasses on each side of the gorge came to her as dual perception—her own, and the now familiar Takora, to whom it wasn't at all threatening. She cloaked herself in that calm, and forced herself to look down at the frothy torrent.

Suddenly, with a loud snap, one of the cable moorings came loose, and in graceful slow motion its cable subsided into the gorge. The sled tipped and wobbled, its mechanism feeling for the correct height above the ever-shifting water's surface. Cy scrambled to the edge controls and lay prone to make an adjustment while Storm worked at the front end.

Krinata clung to her safety line, paralyzed by phobic terror. There was nothing holding them up. Nothing!

"Krinata, I said grab those rear controls and level that end." It was Cy, yelling over the roar.

I can't! She twisted in place, looking at the control box. The platform tilted, and her hands clamped onto the safety harness with new strength.

"Hurry!" urged Cy, not even looking at her.

I've got to. Only this time she wasn't reacting to protect Jindigar, all fears held in abeyance. Nightmare terror froze her in place as death loomed. Refusing to give up, she struggled against the terror, reaching toward the control box at the very edge of the platform.

Gradually her muscles began to cooperate, and she slid along her safety tether, her hands closing on the controls. Her eyes slid past the control box to the frothing water below, but her hands moved steadily over the controls they knew intimately from so many emergencies, night and day. As the sled righted and began to move again, she breathed easier. The stark terror gave way to mere trembling, which dissolved to ordinary fear. And by the time they'd reached the safety of the bank, even that was gone.

She realized the terror she'd felt this time hadn't been the phobic panic at all but only the fear of panic. The phobia itself was gone. She hadn't had a falling nightmare since she'd banished the Desdinda Loop. Nor had she, since the tornado, wanted to reach for Darllanyu's triad and Invert just because she was afraid.

Happy, but shaking in adrenalin reaction, Krinata stepped off the sled to be greeted by Terab and Viradel.

"Nice work there!" complimented Terab, then, oblivious to Krinata's pale face and trembling hands, said, "Cy, do what you can to retrieve these lines. Storm, Darllanyu's finished with Jindigar and ready to go foraging. Krinata, help dig the latrine pit, then join the firewood detail."

Krinata wiped her clammy palms on her trousers, nodded, and went to find a pit-digger. She hadn't pulled latrine detail before, and it never occurred to her to argue. It was only an hour later when she was hauling a sack of degradant to the pit, that she saw Viradel looking at her—thoughtful rather than gloating at an aristocrat doing the dirty work.

It was after dark when Krinata brought in her last load of firewood, on a rack Cy had built from bent stems. She was carrying almost half her weight and had to have Shorwh unload her as he did the other gatherers. But Viradel was watching, again with a neutral expression, considering.

Supper was root soup, and roast bird, on edible leaf plates. As tired as she was, she didn't dare sit very long before she went to wash her hair, then tend Jindigar as she did every evening, often quietly reciting her adventures of the day, hoping to lure him back to reality.

Once, Darllanyu had found her slumped into a doze over the unchanging body and had asked, sympathetically, "Why do you sit here? He doesn't know—"

"I think he does. And—I'd hate myself if I gave up." Then she'd confessed that she'd heard Darllanyu talking to him. "Why do you do it?"

"Guilt, I suppose," admitted the Dushau. "We shouldn't have been ambushed—we should've made friends with that hive before you got there. When an Oliat fails—not that we were so much of an Oliat..."

"Don't be too harsh on yourself. As Jindigar says, if your decisions limit our options, ours limit yours. There were any number of things we might have done differently."

"So he *was* teaching you!"

"I wouldn't call it that." *But*—she thought at Jindigar— *if you recover, maybe we can renegotiate?* She hardly noticed Darllanyu's parting glance, weighing her. She was busy taming the wild hope thundering in her breast. She'd whipped Desdinda. If Jindigar survived, maybe...

In the following days Darllanyu accepted Krinata's vigils at Jindigar's side, and between them and the Lehiroh, somebody was always with him. Even so, he developed sores, and the skin seemed loose over his giant frame. His teeth faded to a chalk white, and the normally springy nap of his skin became limp and unpleasant to the touch.

On the other side of the river they found themselves in the neighborhood of the settlement. Here the rolling hills flattened, dotted with clumps of a new kind of short tree, clinging to the banks of the numerous streams. And they saw the first of the gargantuan herbivores—about as large as a land animal could be under this gravity and seeming larger by casting an illusion of size. They roamed the plain in groups structured like a hive, symbiotic to stationary hives.

They moved in groups of a hundred or more, munching

the tops of trees, females with nursing calves at the center of the herd. But Darllanyu explained, "They return to their habitat at night, carrying food for those who don't forage. The calves are not borne by the ones suckling them but by bearers who stay in the habitat with others who defend it. The habitat isn't a constructed dwelling, just a portion of land. And they migrate with the seasons, almost never returning to the same locale the next year."

The Dushau advised their party to stay well clear of the herds, as they seemed restless, and the triad distrusted them. Once or twice they saw members of different species traveling with large herds, and Cy remarked how unusual that was. Darllanyu said, "We think this's the echo of the Squadron's activities. Ever since their camp was hit by the tornadoes, the Squadron has become more vicious—destroying hives of all sorts. These creatures are forming alliances, preparing to fight a common enemy headed in this direction."

"But they're just beasts!" objected Fenwick.

"Yes," agreed Darllanyu. "Beasts of Phanphihy."

One midday they came across another kind of oversize herbivore, a single shaggy brown animal. The caravan stopped, for the loner was being stalked by a pack of wolf-like creatures. Darllanyu narrated the stalking ritual with the detachment of a naturalist shepherding tourists, the flatness of her voice showing that she spoke for the triad as she ended, "Those hunters could turn on us if they don't get their prey, and we *don't* want to attract the attention of this growing network of hives."

Settling her sled into place, Krinata climbed up to quiet the children, who clung to her more now. They were riding with Jindigar, keeping the piols from inadvertently smothering him. No sooner had she topped the edge of the cargo than Imp tore loose from the Cassrians and ran down to the

ground. Before anyone could act, the piol had dashed head-
long into the stalkers' pack, screaming dementedly.

Krinata was sure that in moments there'd be nothing but
shredded piol fur where Imp had been. But the stunned
creatures eyed the mad furball and broke ranks. In moments
the hunters had disappeared, the grass waving in their wake.
Imp scrambled up the herbivore's shaggy brown pelt and
perched atop its flat head, chattering for all he was worth,
as if trying to steer it away from them.

"Wait right here!" Krinata commanded the Cassrians.

She climbed down and ran to the front of the caravan
where Darllanyu and Cy watched the performance. As she
came up Cy was asking, "What made him do that?"

Darllanyu said, "There's one possibility—" And she
pushed past Krinata to head for the sleds.

Krinata asked, "How are we going to get him back?"

"Good question," said Cy. "I'm not going out there. I've
seen those things squash critters bigger than I am."

Cy had not had his life saved by the piol, nor did he
know how Jindigar could be revived by the small beast's
loving. "Well, then, I'll go!" said Krinata, tucking her shirt
into her trousers as she breasted the tall grass.

Cy started after her. "No! I—"

Krinata was halfway to the beast when the herbivore
tossed his head, causing Imp to clutch with sharp fishing
claws. Enraged by the pain, the huge creature roared,
stomped, then reared back on squatting hind legs, two cloven
hooves pawing the air. As Krinata tried to retreat, a front
hoof caught her on the side of the head, and she went down.

Shouting, Cy distracted the beast from its intent to pound
her to death. Through the ringing in her ears and the roaring
beast, she heard Darllanyu call, "Cy, Rita's pregnant! Imp's
protecting her!"

And then everything receded into blackness.

* * *

"Krinata!" Terab's voice, furry Holot hands and face.

She came to in a bedroll, camp fire lighting their usual shelter, bandages around her head. The huge herbivore was gone, and she thought she'd dreamed it until she remembered it had clobbered her with a hoof. "Imp? Is he all right?"

"Of course," scoffed Terab. "He's indestructible. But you're not. Had to carry you all afternoon. Irnils!" she bellowed to her mate. "Bring Krinata some soup."

Remarkably, after that and a double dose of medicine she was able to get to the latrine, and the next morning, despite a crashing headache, she pulled her sled, though not the tandem rig. She was determined that her stupidity wasn't going to delay getting Jindigar to the help he needed. They had told her how Darllanyu had gotten Rita to call Imp back, and then the herbivore had simply left. She hoped she'd learned her lesson. *Next time trust the triad!*

Oddly, in the next couple of days, she saw Adina and Viradel watching her, not at all contemptuous, though she'd made a fool of herself. She didn't understand those people.

On the seventeenth day after the hive they came to the cliff overlooking the settlement. A strange sense of déjà vu haunted Krinata as she surveyed her new home. They were standing near a rope-and-board elevator rigged at the edge of the cliff, and below them the settlement spread out between the base of the cliff and a broad, winding river. Up on the cliff edge, far to their right, Dushau and ephemerals were constructing something near a waterfall.

Darllanyu pointed to the waterfall. "Our power station. The water wheel is going already, down below. We'll have our generators in before winter, but we've shut down all ship's power until the Squadron leaves." She gestured to their left where, in the shadow of the cliff, metal hulls gleamed.

Across from where the waterfall spilled into the river, there was a gravel mine. Roads had been laid out around groups of buildings and out to distant plowed fields. All around, crews of Dushau and ephemerals were graveling the roads, building, hauling, plowing. To their right a large log stockade shaped like a tilted parallelogram surrounded some log buildings, mostly still under construction. All those within the stockade were Dushau.

Darllanyu pointed out the two largest buildings within the stockade, the Aliom and Historians' temples, saying, "We've had to exclude ephemerals already because some of us have been thrown into Renewal by the repeated shocks of the last year." Then she identified the clay mine on the far side of the river, downstream from the gravel pit. "It's not the best grade, but it will do for a while." On one beach at the edge of the river, a kiln was rising. Beyond a cluster of foundations for houses and barns was a corral where local animals were being trained to pull wagons, and already some teams of beasts were dragging logs in from the stand of tall trees beyond the river.

There had to be at least a thousand people working below them. Krinata asked, "How many Dushau altogether?"

"Four hundred thirteen," answered Darllanyu.

"Humans?"

"Over two hundred. Cassrians, Holot, and Lehiroh account for several hundred more."

Before Krinata could ask about children, they were spotted, and a group of humans and Holot gathered. They harnessed a beast to a horizontal wheel and pulley to power the elevator. Once down at the settlement's level, Krinata, like everyone else, was caught up in the exuberance of a warm greeting. She saw the Cassrian children welcomed by a Cassrian couple, the children thrilled by the unbridled curiosity of others of their own species.

Krinata was drawn into a group of six human young women fussing over her scrapes and bruises, insisting she be seen by their physician. As she was swept away from Jindigar, she looked back and saw Darllanyu accompanying his litter toward the Dushau compound, two other Dushau clustering about them.

She smothered an urge to break away and run to Jindigar, knowing she'd be barred from the private compound, and with good reason. But her mind refused to focus on those welcoming her to the unattached women's house.

They'd built their house larger than a family cabin, and as yet it lacked glazing in the windows, interior walls, and furniture, though they had indoor water taps and would soon have toilets.

"We have to haul the water into the cistern on the roof, but we can have a warm shower when the sun's up. Wait until we get the solar heaters made and the power pumps in!"

As they regaled her with their plans they insisted she shower. Then the doctor arrived. She was a middle-aged woman with a dark chocolate complexion and bright black eyes that saw everything in a flicker. Her hair was cropped painfully short and clung to her head tightly. She wore the same tough cord trousers and tunic as everyone else but with the effortless elegance of the born aristocrat. Poised and unruffled, she examined Krinata without instruments, then corroborated her findings with field sensors. "Practicing against the day when these are gone. Even though they're Dushau manufacture, they'll wear out someday!"

The results tallied, and the doctor announced, "You're one lucky woman indeed. No concussion, no broken bones, no permanent internal injuries. You'll be fine as soon as the bruises heal." She rebandaged Krinata's head and left a locally grown herb potion for pain. "Our pharmaceuticals won't last long, so we'd best get used to these."

Krinata surveyed her body as she dressed in the clean clothes the women provided. Leaner than she'd ever been, she had muscles she'd never have believed before, and the exposed skin areas were incredibly dark compared to her untanned skin. She was no office worker anymore.

The other women had gone back to work, but the cook, an older woman who reminded Krinata of her mother, insisted she eat a hot meal—native foods, but cooked with familiar spices. She couldn't enjoy it, though, her mind plagued with thoughts of the risks Darllanyu might be taking right now to save Jindigar. She was gnawing on a fruit when there was a sound at the door, which stood open in the heat of the day.

A male Dushau voice asked, "Is Krinata Zavaronne here?"

"Who may I say is asking?" inquired the cook, trying to sound like an important servant of a Lady.

Krinata, recognizing Dushau tones, went to the door, heart pounding in sudden anxiety. *He's not dead!*

The Dushau replied, "My name is Zannesu, and I've come with a message from Darllanyu."

"I'm Krinata Zavaronne."

"Darllanyu requests your presence."

"Jindigar! Is he—"

"When I left, he was alive. Darllanyu wishes you to understand that you will not be welcomed by all but that your presence is necessary."

Krinata handed the half-eaten fruit to the cook, mumbling, "Thank you—I'll be back," and plunged out into the afternoon sun, taking the trail toward the Dushau compound before her escort could show her the way.

After the brief taste of acceptance the human women had

shown her, Krinata was doubly chilled by the stares she gathered as Zannesu took her through the gate of the Dushau stockade. Evidently her involvement with the triad had quickly become common knowledge, for everyone they passed—road crews, wagon drivers, loggers, carpenters, miners, fishers and hunters—stopped to inspect her with the curious apprehension usually reserved for a new species.

They entered the stockade at the acute angle of the parallelogram closest to the clusters of dwellings of the ephemerals. There was no actual closable gate. Instead, two walls curved out to embrace each other creating an S-shaped, open portal that blocked all view of the interior. Beyond the portal, walls were being built out from the stockade walls to form an inner chamber. Here foundations of stalls—perhaps a market or visitors' area—were being laid.

All the workers were Dushau, young and old, male and female. She spotted several Dushau races with distinctive features or mottled coloring. As Zannesu led her through the inner walls, a murmur followed them. She felt a chill of unwelcome she knew wasn't Dushau hauteur but rational fear.

Dushau entering Renewal were not emotionally stable. Even Dushau children under a thousand years old were not permitted to travel off-planet because they, too, were not to be trusted to deal rationally with ephemerals. Only after first Renewal could they earn passports by meeting stringent requirements. Krinata walked close to Zannesu, keeping her eyes down, determined not to offend anyone, no matter what.

They came out in the wide area of the central compound, where already there were foundations of another pair of interlocking walls built out from the oblique corners to divide the main compound in half.

Zannesu took her elbow firmly. "With your permission, Lady Zavaronne, we must go quickly through here to Aliom."

She yielded, lengthening stride as they turned into a graveled path among long buildings and cabins with closed courtyards. They had the same steeply pitched roofs as the ephemerals' cabins, but the walls rarely formed right angles, most windows were round or oblong, and doors were concealed. Small gardens had been tilled, but only tiny brown shoots had broken the russet surface. In one building a skylight was being installed—the first glass she'd seen.

At her question Zannesu explained, without slackening pace, "The first attempt to make glass produced very low-grade material. We've found a better sand now, so the next batch should be good enough for windows. This must be accomplished before winter."

"Are the glaziers Dushau?" asked Krinata.

"Some are. We've gathered here artisans in every trade. That's why Jindigar's so important to us, for he'll be our greatest expert on Sentient computers, as well as our Active Priest to form a new Oliat—if he survives. With an Oliat we might achieve the industrial base for orbital flight in a thousand years, and Sentient computers within fifteen hundred—by the time the new galactic government discovers us."

Krinata couldn't help contrasting this with the women's ambitions for a water heater and power pump to fill the cisterns. The Dushau perspective was dizzying, yet familiar. For the first time in days Takora was with her, quietly, without fuss, making this alien community seem like home.

They emerged into an open court circled by a cultivated area where Dushau were transplanting saplings that would, in the blink of an eye, perhaps only a few centuries, grow into a circular wall of trees shading the two buildings within.

Two large buildings, virtually identical, faced one another. Each was half-roofed, a pile of shake shingles beside the longest wall. Zannesu took her to a front entry of one building while the gardeners peered at her unhappily.

There was scaffolding over the entry they took, and a craftsman was carving words beneath a replica of the lightning flash over the portal. Krinata was a slow reader in Dushauni but had seen that particular quote before.

SIXTH OBSERVATION OF SHOSHUNRI

Fidelity is the most demanding Law of Nature, thus the most highly rewarded.

From: *Purpose and Method*
by: Shoshunri,
Observing Priest of Aliom

Now she knew Shoshunri's title meant he had once been an Oliat Center. Her eyes lingered on the quotation, as if Takora felt it was important.

As she followed Zannesu between the overlapping walls of the entryway, it suddenly dawned on her. Jindigar had never, ever been loyal to the Emperor, the Empire, or his friends, as she had always thought. He strove for a higher virtue, fidelity. It explained so many of his contradictory actions; he kept his oaths, regardless of how he'd misjudged a situation. He'd abandoned the Emperor only after the Emperor had broken fealty. If she knew all the Aliom oaths a priest took, she'd have understood his reticence.

With that insight came a deeper one. Aliom rejected Inversion because it was resorted to when one had lost the fidelity between one's internal model of the universe and the external, objective reality, and thus could not find one's place in the overall pattern. After having misjudged the pattern, a person was tempted to Invert to correct that mistake by forcing the pattern to conform to their presence.

If fidelity was a law of nature, then Inversion was a breaking of that law, *unless* one's internal model of reality had absolute fidelity, and one was in fact *in* the proper place—and the pattern had become distorted. One might then Invert to restore the pattern expecting to survive it, as Jindigar had.

She rounded the last curve into the Aliom temple, desperate for time to think, but about two dozen Dushau were looking at her. They sat on the floor in a circle, most holding strange Dushau musical instruments. Jindigar's whule reserved a place just before Krinata. Beyond the circle, where the roof was still open and sunlight shafted down between uncovered rafters, a huge carving that would eventually be the Oliat symbol, the X supported at the crux by an arrow, stood half-finished. Piles of construction debris had been swept aside to clear the floor.

In the center of the Dushau's circle under the finished roof, there was a fireplace and chimney of smooth river stones. Despite the warmth of the day a fire burned in the center of the raised hearth. She saw Jindigar lying on his side under a thermal blanket, surrounded by Darllanyu and several others.

"Jindigar!" she gasped, and dashed to him, heedless of protocol. Kneeling, she took his hands, which were clenched to his chest, and felt the tremors shaking him, as bad as when Desdinda had died. She glanced around at Zannesu and accused, "You didn't tell me he was like this!"

A male who sat opposite the door stood and said in Dushauni, "You see, she's not stable enough to attempt duad-grieving. This is no time for dangerous experiments with ephemerals. I can't permit this. That's my final judgment."

Krinata understood him and the general murmur of agreement from the others but was certain he didn't know it. She fought the splash of cold needles that prickled her skin at the vision of Jindigar dying, because his peers rejected him—because of her. Then she blinked aside a dizzying sense of déjà vu, more Takora's than her own, though it seldom seemed that Takora was really a different person anymore.

Darllanyu put her hand over Krinata's and searched her eyes, whispering, "What is he worth to you?"

"My life," she answered without hesitation. "Tell me what to do!"

Darllanyu squeezed the human hand with soft, napped fingers, rose, and faced the others. "You have the right to refuse to risk your lives for the community Raichmat's zunre have started here. Perhaps you can constitute an Oliat without me or Jindigar, but it could hardly be more than a heptad subform!"

"Even properly grieved and freed of the Archive, Jindigar would still be an Invert," answered the leader. "Who here is willing to balance with an Invert Archivist?"

Someone challenged, "Jindigar's no Archivist." The man came around the circle to confront Darllanyu. "That was settled when I tapped Grisnilter's Seal and discovered it had been breached. We all know what Jindigar is and what he's done. He should be allowed to go to dissolution/death without taking anyone else with him."

Darllanyu replied, "Your own grief for Frey colors your feelings, if not your skills, Threntisn."

"You will leave my son out of this! I'm Senior Historian here, and—"

Not Frey's father! The Historian Darllanyu had expected to lift the Archive from Jindigar was Frey's father.

"You're in first grief," countered Darllanyu. "You're forgiven. Perhaps you truly can't do anything for Jindigar."

"Darllanyu." It was the leader. "He *is* Senior."

Another man rose to stand beside the leader, who seemed to be about to walk out. "Threntisn is right. If we try this, we could all be lost in the Archive—and with an ephemeral, there's hardly any chance of success."

One of the darker indigo, thus older, women scoffed, "Who told you pioneering would be safe! Ephemerals have been doing it for millennia, without complaining of the risks. What are you, a bunch of duomorphs? Can't you see we need Jindigar?" Her eyes stopped on Krinata, and she shifted languages. "Do you know what the dangers are? What it could be like to be lost in such a large Archive?"

"Not exactly, but I'm willing to risk my life—which is not the same," she granted, "as you risking yours." Under questioning she told them all she remembered of her last brush with the Archive, the banishing of the Desdinda Loop, ending, "And I died with Takora—I really thought I was dead until I woke up." —*and found Jindigar dead.* "I'm still not sure what was real and what wasn't. I'm not sure how Frey died."

"We'll have to go through that with Jindigar," added Darllanyu. "Find out exactly how Frey died."

Find out that I killed him? She swallowed and knew she'd do even that public penance to revive Jindigar. *Will they label me zunre-killer and shun us both?*

Darllanyu cut through a general dissension, saying, "Jindigar is in crisis. Krinata came to help him, even though she doesn't need to grieve Frey to survive this. I won't let her stand alone! I'll grieve with them!"

Krinata was sure Jindigar's tremors were increasing, his whole nervous system in chaos. She pled with one of those still kneeling beside him. "Can't you do something?"

"He's had all the medication we dare use. At least it stopped the convulsions."

Zannesu came across to Darllanyu, saying, "And I'll grieve with them."

That started a general movement as one and then another rose and came to Darllanyu, saying things like, "I don't approve of him, but I can't desert him for bad judgment."

And, "He's our only priest after all." Or, "I'll never balance him, but we can't allow him to die."

Finally eight people stood with Darllanyu, including those who'd knelt beside Jindigar, trying to help him.

Then her heart sank as the leader confronted them. "Ten of you? It's much too dangerous. This community can't afford to lose so many. I can't permit it."

Krinata loosed Jindigar's knotted fingers and stood up, indignation welling up as she drew breath. A silence fell that let them hear every shovel of dirt pitched by the gardeners, every echoing hammer blow from far outside the stockade, and every cry of the half-tamed beasts of burden.

"It says there"—Krinata pointed to the portal where the artisan had ceased carving—"Fidelity is a Law of Nature. That's carved over the lightning symbol of Aliom. The carving's not even finished yet, and you're all acting as if familiarity had blinded you to the real meaning!

"Jindigar opened my eyes to the life force connecting all living things, and I learned that as created beings we're much safer using created implements, rather than daring to manipulate the force represented by the lightning. But twice Jindigar has Inverted to save lives, seeing how the life force running in him belonged to all. Twice he survived it because he was right. If you reward his fidelity with your cowardly betrayal, then by your own law—by the very Law of Nature you believe is destroying the Squadron as it fights this planet—it is *you* who will suffer, not him!"

She hadn't known she'd ever had such thoughts, but just for that instant she'd understood their alien viewpoint and framed the thought easily in their own language. When she finished, a breathless silence fell.

The old woman said, from her seat, "Jindigar's always been eccentric, but he fears Inversion as much as any of us. I think Lady Zavaronne represents one of his more resounding coups. At least, *I* will grieve with her." She came to Krinata. "If she will permit?"

"If numbers help, I'd welcome anyone."

There was a silent shuffle as more came to Darllanyu. Finally only a handful clustered around the leader, who said, "This is irresponsible. Come, at least some of us must survive to transmit Aliom." He turned to the door, taking his musical instrument with him. A man and a woman deserted his group for Jindigar's, and only five left the building.

Darllanyu knelt beside Jindigar, putting one hand to his forehead. Krinata said, "Do you all know he's never considered violating his priesthood to become a Historian? He fought Grisnilter until it would have been a violation *not* to take the Archive." And then she noticed that Threntisn had remained, standing a little apart, listening.

The Historian came to look down at the trembling form amid the blankets. "I thought to remain to Archive the end of this matter, but—" He scanned the group, weighing them each, and Krinata saw the lines of tension around his eyes. "May I join you? I need to grieve my son."

"Grieving is not a private matter," answered Darllanyu.

"But I won't touch Jindigar—or what's left of Grisnilter's Archive."

"Your choice," agreed Darllanyu. "Now let's get Jindigar over to the fire, and somebody get his whule." There was a general shuffling as several of them moved Jindigar, then placed Krinata beside him, his whule on her other side. She grasped his trembling hands again.

In moments they were all settled in the circle around the fire, Darllanyu poking it up to a blaze while Zannesu stacked on more logs and kindling, muttering how the open roof was going to make this cold work.

The late afternoon sun had abandoned the angle into the building, so they sat in shadow. Darllanyu took the place near the door, opposite Jindigar, and put a pipe to her lips, producing a high, bittersweet note. Krinata heard a general wail rise up outside, and the sounds of work ceased.

Darllanyu piped a simple melody, ending in that same poignant note, and Krinata sensed that those outside had moved away. Other instruments joined now, and the music began to fill the room, a tangible substance.

It wasn't the same as Jindigar had played in the small canyon that night near the river. But it opened vistas and brought instant tears to her eyes with the solemn finality of the dirge reserved for the Emperor, and Kings, representing an irrevocable turning of the times and seasons. There was no going back, no second chance. The clarion voice of Darllanyu's pipe called out over the strings, good-bye to the souls departed, a day and a life ended, a season and a generation turning.

She'd never heard the melody before, yet instantly it drew to mind all the deaths that had ever touched her life, all the people gone forever. Her eyes and nose were running as the last note died away to a silence that seemed now to grip the entire community around them.

Halfway around the circle, Threntisn sat tailor-fashion, eyeing Krinata as if surrendering to an inevitable fate. On Jindigar's other side Zannesu knelt, hands on his knees, eyes lowered. As the silence stretched he glanced expectantly at Krinata. She blinked, sniffed, and queried with an eyebrow. He leaned over and hissed, "Duad!"

"I can't!" Sudden fear lanced through her. They expected something she couldn't do. "Jindigar always did it! I don't know how I did it when—" *But even so, I couldn't!* It felt as if she'd been asked to thrust a recently burned hand into an open flame.

He took her hands and placed them on Jindigar's face. "Lean into his inner vision. Follow aliom *in*. What a triad has lost, the duad must grieve. Must, Krinata. We can't do it without you."

She remembered how the river gorge had intimidated her, but she'd whipped it. What was the Archive but another kind of void? *Oh, Takora, where are you when I need you?* "I don't know how!"

Zannesu appealed to Darllanyu, who replied by sounding another note on her pipe. A murmur rippled around the circle, then Threntisn nodded and moved closer to the fire, the circle closing behind him. The music picked up, filling the dusky shadows with eerie life. Threntisn took two long-handled paddles of some reflective material and thrust their flat ends into the fire, flipping them over rhythmically, causing a whirling pattern of lights to dance above the fire.

To Krinata's heightened senses it seemed that the sparks of light coalesced into a form, wavering in the heat shimmer above the fire—*Frey's face!*

No! She'd felt him dissolve. He was dead. He couldn't be here—completing the triad. But he was there, tangible to her mind. The Jindigar-Frey axis called to her—and suddenly she was in triad again.

NINE

Grieving Is Not a Private Thing

Frey screamed, voice and mind echoing hollowly. *This is what it's like to be raped. This is what drove Desdinda beyond help,* he thought as his awareness constricted, chipped away by the monstrous, alien mind that forced him into contact with Desdinda. Her searing hatred raced through his nerves like burning oil, etching channels of fire that consumed more of him. He felt himself wrapped around himself, squeezed to a point of nothingness. *I can't!* he begged. *Let me go! I can't!*

But the monstrous, ancient multimind was unmoved. He was a specimen, exotic, fascinating, but his individual pain and fate meant nothing to them. His zunre's frantic pleas meant nothing to them. All Jindigar's might was nothing; all Krinata's passionate pleas were nothing. Death meant little to them, for they weren't truly individuals.

He wept for Jindigar's pain at the loss of a student, crying out in his last moment, "This's not your doing, Jindigar. I wanted to learn too much, too fast. Save Krinata!" Torn to shreds by pain, he dwindled to nothing and was gone.

Krinata, stunned by the sheets of fiery pain, clung to the triad bond to the very moment of its snapping, certain that she would be sucked into dissolution/death too. There was nothing she could do to stop it.

She sensed presences around her, fleeing the pain like particles flying from a disintegrating nucleus. But she clung, determined to accept the fate she'd brought on her zunre. She felt a touch—a light, nap-skinned whisper.

//Krinata?//

She was clinging now to a cold, hard, faceted pinnacle, her hands touching— //Jindigar!//

Jindigar clung to the other side of the chipped flint pinnacle, his hands barely able to reach hers. Around them was blackness, a starless void. She knew, with his knowledge, that in the pit below was the Archive. They clung to the highest apex of his memory, but it didn't reach to outside reality. The memory between them, tapering up to a sharp point, every facet lacerating their flesh, was the memory of Frey's death.

He knew, with her memory, why her human pride had insisted she deal with Desdinda alone, and though that decision was far down this pinnacle, it wasn't the base, for knowing her character, he should have predicted her behavior. Always she'd coped with her problems without leaning. She was independent, and thus what she did, felt, and decided didn't have to affect everyone around her.

She knew, with his sense of Purpose behind the Laws of Nature, that her independence was an illusion arising from the ephemeral existence in which all memory was lost at each Renewing Birth. Any Dushau could see that everything was a manifestation of the energy represented by the flicker-flash of the lightning bolt. Living and nonliving were all part of one fabric. Every thought and feeling, conscious and unconscious, registered permanently on this substrata, which supported all manifestation and affected all reality.

She defended herself against this idea, unable to face the weight of responsibility for every tiny feeling she'd ever had, every moment wasted indulging in the simpleminded diversions she mistook for pleasure. The abyss below held less terror than this dread truth.

Anxiety rising, she thought, *We can't stay here, at the point of Frey's death!* She shinnied around the pinnacle, grabbing his hand in both of hers, and tore him off his perch, sending them both into a swan dive toward the abyss.

Only after it was done did she remember her fear of emptiness. *But Grisnilter taught me about this. It should be easy.* She peered with eyes that saw above her head and below, to left and to right, all at once, Dushau eyes, normal eyes. She felt with the nap of her skin sensitive to a thousand signals from her environment. She heard with twice her audible range. She remembered deep into the past and could see patterns imperceptible from the perspective of an ephemeral.

//There!// she told Jindigar. //An unSealed Gate!// Gleaming in the darkness, a tesseract form warped into other dimensions. Faceted sides twirled, showing scenes from within, like windows enticing the unwary. To enter by any of those scenes was certain death, for it would lead them only into the vortex at the center of the Archive, the point of contact with Infinity, the Gateway to Dissolution, the Archive's Eye. A Sealed Archive was a self-contained maze with no exit—but no entry, either. A partially unSealed Archive was a deadly trap for those lacking the key. No key would work on a Tampered, Mal-edited, or Distorted Archive. Such an Archive was an abomination capable of closing the Gate to Completion for an entire generation.

//No!// He pulled away from her grasp, hand trembling with fear. //Takora! No! We mustn't Tamper— //

//Not to Tamper! We can't get out through Frey, because he ended inside. We have to search for a contact point. There must be several that anchor the Archive to you.//

The logic was impeccable, but still he resisted with the stubbornness of the superstitious. A horrifying thought occurred to her. //You haven't dared to interact with that Archive, have you?//

//No! I swear it, Takora, by my Oaths and Offices!//

She believed him. //Then there's no prob— //

They were almost at the unSealed Gate, a black panel amid the brightly colored ones. At the last minute, before they breasted the Gate, Jindigar screamed, //No! I swore to Grisnilter—I'll take the Archive to Dissolution rather than risk an alteration!//

He wrenched and twisted, pitching them into a panel showing a lavishly appointed, royal sickroom.

An old, old human woman lay shriveled and nearly invisible among sumptuous covers on a bed sheltered from drafts by a gorgeously embroidered canopy, Jindigar's crest on the Dushaun colors. The room was close and humid, yet the old woman complained bitterly of the chill.

Jindigar, trembling visibly, adjusted the thermal currents for her. He still glowed with the vital luminosity of Renewal, the brimming energy of returning youth. He had decades yet to go. Grisnilter knew now how integral the human had become to Jindigar's Renewal. Her death would leave a gaping hole to be filled by scar, leaving the youth handicapped when he finally came for Historian's training. *A scar acquired mid-Renewal. How will I ever train him around that? But he's too talented to abandon.*

"Ontarrah, you won't suffer long now," said Jindigar.

"You shouldn't have come. I never wanted you to see me like this. You must remember me forever young as you are."

"Not forever, Ontarrah—there's only a minor discrepancy between our lifespans."

"I believed that once. I was wrong."

Jindigar edged onto the bed and took one wandering, skeletal hand in his.

She smiled up at him, a spark of youth in her eyes, her teeth pearly, her hair ashen blond, but her skin old beyond numbering the years. "If I hadn't decided to chase you all the way to Dushaun, I'd have taken my own life long ago.

I know that now, but I also know I'm leaving you to tens of lifetimes longer than I'd have faced. I was selfish, Jindigar. That's no way to Completion."

Eyes bright, he whispered, "I pay the price of your company these years gladly." He leaned over and kissed her forehead gently as her eyes closed. He stayed that way a long moment, waiting for Ontarrah to draw another breath. Then he sat up, and Grisnilter heard him whisper, "I loved you. I hope you knew that. I hope it helped."

When at long last he rose and turned, his face showed the unmitigated desolation possible only in Renewal. His wife was behind him, and both their children. The moment of payment was upon him, and Grisnilter felt he should leave, his job as Recorder completed with the death of the first ephemeral to join a Renewing household.

For the first time Grisnilter noticed the family's obvious pain, betraying how they'd valued the human too. *What has the youth done?*

With tender candor Jindigar's wife said, "I envied her what you could never give me. Only now, I've realized I loved her as a sister." She collapsed to the floor at the foot of Ontarrah's bed and commenced a Renewal's kindred mourning.

It was only then that the children understood. His son said in a voice that hadn't hardened yet, "Dissolution/death?"

"I think not," Jindigar articulated as if his throat were clogged. "She'll return. Ephemerals do, you know. But even more changed than a Renewal, and with total amnesia." He spoke kindly to the older girl. "It doesn't hurt them. Only we suffer the pain. Don't deny it to yourself—it's not healthy. She's gone from *our* lives, if not her own. If we see her again, she won't know us, and we won't know her."

Luminous eyes met his. "I didn't hate her, Father, not really. I came to tell her that. I was too late."

"Come. Let us mourn together, and I will teach you to

grieve. After all, what's the use of having an Aliom priest in the family, if not to teach the overcoming of the pain he causes!" Overwhelmed afresh, he went down beside his wife with his two children and set about the aching business of accepting a scar that would never heal. For in granting himself a moment of fulfillment he had brought Ontarrah to a lonely life on Dushaun where no other human ever came. He had inflicted a searing soul-agony on his new wife. She'd agreed to have the ephemeral in the house without knowing what it would mean. Ontarrah wasn't a pet. She was a person. And he had condemned his Historian-talented children to suffer premature grieving scars that would hamper them all their lives long.

His integrity, thought Grisnilter, *will one day teach him that what he's done is worse than Inverting. And on that day I'll be there.* He went to tender the report that eventually became the key argument in pronouncing exile on Jindigar, until he learned. But as he backed out of the grieving room's door, he fell, plummeting into nightmare.

She was spinning in space, panels of every shape and color, scenes culled from the lives of uncounted Historians who'd carried this Archive, closing in on her to crush her out of existence. All trace of Grisnilter's supreme mastery of this filing system was gone. The system itself had been scrambled according to a key well hidden within the Seals by a method only a Senior Historian could hope to apply. Takora knew there was no way she could stop her mad plunge into the Eye of the Archive—*she* was not Grisnilter.

She clung to Jindigar's arm, refusing to cry out. They were living the oldest and most feared Historians' nightmare—falling through the Gate to Dissolution at the Eye of the Archive, with the whole Archive collapsing around them, squeezing them out into nothingness, imploding to its own destruction. *I gambled—and lost.*

Then, with the hysterical laughter that only comes in the

freedom beyond death, she shouted to the cosmos, "Ah, Threntisn, were you ever wrong! Now you've lost the whole Archive, and your chance at Completion, for your cowardice!" She was not coward enough even to consider grabbing the duad link and trying to Invert within the Archive. That would surely Distort the Archive—better to ride to Dissolution. At least then they'd still have a chance at the mythical postcorporeal Completion.

Jindigar's arms enfolded her, and she felt his love like a tangible energy vibrating in her bones, making her want to live so much that the agony of slow death redoubled. //I'm sorry, Takora—I wish it could have been otherwise.//

"//Look!//" She freed a hand and pointed, both sending the alert via the duad link and yelling with her voice.

One of the panels had detached itself from the maelstrom and was arrowing toward them. It twirled on several axes as it melted away, leaving a three-dimensional image spinning toward them. But she saw a familiar face. "//Threntisn!//" *Oh, no! He'll die with us!* But she called, "//Over here!//"

Spotting them, he swam toward them, body glowing with an odd indigo light. Without preamble he grabbed them by the upper arms, shoving them before him as if he wore a free-fall maneuvering pack. Within the Archive, his own element, his naked will had the power of a ship's drive. In seconds they were speeding between panels of exotic scenes too bizarre to comprehend. After dizzying twists and turns he propelled them toward an oblique corner where black borders between panels joined and warped into another dimension. "Go!"

They slammed through what felt like a soap bubble membrane and popped out over a narrow ledge cut into the side of a sloping pinnacle of chipped flint. They landed in a heap, facing a triangular archway cut out of a single, huge square etched into the flint.

Jindigar picked himself up, assessed the portal, and announced, //I know this place! It's the Guardian of the Primary Oath! Come on! This way out!// He strode off through a white mist that occluded the entry.

She knew what had happened then, though her memory seemed to be blurring. Somehow Threntisn had heard her and had decided to risk himself to save them and the Archive—by throwing them out through one of the anchor points she'd planned to search for. Ahead of them Jindigar's memory led to the outside world, a trail familiar to him, but which she couldn't possibly negotiate alone. She ran after him.

Squinting against the searing light, she forged ahead until she fell over a ridge and into knee-deep water. On hands and knees she managed to get an eye open and saw the water stretched ahead into the dark blue of ocean deeps, but a plume of spray rose from its center, spreading mist between her and the figure standing on the far shore, tall, white-clad, filling her vision, impossibly bright—seemingly a figurine lit from within. Flanking it crouched two ferocious-looking animals. As she scrambled to her feet mist and light cast rainbows around the figure.

Jindigar was standing on top of the water before the figurine. "Who are you?" challenged the odd being.

"All and none," answered Jindigar. "There is only one identity, of which I am an infinitely small increment. Yet I contain the pattern of the whole."

"What do you seek?"

"To practice the Laws of Nature."

"Sufficient, though you may find it more difficult than you expect."

Jindigar sighed. "Don't I always?" And he trudged past the figurine onto a white, crushed gravel path that led into the distance where grass and trees dotted a peaceful landscape. He turned and beckoned to Krinata, and she started toward the Guardian. Before she'd gone two steps, he challenged her.

"Who are you?" asked the figure.

"All and none," she said, and started on past.

"That's not your own answer." The figure raised a hand, and she was held in place by an invisible force. "Who are *you?*"

"I'm not sure. I have many names. Takora, for one."

"I didn't ask your name; your identity."

She suddenly felt on the verge of tears, like a small child caught fibbing about her name. "So call me Krinata if you prefer! I'm not even sure what identity is!"

"What distinguishes you from all others?"

She searched the far reaches of memory and was astonished when a black wall barred her from questing more than a few decades back. She swallowed sudden fear and answered, "I'm the first human to join a Dushau in an Oliat subform. I was with Jindigar in duad. He's right there." She pointed.

"Ah, then do you define yourself in terms of what you do or of who you know?"

The stupidity of her answer crashed in on her, and she chewed her lip, perplexed.

Patiently the figure asked, "If I took what you do and who you know away from you, who would you be?"

"A believer in peace. I wouldn't torment you like this!"

"So you define yourself as different from others by what you believe about right and wrong."

Way out on the plain, Jindigar turned his back and began to walk away, shoulders slumped, head bowed, failure and dejection in his every move. In a sudden fit of urgency she threw a fistful of water at the figure, though the drops fell short even of the fountain between them. "If you don't let me pass, I'll go around you!" She cupped her hands around her lips and whistled piercingly. "Jindigar! Wait!"

"You'll have to travel the other ways eventually, but those roads are much harder." Gently the figure asked, "What is it about your identity that you fear so much?"

At wits' end, she snarled, "Losing it, you fool!"

Reasonably the figure replied, "But if you don't know what it is, how do you know you have it?"

"What is this, the riddle of the Sphinx? I've got to catch up to Jindigar!" She waded into the water, determined to swim across and force her way by the figure onto his path. But she sank like a stone. Mentally she cried out in frustration, *So I don't have an identity! I'm nobody!*

She began to float to the surface where light beckoned, and a suspicion seeped into her consciousness. She surfaced on the other side of the fountain, close to the figure. Furious at being tricked but triumphant at having seen through it, she declared, "There's no such thing as identity! That's the answer to your riddle!"

Something solid hit her feet, and she stood, waist-deep.

"Your attitude is not optimal, but you may essay the journey—at your own personal risk."

Crazy Dushau! If there's no such thing as identity, how can anyone take a personal risk! But she kept her thought to herself and trudged up out of the water, right through the figure, as if it were a projection, and out onto the trail that snaked away toward the distant mountains. She hurried to catch up to the indigo form that scuffed along the path far ahead of her, shoulders bent in defeat.

Almost as she willed her feet to move, she was beside him. He looked around startled. //Ontarrah!//

//I wish you'd stop calling me strange names. I know your silly Sphinx doesn't think identity exists, but I'm a bit attached to mine. I'm Takora—I mean, Krinata.//

//Yes, Ontarrah, anything you say. But walk a little faster. We've got to get to the concert before it's over.//

She was so disturbed to be mistaken for Ontarrah, she strode off ahead of him, trying to outrun the knotted tangle of emotions that mistake evoked. But Takora knew that that particular grieving scar stood at a crossroad of memory Jindigar had to travel in every farfetching. Familiarity didn't dim its bright pain. She had only viewed Grisnilter's recording of Ontarrah's death. Jindigar had to relive it all, every time he wanted total recall of something that had happened before Ontarrah.

She slowed the pace of her irrational flight, waiting for him to catch up to her. She heard the music then; it was sweet, with a strong, triumphant beat, a thrill of gratitude, and a celebration of truth. As she got closer she could grab hold of it and shape it, guide it, infuse it with the energies gathering within her that had no other outlet. Her heart was made of music, and music filled reality. It became the substance of identity, pulsing back and forth within her body, leaving reawakened senses in its wake, defining the meaning of life.

"Krinata!"

Icy Dushau hands grabbed at her slick fingers, trapping them. Her vision spun, her heart thundered in shock. Dushau voices gabbled incomprehensibly over the final crashing chords of atonal Dushau music. A whisper somewhere beside her: "I lost Frey. I lost your son. It was my fault, Threntisn."

"I couldn't keep him from going to you. He said he'd search for you a thousand years and follow you the rest of his life. In the end he didn't feel you'd failed him."

A heavy sigh was the only answer.

Krinata felt pulverized, aching in every muscle and joint as she hadn't since they'd first left *Truth*. She pried her eyes open, discovering she was sitting cross-legged, leaning on the whule in her lap. She raised a hand, twisting it free of a Dushau grip. It was wet. Sticky. "What happened?" The fire had burned low, chill darkness engulfing the unfinished hall. People were moving around.

"Here," said someone, and a wet cloth was pressed into Krinata's hand, reeking of antiseptic, stinging her flesh.

She felt ice-cold, stiff. But she forced her eyes to focus on her hands. Blood. They were covered with dark red blood. The finger board of the whule in her lap was also smeared with it. "Where—how did we—" She vaguely remembered setting out to grieve for Frey, to lure Jindigar out of himself—but nothing after that.

Seeing her eyeing the instrument, Darllanyu said, "You played Lelwatha's whule as well as Takora ever did—though how you could with only five fingers, I don't know."

The whule had been left to Jindigar by Lelwatha, the eldest member of Kamminth's—Jindigar's last Oliat. She'd met Lelwatha only minutes before he died protecting his zunre. He'd been dark, emaciated, elderly, with deep, wise eyes. But some other part of her remembered him as lighter-colored, jolly, wickedly humorous, intense at composing for whule and durichord. He had taught her to play on this very whule, painting her fantasies of how she'd take Dushaun society by storm at her next Renewal if she could learn a few chords to accompany her splendid singing voice.

Dizzy with the doubled vision, Krinata fought clear of fantasy as her eyes came to Jindigar.

He was lying beside her, the blanket pulled up to his chin, Zannesu holding his head up so he could drink from a steaming cup. His eyes were open. "Jindigar!"

He blinked at her, then smiled languidly, whispered, "It's all right now, Ontarrah." He pushed the cup aside and struggled to sit up, barely able to move without Zannesu's help. "I mean Krinata," he corrected himself, and seemed almost normal. "Where are we?"

Everyone began to talk at once. Finally Darllanyu summarized recent events, and he focused on her, enchantment suffusing his features as he croaked, "Don't I know—Dar? Is it really—I thought I contacted—but—" Enchantment faded to puzzlement. "Avelor?"

They all told him of the deaths, Darllanyu ending with, "We're only a triad now, and since Sarvesun won't balance you, I don't know how we can constitute any sort of Oliat."

"This community needs an Oliat," declared Threntisn, eyes narrowed as he surveyed them all. "I will modify my position. If you'll accept Jindigar as your Center, and he survives it, I'll take the Archive from him—and take my chances with it."

That was met with an uproar, Darllanyu's voice cutting through it all. "You don't know what you're asking. It's much too late for him to Center. He's a priest—"

"I know what a priest is. It's no more than you're asking of me. And we all have the whole community to consider. I leave it to your professional judgment."

He dusted the knees of his trousers and pushed through the group to the door. Someone started to go after him, but Jindigar raised a hand, panting with the effort but seeming to have sorted out the realities of the situation very quickly. "Let him go! His suggestion won't help, anyway. Is there anyone here who'd work with me?"

Eyes suddenly inspected the fire, faces going stony. Finally Zannesu said, "Most of us would prefer not to."

"Then, while someone goes for your Active Priest, we will leave—though I think I'll have to be carried."

Krinata began the slow, painful business of getting her stiff, numb legs under her. When she was sitting on her heels, Darllanyu said into a breathless silence, "Jindigar, we *have* no Active. You will have that office in Renewal."

Jindigar stared. "No Active? What happened to—" He rapidly named off a list of Dushau.

Answers came from different people around the circle, until in the end Darllanyu said, "None of them are here, though some may still be on their way. We have so little talent left, we dare not attempt another Oliat without guidance." She told him of the way Avelor's bad judgment had led them into ambush. "Avelor's wasn't adequately balanced. But if you would take Active, I will work with what we have."

An Aliom priest was "active" only during Renewal. Knowing Darllanyu wanted to spend Renewal with Jindigar, Krinata appreciated the woman's sacrifice. But Jindigar said, "No, I can't do that while Threntisn's offer stands and while the community is threatened." He sounded weaker as he added, "You haven't mentioned the Squadron." When they'd filled him in on what they knew, he mused, "Tornadoes? Well, even so, it can't be much longer until they find us. Tomorrow—tomorrow we'll see if I can constitute an Oliat. Tomorrow. . . ." He fell asleep in mid-word.

But it was three days until Jindigar was strong enough to sit in a chair for more than an hour, and two more before he was walking. Darllanyu kept Krinata informed, often by sending Cyrus with a daily bulletin. She hardly needed the news, though. There was an awareness in the back of her mind, a growing strength that kept a smile on her face. She accepted the residual link, far short of a duad, and never thought she was responding to it when it suddenly occurred to her that Jindigar would love to see Imp.

She had been lying on her back in bed, drowsily realizing it was getting light, when Imp leapt in through an open window and deposited a still flopping fish on her chest. Stifling an outcry, she dried the piol off and took him and his fish to the Dushau compound, trying to convince him to gift Jindigar with the fish. The Dushau who met her looked dubious, but Imp took his fish and scampered past the gate as if homing on a scent. Much later Krinata learned that Imp had found Jindigar's bed and had deposited the cold, wet fish under his nose, making him laugh for the first time.

Later she sent Jindigar word of how their Cassrian orphans had been adopted by a childless Cassrian couple who were giving them the kind of love they needed, while Terab and Irnils were accepted by the Holot community.

She hardly saw any of the other refugees. After being cooped up with each other for nearly a year, it wasn't surprising that they didn't seek each other's company.

Nevertheless, she was enjoying an upwelling sense of health and vitality. The nightmares had stopped. All pangs of guilt and shame over Frey's death were gone, and she no longer wondered which passing Dushau avoided her eyes because she was a zunre-killer. She went about her duties in the fields, filling in for people sent to dig defense trenches, bunkers, traps, and deadfalls with more cheer than their situation warranted.

The settlement's scouts had observed the hives on the plain above the cliff becoming ever more touchy, and a skywatcher had reported three orbiters passing overhead the previous night. Artisans redoubled their pace, fashioning crude weapons from native material; labor was pulled off the job for target practice with stunners and bush-whips.

Irnils turned out to be the champion shot with a stunner, with Terab a close second, because the Outriders disqualified themselves. The Holot community was inordinately proud, their rousing nightly celebrations entertaining the whole camp.

Cyrus took Krinata to the dancing on the fifth night, after her hands had healed. They had to wait for the six-legged Holot to finish before two-legged rhythms were played, the dancing becoming a competition among species, in strength and endurance as much as grace and warrior spirit. But it also seemed to bind the community, for every night a few Dushau joined in as musicians and dancers.

Studying the indigo figures, almost invisible in the dark firelight, Krinata noticed how they eluded all direct confrontation, not flaunting their strength as the Holot did, nor displaying their grace and speed, as the Lehiroh did. Dance was not to them, as to the humans and others, the quasi-sexual ritual of female preening to waken male prowess and lead to sensuous intimacy.

No, there was another energy the Dushau were raising, another way of living symbolized by their dance. They moved among the aggressive shouting and stomping dancers like wraiths, near but not touching, apparently in danger of collision but escaping unhurriedly. They understood the pattern of the dance and wove themselves through it without disturbing it—without leaving a trace. And when they left, the dance was over.

Krinata dreamed of that dance, and what it might become when danced during Renewal, and woke chasing the memory with a tantalizing sense of near understanding. Later that morning, the seventh since they'd arrived, Darllanyu sought her out where she was helping weed a field.

By this time Krinata didn't even notice the curious stares that followed the Dushau visits. Those who accepted her odd connection to the Dushau had asked their embarrassing questions and become friends. Those who couldn't encompass it just left her alone.

"You look as if you've already done a day's work," said Darllanyu as Krinata leaned on her hoe, stripping off gloves.

It was only mid-morning, but Krinata had been out since before dawn. "It's almost quitting time. Too hot for humans to work. The Lehiroh crew will be out in a bit." She was supposed to go with Cyrus later, to gather medicinal herbs for the field hospital, in case they survived the battle.

"The roof on the temple is finished, and it's cool inside,"

offered Darllanyu. Krinata raised her eyebrows, and Darllanyu interpreted that correctly. "Jindigar is going to try the constitution now, and he says with the duad link, it's distracting if you're focusing on this ecology while he's trying to pull an Oliat out of thin air."

She was speaking colloquial Dushauni, and though Krinata didn't follow it all, she asked, "What duad link?"

"The one you're holding with Jindigar."

"Oh," said Krinata, some things coming clear. "Duad."

"Will you come?"

All morning she'd been suppressing an urge to go to the Dushau compound to see Jindigar—knowing she'd be brusquely turned away at the gate. "Duad," she repeated, hacking her hoe into the ground to mark her place. "Can I shower first?"

"Don't take long," Darllanyu admonished, and started back along the furrow. "I'll send Zannesu for you."

The Aliom temple was indeed cool inside, and they even had a fire going. They had plugged all the windows with some fine, dry moss and trickled water into it from a cistern on the roof. The air that came through the windows was several degrees cooler than that outside.

A new ceiling was in place, forming an insulating attic space above rough hewn roof beams, and the giant Oliat symbol had been finished, an X supported at its crux by an arrow point. It stood away from the back wall, taller than a man and twice as broad. Piles of debris still littered the floor, and heaps of lumber for furniture were stacked near the walls. The astringent smell of sawdust from Phanphihy's woods filled the air.

As she came in with Zannesu, people stood talking in small groups. She saw Jindigar sitting on a pile of boards close to Darllanyu, and there was something different about him—a vibrant sensuousness that echoed through the duad link—as if a totally different personality with different values and goals was struggling to emerge. He brushed his fingers across Darllanyu's cheek in a clearly intimate gesture, whispering to her. Her hands drifted to his neck, but he caught them and returned them to her lap, a firm negative.

Then he saw Krinata and rose to come toward her. He moved like an old man, carefully on top of his feet. She was shocked at how he seemed to have aged. His nap even seemed darker. "I'm glad you decided to come," he said. "I should have come out to see you—"

"No," she denied. "It's all right. If I can help—"

"Well, I don't know. But let's get started and see what happens." He turned to look around the room and gathered attention by calling out the first line of a chant, which everyone answered. The groups coalesced into one, a form that changed constantly, Dushau dance without the structure of the aggressive species, yet bursting with triumph, vigor, and the joy of celebration. Her feet wanted to move in the patterns, but she held back, for they were doing more than dancing. They were presenting themselves to Jindigar for his judgment, displaying skills, announcing talents. Eventually they ended in a single movement, all facing the Oliat symbol.

At the base of the huge symbol was a larger-than-life wood carving of a Dushau hand, the end of each of the seven fingers tapering into a stylized flame while the palm, cupped upward, became a bowl filled with water in which a tiny fish swam. The carved hand was set on a stone tray filled with dirt, and planted as a miniature garden. On another tray hewn from a gorgeous pink stone from a local quarry was an array of local fruits. She'd heard that the Dushau eventually planned to use that stone for permanent buildings. They were uncomfortable with wooden structures, which wouldn't last long enough to raise a child.

Jindigar gazed at the ensemble of symbols. "Well, pioneering does require improvisation. The test is whether it works." He motioned to Krinata to stand to one side, asking, "Can you focus your whole attention on these symbols?"

"I can try," she said without much hope. She was much too interested in what was going on, but he was attempting a job he wasn't qualified for, and she wanted to help.

"Do your best," he replied, and turned and went into the space between the carved X and the wall. Singly, the others went behind the symbol to face him. Sometimes their low voices could be heard, but she was more fascinated by the hand growing from the tiny garden, turning to flame. The duad link vibrated, tantalizing her with near insights from time to time, a pattern trying to form, delicate, unstable, guided by that symbolic hand beneath the balanced X which formed the shape of the Oliat array:

Protector   Receptor

                        Center

Formulator   Emulator

                        Inreach

                        Outreach

At one point it seemed that the carved hand had turned from wood to polished indigo agate, and now real flames rose from the fingertips, casting light and warmth on the world cupped in the palm and growing in the soil that nurtured the hand. The plants around the hand had matured, become vines twining around the fingers, shading the pond. Each of the seven flame jets emitted a single musical note, forming a chord.

She had just begun to see how the flames both rose from the fingertips of the hand and descended from the X, tracing out a branched path like a lightning strike, depicting the way all things were of one fabric, when the last of the candidates emerged, followed by Jindigar, and the whole vision shimmered back to reality—a wooden hand, no flames, no obvious significance.

As the candidates had returned they'd divided themselves into two groups. There were six in the smaller group, everyone else in the larger, as the last man came around to the front. He looked from one group to the other as a total hush fell. He turned to the array of symbols and chose and ate a piece of fruit. Then he picked up the platter of fruit, offering it to the group of six, who had drawn closer together. Krinata had learned to recognize fear in a Dushau, and she saw it now as the last man faced them.

Jindigar announced, "Indito will take your Center."

Indito proffered the tray of fruit to each of the other six, and each hesitated as if his life depended on it before selecting and eating a fruit.

When the tray was returned to its place, Jindigar addressed them. "You will be a very substandard Oliat, in great danger from your own lack of experience, but if you survive long enough, you'll gain skill and serve this community well. I'll speak to the Outriders I brought with me, and to your own Senior Outrider. They'll be waiting if you can Temper and Balance."

Zannesu was with the new Oliat, as was Darllanyu. Jindigar's gaze locked to hers for a moment, then he added, "Indito, if you're very clever, you'll set Dar as your Outreach, and Zannesu as Inreach." He named off the other Offices but added, "Of course, it's your Oliat, and not my place to advise further."

Jindigar swept Krinata toward the portal, leading an exodus. The oppressive heat of late afternoon made Krinata's knees sag, and from how tired she was she realized how exhausted Jindigar had to be. The others dispersed, and Darllanyu caught up with them near the Historians' temple, where Threntisn was sitting on the porch, at a makeshift table, eating fruit and sipping from a canteen.

Stopping Jindigar, Darllanyu said to Krinata, "I must thank you for grieving Avelor's with me. If we never speak again, I want you to know you've given me a Law of Nature I could never have apprehended without you."

Krinata was nonplussed. Jindigar explained, "Dar, I suspect Krinata doesn't recall peripherals."

"But when she saved me from Avelor's beasts, she—"

"Avelor's *beasts?*" asked Krinata.

"You don't remember," stated Darllanyu. Bewildered, she complained, "Jindigar, what good is a grieving she can't remember?"

"Humans are like that. It doesn't worry me."

"Nothing ever worries you."

"Let's not quarrel. This may be an ending for us."

"You chose to send me into Indito's."

He riveted her with a peculiar gaze, a ragged tone to his voice as he said, "If I'd been an *Active,* I probably couldn't have. Is that what you wanted to hear?"

It was Darllanyu's turn to manifest some *other* personality, ready to shuck off all the affairs previously important to her and turn in a different direction. Those two personalities warred within her as she locked eyes with Jindigar.

Then, suddenly, choosing duty above gratification, she whirled and strode back to the temple.

Jindigar watched her go, one hand almost beckoning her back. But, resolutely, he turned away, gripping Krinata's arm as Zannesu had—repressed tremors pulsing through him. *Could Dushau seduce each other into Renewal?*

As they made for the street of houses that led to the gate, Threntisn called, "Jindigar!"

TEN

Farfetch

Jindigar stopped, paused before turning as if summoning strength, and then called back to Threntisn, "Yes?"

Threntisn beckoned, and Jindigar glanced at Krinata. She offered, "I could find my own way to the gate...."

"This can't take long. I must find the Outriders. Can you wait?"

"Sure," she agreed, and expected to park herself near one of the newly planted saplings. But Jindigar kept his hold on her elbow as he headed for the Historian's porch.

As they approached, Threntisn piled up two more stacks of lumber and laid out some more fruit from a net bag beside him. "Come—there's fresh—whatever these are. We must name these things, you know."

Jindigar remained standing. "Your department. I'm on an errand, Threntisn."

"Bluntly, do we have an Oliat?"

"Maybe, though anywhere else they'd be called a heptad."

"Not my business to assess your risks—"

Jindigar tensed. "But it's your business to set them."

Krinata had never seen Jindigar's anger before, and she well understood it, for Threntisn had set impossible conditions for taking the Archive from Jindigar.

"Sit down," urged Threntisn. "I'll have someone escort Krinata to the gate. You and I must speak frankly."

Jindigar looked to Krinata. "This concerns my apprentice

too. And, if I were her, I wouldn't appreciate being disregarded."

"If I were you," said Krinata to Threntisn in her best Dushauni submission-mode, "I wouldn't assume that the senior Oliat priest had been detailed to escort a visitor to the gate."

Threntisn gazed at her in astonishment, then a smile lighted his face and he stood, sweeping her a courtly bow. "My apologies. I hadn't realized you were so deeply involved. Jindigar—please. I won't keep you long."

They took seats, and Threntisn handed Krinata one of the nicest yellow fruits, which could be eaten skin and all. It was cool and juicy, and she was thirsty. "Thank you."

Jindigar likewise accepted a fruit and idly toyed with a very large loop of string on the makeshift table. "You may speak freely in front of Krinata."

"I saw you with Dar. I'm sorry it doesn't seem to be working out. She's so much closer to Renewal than you are."

"There's no telling how long Indito's will last, if it ever forms. But—I can't make plans until I've delivered the Archive. I can't even train Krinata. The Archive's unaltered now, but my every thought sets it resonating. Every association—even references to people I've known—every personal memory leads me to it. I wouldn't dare try to Center even if they'd have me—Threntisn, didn't you see how I almost pulled the entire grieving zunre into the Eye with me? I didn't mean to do that! I could inadvertently pull an entire Oliat in there with me. The thing's a giant trap now. Take it, and let me use my talents for this community."

"I can't. My oath forbids."

"Couldn't you see the Archive is unaltered? You came into it to rescue us."

Krinata listened, haunted by echoes of memory—suddenly unable to sort dream from reality. Did she remember being sucked down into a whirlwind called an Eye, or had that been a nightmare from the bad times out on the plain?

"With Grisnilter's Seals broken there's no way to test his Archive. No one could check every record in it against other Archives. It would take more than a lifetime! But we were all able to get out, which clearly indicates that the structure is undistorted. Your zeal convinces me that the contents are probably unedited. That's why I made my offer. I'll chance it, if I have proof of your fidelity to satisfy our Criteria. Surviving Centering would be sufficient."

"But that's impossible. You saw that at the grieving. My identity is pledged to Raichmat's multicolony just as it is to delivering Grisnilter's Archive. Since the Archive will destroy any Oliat zunre linked to me—in fact, it prevents my completely dissolving the duad I'm holding with Krinata, and so it endangers her too—I can't fulfill either pledge.

"Shoshunri Observed that it's impossible to achieve Completion by forsaking fidelity or to achieve fidelity by forsaking Completion. You're demanding I choose between two vows of equal force. Either choice is a forsaking of fidelity. So you're asking me to forsake fidelity to prove fidelity."

He knew something like this could happen, thought Krinata. *That's why he fought Grisnilter so hard.*

"That's a good description of what you're demanding of me," the Historian replied. "I'm pledged to protect the accuracy of our memory. I dare not introduce a questionable Archive into our colony's permanent record. This is now my community. For a Historian, the community becomes Identity. I wouldn't expect an Aliom to understand Identity, but you come of a Historian family. . . ."

Jindigar seized on that. "Yes, and so I know this community must have this Archive—the risk of taking it is less than the risk of delay, for I *will* fail eventually."

"I don't know that you haven't failed already. With the

Seal broken I've no way to test it, short of absolute proof of your fidelity. How did you break into it? Inverting?"

Jindigar held himself very still, but his confession when it came held neither guilt, remorse, nor pride. "Yes." Jindigar recited the events that led to Desdinda's death as if telling off memory beads on a well-worn string.

Finally he added, "We were a very hasty, unbalanced triad, and I did Invert them—but only to affect the Emperor's machinery, which was being used to keep us from our proper place in the pattern—I wouldn't expect a Historian to understand. We did survive, so I was right. But Desdinda's death left us all injured—so I was also wrong. Frey eventually died as a result of a train of bad judgments, for which I'm also responsible. If Krinata and I die because of the Archive being unSealed, then it will confirm the injunction against Inversion, for it will be clear that Inverting has impaired my judgment, preventing anyone associated with me from attaining Completion."

"And if you survive?" Threntisn prompted.

"It won't disprove the theory, for the dangers are as formidable as reputed. Threntisn, I didn't Invert originally to disprove the major tenet of Aliom! It was a 'strike,' an unpremeditated action, an expression of the primal desire to survive to Completion. I believe I still have a good chance at it." He explained how Desdinda's death had left a Loop impressed on Krinata, and how she'd finally dealt with it in the hive. She hardly recognized a single image. But it brought back the stark terror, the forced confrontation, and the infinite relief she'd felt. Those had become such an integral part of her identity, she didn't know they were there anymore.

He finished his account, adding, "I couldn't help either Frey or Krinata because of the Archive. Krinata healed herself, despite the hive's Long Memory, while Frey failed."

"You put the Archive above your zunre's lives?"

Jindigar hung his head. His sigh was a long shudder. But when he raised his eyes, he said firmly, "Yes. And I will always, because if I break my pledge to Grisnilter, what good is my pledge to my zunre, and if I forsake fidelity, how can I or my zunre achieve Completion?"

Threntisn turned to Krinata. "How do you feel about that?"

"Maybe I can't ever know how a Historian regards Identity, but I'm beginning to believe mine includes Jindigar, and that's why we're linked. But I'd rather die than see him go to Dissolution, which is what ruining the Archive would do to him."

Astonished, Threntisn asked Jindigar, "Is she another Ontarrah? Is that why Darllanyu—"

Ontarrah. Images of a sumptuous bedchamber flooded into her mind, and suddenly she knew who Ontarrah was, though the memory had that same maybe-not-dream quality which so confused her these days.

"No, she's not," Jindigar answered levelly. "We won't make that mistake again. But I owe her my life, many times over. She's zunre to me, and your son—and so to you. *Take* the Archive, Threntisn—before it does become altered—and let me fulfill my other obligations."

Silently he weighed Jindigar, and Krinata thought he'd do it, but he said, "I *believe* you, Jindigar, and I want to now. But I can't. I must have full-jeopardy, objective proof for the record before I can risk it. Doesn't Aliom have some such law for its Seniors?"

"Yes, of course. I understand, but I disagree. There must be some law you are breaking by forcing this choice upon me." He glanced at the sun. "We must go." On the stairs he turned and added, "After you fished us out of the Archive's Eye, I thought you'd understand."

"I do, Jindigar. You chose Dissolution with the Archive, rather than break either oath. You'd have made a great Historian. That's the only other choice you have, you know." He gestured to the portal behind him. "Come in and let me teach you to reSeal it and foster it yourself."

Jindigar looked up at the other man with an ironic smile. "I will—on the day you become an Aliom priest."

"Then we may go to dissolution/death together, each clinging to our own path to Completion and failing."

Jindigar sighed, shook his head, and took Krinata off toward the street that led to the compound gate.

Eye of the Archive. The image awakened vague shuddering terrors for Krinata. "It seems everybody else remembers what happened in that grieving. All I seem to have is a determination never to try it again!"

"Grieving itself isn't a fearful experience; being dragged into someone else's attempted suicide is. I'm sorry, Krinata, but you left me no choice."

When she asked what he meant, he drew her a vivid word picture of the Archive swallowing them. She recalled the jagged black pinnacle, and a pond with its ludicrously fearsome guardian, and described them, saying, "I cast us off and limited your options. If I'd understood then, I might not have done that. I'm sorry."

"It was the only way out for me. The problem, of course, was how many other lives were risked for my sake and what I owe them all for that."

"I didn't know anyone else was involved when I did it."

"No?" He shook his head. "Pinnacles, fountains, and luminous statues, of all things—the imagery of the human mind is astonishing. I wonder how I can possibly train you in duad across such a gulf. But I know I heard you play the whule—and beautifully too."

"I hope my blood didn't ruin the strings."

"I cleaned them easily. Such an instrument doesn't survive by being sensitive to moisture, remember?"

The memory of the waterfall in the small canyon rushed at her through the duad link. All the reasons he shouldn't come to care for her flooded into her mind. "Jindigar—"

"I hope you'll play for me, now that your fingers are healed. It could help you recall Frey's grieving and make it useful to you." They were at the portal, and he said, before she could answer, "Come, let's alert the Outriders, then go down by the river and watch the piols fish."

The Outriders were camped just within the walls that enclosed the entry to the Dushau compound. Clearly this outer area would contain small cabins to house the Outriders—who had better sense than to intrude on the inner compound and who could then deal with ephemerals on behalf of the Dushau. But only a few of the cabins had walls as yet. The four Lehiroh and Cy had a cook fire blazing and dinner roasting while they cleaned stun rifles.

Cyrus turned. "Jindigar! Come, sit down! Krinata—"

"Oh, no! I forgot, Cy! I was—"

"It's okay. They told me you were on another job."

Jindigar lowered himself to sit on a pack beside the fire, and Storm fussed over him, insisting they stay for dinner. "You've got to get your strength back."

"I'm fine now, really. Thank you," said Jindigar.

They served a haunch of meat, with eggs and fruit, saying, "We'll be laying in supplies for the winter as soon as the smoke pits are ready."

"Good," said Jindigar. "This community will survive." And he explained the needs of the new Oliat—how much more delicate their balance was than the groups who worked for the Allegiancy. "Ordinarily such an Oliat would work only on Dushaun, using Officers as Outriders. Here, we need you to relate them to the ephemeral community."

"We'll keep ephemerals away from them until they're ready," said Storm.

They talked of the community's plans for defense, then they all went with Jindigar for his first view of the river. While the others splashed about with people just getting off work and coming to bathe, the piols flashed about deviling the swimmers. Krinata and Jindigar found a spot under a tree and sat talking. After a while Jindigar questioned her about how she was getting along. "Does Viradel bother you?"

"She doesn't seem to be spreading rumors. I've met some friendly people, but there are also those who won't speak to me. On the whole, this is an unusually harmonious group."

"Well, they're Raichmat zunre, and Raichmat was of Shoshunri's School of Efficacious Helplessness, so naturally everyone here is biased in—" He sat bolt upright. "That's it! But neither Threntisn nor I have applied it consistently!" He glanced at her. "What's wrong?"

School of Efficacious Helplessness? "I made that up! I made that silly phrase up!" And she recounted her insight while watching the lightning.

"You've done a lot of reading. You must have—"

"No! I'd remember something like that!"

"Takora was trained by Raichmat, and you seem to have internalized her from my memories. It's puzzling, but no human has ever—"

She lost track of his words, assembling fragile threads of memory. Could it really be? The preposterous conviction grew beyond all reason. She told herself the Dushau knew what they were talking about—they didn't reincarnate. She wasn't even sure ephemerals did. *Maybe everybody doesn't always—but somehow, I once was Takora. I was never Desdinda—this is totally different. I'm not Takora now, but once I was her.*

She looked over at Jindigar, who'd fallen asleep waiting for her to reply to something. *I'm out of my mind! He'd never believe it. I don't!*

Other consequences crowded into her head—after being Center, you couldn't go back into the Oliat. There had to be some reason for that rule—had she caused her problem with Desdinda by breaking an Oliat rule? Or didn't the rule carry from one lifetime to another—but Dushau didn't reincarnate, so how could they have multilife rules?

Krinata was still chasing the illogic around in circles when it got so dark, they had to wake Jindigar and leave the river to the nightstalkers. Jindigar walked back to the Dushau compound, weary but seeming stronger. Perhaps tomorrow there'd be time to discuss her wild notions.

But the next morning, she woke to the sounds of women poking up the fire and washing in the buckets brought in the night before and warmed this morning with hot stones from the banked fire, or helping each other bind their hair.

A low rumble shook the building, evoking a babble of comments: "Sounds mechanical!" "No, just thunder—another storm." "Thunder doesn't go on getting louder like that!"

The walls began to rattle, and she was fully awake. The ground shook, the animals in the hive-corral screamed. People poured out of buildings, raising a dreadful racket.

The Squadron!

Krinata had pulled on trousers and was skipping to yank on boots as she ran out the door before any of the women already up and dressed could move. She scrambled across a trench and sprinted toward the Dushau compound, the duad link within her mind ringing out alarm.

At the place where two roads met to feed into the portal, a crowd of Dushau had gathered. Storm and Cy, with a group of Dushau and Lehiroh, surrounded the seven who had balanced in Oliat. Jindigar found Krinata, and she shouted over the rumble, "What is that noise?"

"Look up!" he yelled pointing.

Above the clouds in the morning sky four flat shapes descended, plumes of plasma and vapor spraying from the undersides. The duad linkage made them seem familiar, though she'd never seen one before. "Imperial Landbases," Jindigar identified tonelessly, "fortresses, each carrying hundreds of troops! Once positioned, they could demolish the settlement, even boil the ground down to bedrock." His clinical distance reminded her of how he'd told Threntisn that every memory led to the Archive. *He's more frightened than I am!*

Someone yelled, "Look!" To the west, on the cliff high above them where one of the bases was settling, a line of armored Imperial troopers waited mounted on gravity scooters, weapons at ready, armor scintillating.

Darllanyu separated from the Oliat and shouted to Cy, "Look! Up there!" She pointed to the mounted troopers. "Phanphihy native—hivebounders—a herald, we think, and a little one—mind-gatherer. Prisoners!"

Jindigar drew Krinata away down the road to the cliff, peering up uncertainly. "It could be Chinchee! I wouldn't put it past him to try to communicate with the Imperials. They might have forced him to lead them here."

"How would he know?"

"Phanphihy doesn't need an Oliat—it *is* an Oliat!"

By now the trenches were filling, but the refugees from *Truth* were gravitating toward Jindigar, Terab and Irnils in the lead. Energy weapons, created from the downed landers' drives, had been placed in the bunkers, and now crews rushed to man them. Others, armed with hunting stunners and farming tools, air rifles, and even quarter-staves, assembled.

"Krinata, do you notice anything odd?" asked Jindigar, pivoting to view each of the four fortresses that were now hovering within a few feet of the ground, forms distorted by shimmering waves of energy and plumes of dust.

At her bewilderment he asked, "How many troops do you suppose are really up there?"

One of the fortresses was settling right on the far edge of the east field, the sun rising behind it. Another was due north of the corral, while the third came down to the south of the stockade on the flat area around the gravel mine. The fourth, on the escarpment above them, cut off all hope of escape. "Eight—maybe twelve hundred in the fortresses. Another hundred or so mounted and ready to move in on us."

"No," he said slowly, pivoting. "No, it's a trick!"

He whirled and strode back to the Oliat where a crowd of the settlement's elected defense managers were clumsily questioning Darllanyu over Cy's objections.

Jindigar singled out the ephemeral leader. "I believe I can extract the information you most need."

He motioned Cy to move the defense committee back and turned to Darllanyu. His demeanor was shockingly distant, impersonal, as he addressed not Darllanyu, but the Oliat. "Does Indito's notice anything odd about the eastern fortress?"

One of the Officer's eyes snapped to the east where the descending fortress was still barely visible. The Outreach answered, loudly enough for the committee to hear, "Indito's judges there is no fortress there, nor to the north, nor to the south! The western one is solid. And manned." There was a hesitation, a silent communion among them. "Indito's estimates the western fortress is sparsely crewed—perhaps only three or four hundred."

A runner was dispatched to concentrate forces in the

west, and jubilation spread through the defenders. They numbered nearly a thousand, and the enemy only four or five hundred. Without the Oliat they'd never have known, and the ruse might have made them surrender.

Jindigar fired more carefully worded questions at the Outreach, and gradually the defense command saw how the Squadron had been decimated already. The fortress was barely functional, malfunctions plaguing them where native sand or even air had gotten in. A nasty fungus had ruined the air purifier, and something vile was growing in the water. They'd lowered their ambient temperature to try to kill the microorganisms, and as a result, many of them were ill.

Exposure to the hivebound had left them all seeing horrors crawling out of solid bulkheads or lurking behind every tree or hill. Transfixed within their hallucinations, the crew made irreparable errors with precious equipment. They wanted nothing more than to get off this uninhabitable planet before their ships were no longer spaceworthy.

Jindigar traded a glance with Krinata, and she knew this was indeed what had happened to Raichmat's Outriders. It hadn't happened to *Truth*'s passengers only because Jindigar and Frey had kept them treading lightly through this world's ecology. Her sledgehammer attacks with Inverting the triad could have destroyed them all.

Indito's Outreach proclaimed, "The whole fortress rings with resentment and anger covering fear and revulsion. They must attack soon, for we stand between them and home."

Indito's prediction was hardly made when the mounted cohort on the cliff above rose in a maneuver clearly intended to be parade-ground-precise and impressive. But three stragglers, one scooter failure that sent its rider tumbling into the river, and a midair collision spoiled the effect. As if to divert attention from that, the fortress extruded a beamer-cannon and fired at the row of abandoned landers parked to the north of the corral. The loud crack-whump sound deafened them, and shards of shredded hull and circuitry rained down, forcing all the unarmored to duck.

Then the cannon turned and bombarded the corral. The animals huddled together in terror. The densely packed flesh exploded. Blood and chunks of sizzling meat rained onto rooftops and defenders to the north.

Then battle was joined, and people were screaming and dying on all sides as armored troopers descended toward the Dushau compound.

"Why don't they just obliterate the settlement?" asked Viradel, who was holding a stun pistol, standing among the other refugees who'd come with Jindigar.

Jindigar answered, "They want us alive."

On the cliff top more troopers were pouring out of the fortress—some jumping down the cliff using their armor's repellers, others on grav-scooters or huge, round flying gun platforms. The defenders, pulled out of the north trench and from the riverside emplacements, had regrouped to defend the Dushau stockade, forming a line about a hundred meters away.

Krinata watched horrified as the fighting came at them like a wave and was stalled by the defenders. Five scooters were downed by Lehiroh farmers, but more armored Imperials descended from the cliff. The Outriders urged the Oliat toward the river. Jindigar called, "Cy, it's pointless to retreat. We can't outrun them."

"Then let's surrender!" said Krinata.

"No use!" replied Terab. "All of us here are guilty of consorting with Dushau—an automatic death penalty."

Krinata could see no pattern in it, no right place to be, no way to efficacious helplessness. All her insights deserted her, except the one determination never to try to solve a problem by Inverting an Oliat subform. "I don't know about you," she said, "but I can't just stand here and watch people be slaughtered defending me!"

She charged down the road toward the battle, pausing only to grab a stunner from a dead defender. Crouching low, she zigzagged, firing the stunner at coruscating Imperial armor. She was amazed to be alive when she reached the place where six Holot had downed three troopers. Riderless scooters floated overhead. Beyond her, defenders stole weapons from the dead bodies and fired on the next wave of troops. Their crisp formation dissolved on contact with the defenders. The professionals had lost their nerve. Still, many defenders went down before overwhelming force.

Krinata saw a Holot engineer she recognized fire at a mounted trooper. The trooper, armor sparkling with protective fields, fired back. The Holot went down, and the rider zoomed over him, still firing at his victim.

Krinata tossed her stunner aside, dove at the Holot's body, and snatched up his beamer to fire at the trooper, as she rolled for cover behind a boulder. As she moved, the Holot's head came away from his shoulders and rolled to her feet. She screeched, gagged, and almost retched. But then she saw the scooter returning, its rider aiming a beamer at her, but his armor was gray now, not scintillating.

With a coolness that astonished her she rose to her knee, aimed at the professional who was aiming at her, and squeezed off the neatest shot she'd ever put into a moving target. The trooper's armored head rolled to one side, his body fell off the scooter on the other side, and the scooter was left riderless, coming toward her on inertia.

She dropped flat, letting it zip over her, blessing Arlai for the hours of weapons drill he'd put her through after each of her injuries.

Prone, she squirmed around and glanced back at the knot of people gathered about the Oliat. As she watched, Viradel grabbed a stun rifle from Adina and broke ranks to follow Krinata. Right behind her came Jindigar. The Dushau were evolved prey, not evolved predators like the other species here, and never fought unless cornered. When they did fight, their style was more devious than vicious.

Behind Jindigar, several of the Dushau who'd grieved Frey also broke ranks and trotted after him. Others joined the movement, grouping around the Oliat and its Outriders in a protective wall of indigo bodies, charging into battle.

As the Dushau moved, another Imperial mounted detachment peeled off and swooped down over them. Firing deadly burners and beamers, they slashed through the defenders. But some Imperials were only armed with stunners. *They're not invincible!* Krinata's heart thundered with the first hope she'd felt. Some fallen defenders had to be alive.

Grinning, she rose and aimed her beamer at the mechanism of a gun platform already wobbling as it descended. Tracking her target, she burned through the housing, and the platform dropped inertly. She picked off two more scooters and was just beginning to feel effective when a suit of Holot armor, dull gray without its fields, came up behind and snatched her off her feet in a huge bear hug.

Without warning the both of them went spinning into a backward somersault, and the trooper landed on top of her, knocking her breath out. Cy heaved the armor off her, hollering over his shoulder, "Jindigar, that was clumsy. You almost killed Krinata!"

Jindigar sent another trooper spinning and waded toward them. "She's not hurt!"

"That's not the point!" Cy complained. "You should have let me take his head off."

Krinata pointed and screamed, "Duck!"

Another scooter whizzed overhead. Cy came up on one knee, shooting from the hip into the underside. Sparks flew, and a loud explosion flattened them again. The concussion unseated a couple of other troopers, who were summarily dealt with by other defenders, and suddenly there were a lot of abandoned scooters floating around. Krinata knew the best strategy was to outflank and attack from behind.

She beckoned. "Come on!" She grabbed a scooter, swung aboard, and fumbled at the controls. She'd never been on a military unit before. After several harrowing mistakes she found that the controls were backwards.

After that, it was a short hop to the top of the cliff. She angled north across the tall grass to the fortress, sparing only one quick glance back. An indigo flood, carrying a host of other species, rose over the cliff edge behind her. *Hell of a way to surrender, isn't it?*

Streaking low, hoping none of the big guns would fire at them, she aimed for the fortress's scooter-launching platform. A swarm of half-armored troopers—all species— emerged onto the platform, took positions, and fired at them with small arms, mostly stun-pistols.

She flew straight into it, unable to remember how to turn. A shot singed her hair. Another glanced off the scooter's armor. Then one direct hit showered sparks in her face. She yawed and crashed onto the platform, skidded sideways, and smashed the bottom of her scooter into the hatch at the rear of the platform. The heavy machine blocked the hatch, while it pinned her left leg to the deck. Behind her, the other scooters came in, landing with more elegance. Most riderless scooters circled under control of the docking programmer. But the Dushau transferred from one scooter to another in midair, sending their abandoned machines in to crash on the platform, turning it into a smoking inferno, driving the Imperials back through other hatches.

Krinata put her hands over her head. She was trapped, about to die, and it had all been for nothing. She had totally surrendered to her fate, when suddenly she heard, "Jindigar, give me a hand!" It was Cy, heaving at the dead machine pinning her. Indigo hands joined his, and human ones.

"Jindigar! Storm! Viradel!" She pulled her leg free, amazed she could still feel it. Cy pulled her up. She leaned on him, squinting through the smoke, coughing. "Where's the Oliat?"

Jindigar gathered her in, and she felt the duad link clenched down tight, so she could barely feel it. "They've taken losses. We must secure the platform to give them time to recover from the shock."

"Jindigar, you should stay and help them." She grunted as she helped Cy heave the dead scooter away from the hatch.

"No," he said woodenly, dragging at the massive machine.

She froze at a horrible thought. "Darllanyu?" She had to peel him away from the stubborn lump of metal and shake him. "Darllanyu? Is she all right?"

"I don't know! I *must* not go to them now, Krinata, and neither may you!" He yanked free and applied himself to the job. With Cy and Storm they moved it enough to get by. Krinata grabbed a fully charged beamer from a Cassrian trooper. People gathered to follow them, but Jindigar nudged Cy and Storm back. "The Oliat needs you."

Cy glanced at Krinata as she struggled to fit her hand into the grip of the Cassrian's beamer. He said, "Storm, I'll stay with the duad; your group take the rest of the Oliat." Then he forged ahead into the open hatch, beckoning, "Come on before we lose the advantage of surprise."

Krinata pushed ahead, ignoring the sharp yanks of pain that laced her body. Her concentration narrowed to exclude fear, but her heart was pumping hard. She glanced back and thought she saw Shorwh behind them. *No! He's just a child!*

But there was no time. She traded the Cassrian beamer to a Cassrian who could use it, in return for a burner designed for human hands. It could cut through the bulkheads of this fortress if it had to.

They jogged along a corridor to an intersection, rounded the corner, and found a waist-high barricade across the bottom half of the next corridor. Behind that, a line of Imperials stood, weapons aimed point-blank.

When they whirled to look behind, a vacuum bulkhead slammed across the intersection. Retreat was cut off. Along the corridor, status panels blinked alarm/alert. A silence fell as the two groups confronted each other.

Krinata handed her burner to Jindigar and strolled out into the space between them, arms out from her sides, a smile on her face. "I surrender!"

At the center of the line of troopers facing them, a Cassrian, grotesque in scintillating Imperial armor, but wearing Commander's insignia, snapped in a trained voice, "Who are you?"

"Myself," snapped Krinata.

The Commander warned, "Insolence will—"

Jindigar handed away the weapons and drifted out behind her. She didn't turn.

Distracted, the Commander started again, in a more reedy voice, Cassrian outrage growing, "What kind of people are you to bring a child into this?"

"What?" Krinata turned to follow his gaze. Shorwh eased out of the group. His field clothes were torn and dirty, and he limped on his right leg, but he held himself proudly.

"They didn't bring me," he announced. "I came because I must protect my siblings—I'm all they have."

Krinata could never have read Cassrian emotions through the shrouding armor, but she guessed that the Commander's parental instincts had engaged. Shorwh had claimed a sacred privilege. If his brothers lived, he wouldn't be killed.

The Commander of the fortress signaled, and the barricade clanged into the floor. The troops moved up to cut the three off from the group surging forward to help the Dushau. The Commander aimed his beamer at them and announced, "The battle is over. The settlement has surrendered." He ordered his men to put the prisoners in detention. "And get identity checks on them all. We can be off this planet by nightfall."

He turned and stomped away. Krinata stared after them.

They were herded through a cargo bay hatch, beyond which was a long chamber of empty cargo racks shrouded in red shadows under battle lighting. Dushau would be almost blind here. The hatch slammed ringingly.

Krinata saw cargotainers labeled as field rations for various metabolisms. While people sagged to the deck, weakened by the backwash of adrenalin, Jindigar only leaned weakly against a bulkhead. He was shaking, the duad linkage all but imperceptible.

Suddenly he grabbed at a protruding handle and pulled. What came sliding out of a recess looked like an oversize cargo come-along. Jindigar brandished it like a weapon. Then he grabbed it with both hands as he let himself down to sit on the deck, back propped against a bulkhead. "When—"

His stricture on the duad slipped, and Krinata felt the dizzying whirlwind of images flickering through his mind. Alarmed, she knelt. "Jindigar!"

He laid the come-along across his knees and cradled her neck with his broad hands, capturing her eyes. "Yes. Anchor for me. It can't be more than two Renewals!"

From over her shoulder, Threntisn's voice boomed, "What can't be?"

Jindigar looked up at him, blind in the low lighting. "A fortress—just like this one. Don't worry, Krinata can anchor me." And his face went slack.

The duad linkage flowed with scattered images. "Can you?" asked Threntisn.

"I—" The images were claiming all her attention. "I don't know." On the periphery of awareness, she sensed a knot of pain, five bright hot spots of ongoing loss.

//No, not there. The pentad will grab us, and we'll have to contend with the Archive. Concentrate—//

Then she was overwhelmed by rapid-flowing images she recognized, flying at her and through her in rapid succession as if guided by a strong hand, flashing brighter, surrounding her with vivid holos—Ontarrah's death, only this time she was Jindigar—Takora's death, only this time she was Jindigar—and on back before Jindigar knew how to form an Oliat. And suddenly they were in the cargo hold of a fortress, they were walking the corridors, they were in the main control room—lights flashing everywhere. And on the screens of the engineering station—flick—flash—the plans for the fortress.

//Jindigar?// Behind her mind, the lopsided whirling tesseract beckoned with its myriad windows flashing images.

//Takora—I've got it. Can't stay here.//

//All right. Let's go.// But which reality was real? //The cargo bay—Bay Six—how do we get there?//

//This way.// From the control room they raced weightlessly along corridors, but when they opened the hatch of Bay Six, they found it crammed with cargotainers.

Jindigar gathered her in his arms, pressing her face against his shoulder. //No, we're not now, we're then. You're Krinata now.//

//Krinata.// It was a vaguely familiar name, a proud name. //Yes, I'll be Krinata.//

Again they raced through Takora's death, barely time to sob out the horrible agony of knowledge of what they'd done, and Ontarrah's death, eclipsing all the minor losses of those years. And there she was, seated at her desk console, looking up politely at this new Outreach who'd come to be debriefed—"Krinata Zavaronne?"

"Yes."

"Krinata!"

Jindigar was shaking her. Threntisn was peering at Jindigar, one hand on his forehead. "Yes," she said, "I'm all right." The crowding images had receded, and the duad link was choked off again. *That was farfetching? It can't be that simple!*

"You got it?" asked Threntisn.

"Yes," answered Jindigar.

"You're a fool!" said the Historian. "You've no right to risk your life and hers like that!"

"Tell me that after you've Centered—"

Just then the hatch clanged open and another line of disheveled combatants was ushered in. When it shut again, Darllanyu emerged from behind the dirt- and smoke-begrimed Lehiroh Outriders. Leaning heavily on Storm, she made for Jindigar.

Darllanyu shook her head. "Jindigar—I'm sorry—"

He waved her away. "It's all right. I found a block."

Darllanyu wavered unsteadily, and Storm made her lean on him, urging her back toward the knot of Dushau and Outriders who had appropriated a stretch of bulkhead on the other side of the chamber. Krinata counted. Five of the Oliat had survived—a pentad, if anyone was strong enough to hold it. Some of those Dushau had lost Oliat zunre twice in the span of months. It was a miracle any of them survived.

People were breaking open the ration containers, looking for water. "I found the Medic Aide's Supplies!" called someone, and a small stampede flowed to the other end of the bay until someone else called, "A native! No, two!"

Jindigar perked up at that. "Chinchee!"

Krinata followed Jindigar to see what she knew had to be there—Chinchee and one of the shellfolk, a hivebinder. The two were huddled by a stack of first-aid supplies. Chinchee seemed to be feverish and unconscious, more emaciated than when they'd first found him but with no visible wounds. The small, dark creature clinging to his shoulder was unmoving except for a faint trace of respiration.

Krinata cut across the babble. "They didn't know how to open the containers—or maybe even that they are containers. Let's find them some water! And they can eat ration bars."

Shorwh and Irnils wrestled a water container over and began forcing drops into the two natives. After a few moments she realized that Jindigar was no longer beside her. "Cy!" He turned, and they saw Jindigar lurching across the wide, open floor toward the pentad. Krinata raced to catch up with him.

People crowded about them as Darllanyu met them halfway. Krinata began to understand as the duad link wavered, sending disjointed images blinking behind her vision. Darllanyu apologized, "We—I can't stop it, Jindigar." She glanced around, only a trace of the Outreach's distance in her manner. "We've lost our Center and Emulator. But we're still reading the local gestalt. This fortress is doomed—and so is the settlement."

Jindigar swayed, and Cy took his elbow to steady him. "What are you doing to him?"

Krinata took his other elbow. "You've got to stop it, Darllanyu. You'll throw him into the Archive!"

Her eyes widened, her hands coming up to cover her face as if to fend off a horror. Krinata hammered her words home through gritted teeth. "He'll drag you all down into it again, like at the grieving!"

Jindigar seemed to pull himself together, tightening his grip on Krinata to stem the flow of her fears. "They're a constituted pentad and we're a duad," he explained softly. "They can't help it."

The images flickering behind her mind showed creatures, thousands and thousands of creatures, running together in an enormous herd that stretched across the upper plain farther than the eye could see. Below the cliff, far out beyond the river, swarms of huge insects flew and crawled, blackening the trees and grass like locusts. Only something told her these would as gladly eat flesh.

Jindigar turned to the crowd behind them and raised his voice. "This fortress has grievously wounded the network of hive symbioses in this region, and now hundreds of hives have sent their protectors against it. Thousands of animals are stampeding toward the fortress in a mindless, thrashing rage, determined to destroy as they have been destroyed. Billions of insects are swarming toward the settlement. There may be nothing left alive here tomorrow."

Considering the fortress's defenses, it was hard to regard animals as a threat. But the hives of this world had already reduced a proud force of the Imperial Guard to a rather sad state. "Including us," said Krinata.

Jindigar added more softly, "Unless Chinchee and his friend will help us."

Storm peered into the gloom to where the white figure was now stretched out, head propped on a water bag.

"What," asked Terab, "could we say to get him to help? He's seen two hives destroyed by offworlders. And what could he do against thousands of tons of mass?"

"I don't know," answered Jindigar in a thin voice, breathing deeper, as if determined not to faint. "But I'll do my best to find out. We haven't got much time."

Krinata looked around at the bay. Stowage for the standardized cargo crates lined the walls, but in spots machinery blossomed, panels of controls bristling with complex knobs and screens. Cargo handlers.

She was blinded by a sudden light in the eyes. It flashed, and then passed on—the onboard Sentient grabbing ID data on them, no doubt. They hadn't much time. She wouldn't put it past that Cassrian Commander to start ordering executions before they'd finished identifying everyone.

With Jindigar she went back to the natives, sure she could already feel the deck vibrating under her feet.

ELEVEN

Efficacious Helplessness

"Chinchee!" whispered Jindigar. As he transferred concentration to the native he seemed to forget to keep the duad link constricted. His headache pierced her, and the pentad's perception of a living wall of herbivores stampeding at the grounded fortress intensified. Behind that, Krinata felt the kaleidoscopic whirlpool of Archive images enticing her attention. But she'd learned that was deadly.

Jindigar went down on one knee beside the natives. Chinchee was feeding a ration bar to the shellperson on his shoulder, the job seeming to take all his strength. But he acknowledged Jindigar by patting the Dushau's cheek.

Jindigar began gabbling at him full-speed. Chinchee dropped the ration bar and gabbled back, talking at the same time as Jindigar, who never stopped. Soon the shellperson was twittering and hooting with them. The pentad and everyone else gathered to watch this demonstration, and every once in a while, Shorwh put in a squeak or howl.

The duad link gave Krinata the gist. Jindigar was asking him to stop the attack, and Chinchee was objecting that it was impossible. Jindigar insisted, and Chinchee's resolve weakened as the hivebinder rang in on Jindigar's side. Its nature was to bind mind-groupings, and that's what it wanted to do. But Chinchee overrode that with the edict of the plain's hives that the destroyers must be destroyed.

Before Jindigar could point out that the herds would also destroy people who respected the land, the main hatch clanged open, and armored feet marched into the bay. There must have been more than a dozen fully battle-armored troopers surrounding the fortress Commander. "Stand to! Which one of you is in charge here?"

As his troopers spread out to cover them, a few guards accompanied the Cassrian Commander down the center of the bay toward them. Krinata rose. *This is the one who threw Chinchee in here without food or water. He deserves the same treatment.*

The native was still too weak to stand, but the others gathered protectively in front of him. No one answered the Commander. The chairman of the defense committee for the settlement wasn't there. Terab was, but she had not been elected by the settlers.

The Commander surveyed them all, then zeroed in on Krinata and Jindigar, his manner hasty—almost jittery. "Technically a Prince outranks you, Lady Zavaronne, but he's Dushau. So I'll talk to you. Come."

He about-faced and started for the hatch, his guards closing on Krinata. *He wants something from me! He knows who we are—why hasn't he lifted off?* She stood her ground. "Wait a moment!" The Cassrian turned. "First, we don't go by rank. Second, I don't go anywhere without Jindigar. Third, I won't speak for this whole group. You'll have to negotiate with all of us."

"Negotiate? You're hardly in a position to negotiate."

"No? We can stop the stampede."

The silence was profound. Even the faint wheezing of the armored breathing apparatus suspended. "Stampede," said the Cassrian at last. "How did you know—"

Krinata interrupted, keeping the initiative. "Ever heard of an Oliat? They know things about planets—like how to avoid enraging the native species to the point where they turn on you in suicidal attacks. Pity Imperial Squadrons don't employ them—"

"Enraging—?"

She had his attention now. She stepped out from the group. "Now, if you want our help saving this fortress, you'll have to come here and speak civilly to Prince Jindigar and his associates. Put your case nicely, and you could find yourselves with valuable allies."

As the Commander scanned the mass of settlers, then turned to survey the troopers deployed around the hatch, Krinata saw the bulkheads turn to a crazy patchwork of schematic diagrams that momentarily took on a depth as the pentad perception joined. Then it cut off, leaving her gasping. She saw Darllanyu's hands clench. The pentad was as frightened of the Archive as they were.

Jindigar stepped out of the group to stand beside her, whispering, "Sorry, I had to know." Then he addressed the Commander. "On the other hand, now that you've had such a power failure, I could simply ask Threntisn over there to work those three manual override levers and open the cargo bay doors behind us. We aren't your prisoners. We don't have to be your allies. We can all take our chances with the herds. Somehow I don't think they'll hurt us. It's you they're after."

"They're only animals—"

"Animals? Yes. Only? Well, they know what's been devastating their homes. *They* are willing to negotiate."

The Cassrian emitted a derisive hoot, no doubt a profanity. Jindigar didn't react, but a Holot officer behind the Cassrian said, "Commander, I've seen an Oliat pull off miracles. I can believe they could negotiate with a herd of wild beasts. It might be worth leveling with the prisoners. I doubt there's much they don't know already."

From the stir that caused among the distant troops, Krinata sensed that they all agreed. Darllanyu moved close to Jindigar and, in a warning undertone, asked in Dushauni, "You aren't planning to Invert—"

"Of course not. We are where we should be. Chinchee's friend will arrange everything."

The Commander watched that exchange warily. His men had lost heart for suicide missions merely to net two political prisoners. He had to be careful what orders he gave now. He stepped closer to Krinata. "What are your terms?"

What could make a loyal Imperial betray the Empire by consorting with the people who'd assassinated an Emperor? And then she knew. "Your Orbital support is gone, isn't it? They've abandoned you here!"

Krinata saw some of the farther troops move to make mystical signs. Another muttered cynically, "She must be a telepath. A few humans are, you know."

"We only have a few minutes more to live," said the Cassrian. The deck was definitely vibrating now. "I may as well admit it. They detected a large blip heading this way. There's been a lot of privateering in this war, and our ships are considered great prizes. But this planet has left our Fleet undercrewed, and low on spare parts. We're too far from our supply lines to risk an engagement. When the Fleet Captain was told we couldn't lift, he ordered landers down to evacuate us. But the pilots said going down to this planet was suicide with that stampede coming, and not one would volunteer, not even when I reported we had you.

"We've nothing to fight that herd with. Central power systems have failed, and so all our defensive screens are down. There's enough tonnage out there to shove us right over that cliff, and without power to the a-gravs, the fall won't do us any good. We're beaten—by your planet, or maybe by your Oliat."

Darllanyu bristled, but Jindigar said coolly, "The only hand raised against your troops, Commander, has been your own."

From the Cassrian's stiff pride, Krinata knew he'd never

surrendered before, certainly never to his own prisoners.
But his voice was perfectly modulated as he said, "State
your terms."

"Our only terms," said Jindigar, "are that when we've
saved your fortress, you and your troops will join our community, live among us without regard to your origins or
training, as fellow refugees from the crumbling Allegiancy
Empire. We won't single you out as troopers, nor hold the
violence of this day against you. And you won't set yourselves apart from the community but will give freely of
every resource this fortress has yet to give."

Feet shuffled in the background, but the Commander's
second urged, "Accept. I'll get them to agree."

"Done! Adjutant, pass the word!" Then, as if the words
were torn from him, he added, "Strike the Imperial colors."
The Adjutant muttered into his helmet pickup, and the Commander asked, "What do we do?"

"Don't strike the colors, Commander," said Krinata. "Tell
your people to salute the colors and remember they've been
part of one of the greatest glories ever created in our galaxy.
We've served the Empire well, but now it is dead, and we
must bury it and go on with our lives. But we must never
forget the peace and prosperity it brought to the galaxy."

He considered, then amended his order, while Jindigar
turned to Chinchee. A passage opened to expose the tall
white native and his little black friend. Krinata sensed Jindigar's inward uncertainty. They hadn't won the native over
yet. Jindigar knelt and respectfully asked the hivebinder to
come onto his shoulder, stroking the little shellperson affectionately.

Through Jindigar's touch Krinata could feel the hivebinder quivering with the restrained need to *bind*. How could
Jindigar, with his limited command of the language, explain
that those who had gutted hives all across the plain were

now friends of the hives? Did they have wars, that they could understand truce?

Apparently they could.

But no sooner had she sensed their agreement than Krinata felt the hivebinder reaching through Jindigar to her, to the pentad, and into the Cassrian Commander, then out into the troops: war, destruction, honed reflexes, betrayal by faulty equipment, horror rising out of the innocent plains grass; Chinchee's marveling curiosity, images of the armored troopers invading sanctuary hives spouting fire and destruction. All this spun away in every direction into tunnels of hive-memory. It was too much.

Darllanyu crumpled. Krinata nearly retched with sudden vertigo. Jindigar plucked the hivebinder off his shoulder and shrilled a piercing whistle at him.

The whole mental assault cut off, leaving Krinata's mind a black field that was almost worse than the sensory overload. The troopers were staggering about, hands to their heads, moaning and in some cases screaming. Jindigar bent over Darllanyu as Zannesu wavered over to her. Over his shoulder Jindigar mumbled to Krinata, "They'd better leave."

To Krinata it seemed that the scene in the cargo bay was painted into a screen, unreal, two-dimensional. Her voice sounded recorded, and it seemed she only remembered speaking the words she heard. "Commander, it may not be healthy for your troops to stay here while we work."

He spoke the order to withdraw, his voice warbling into the supersonic. As the troopers picked each other up and straggled toward the hatch, Krinata followed the Commander, saying, "Leave the hatch unlocked, and we'll send word."

"How can we survive, trapped on this insane world?"

"It will become a wonderful place to live," she answered. She'd seen the beauty of the planet, but right now she'd rather be back in her nice safe office with only Sentient computers and mad Emperors to deal with.

The Cassrian was still skeptical as the hatch closed behind him, and Krinata turned to see people recovering, standing or sitting around the natives. Jindigar stroked the hivebinder on his shoulder and spoke softly to Darllanyu in Dushauni while intermittently gabbling to the native.

Krinata joined them, sitting beside Jindigar, as he explained to everyone, "The only way the hivebinder can deal with this situation is to create a boundmind from all of us— *all* of us—and use that binding to convince the hives we're not mavericks but controllable neighbors." He speared Threntisn with a glance. "He refused to exclude me. He's intrigued by the Archive; can't believe it's a threat."

Darllanyu said in Dushauni, "We'll all be sucked through the Eye! I'd rather go down to the settlement and be eaten alive."

Krinata squirmed, wondering what she'd do if it came to that, but Threntisn answered, also in Dushauni's technical vocabulary, "No, when Jindigar goes, the Archive will implode after him."

"Jindigar won't *go!*" said Krinata, also in Dushauni, forgetting the others listening. "You're going to take the Archive and Seal it!"

"I told you—"

"'You can't achieve fidelity,'" quoted Krinata, "'by forsaking Completion.' Nobody here is going to achieve Completion by getting trompled or eaten, so what sort of fidelity can you achieve by refusing to risk taking the Archive?"

Threntisn started to object, but she talked him down, suddenly seeing what the Dushau hand growing out of the little garden, harboring a fish bowl, fingers turning to lightning flashes really meant. Certainly, if she could understand, a Historian could. "Listen to me. What is it you're trying to Complete? Your Identity! What is an identity? It's the sum of all experiences. Nobody, not even a Dushau, can live long enough to have every experience! Identities can grow and become complete only by drawing on other organized systems, absorbing them as a plant absorbs nourishment from the soil, integrating even—or especially—your antagonists.

"Threntisn, this Archive is your antagonist because you're the one who's most frightened of it. Do you seek Completion, or do we all die incomplete?"

Jindigar looked at her, as delighted as if she'd solved a Cassrian puzzle-cube using only her soft-fleshed hands. Then he turned a proprietary smile on Threntisn, showing pale teeth. "I only saw it last night, at the river, and here she has the whole solution without even studying the Seven Schools of Aliom. Threntisn, we've been trying to practice Efficacious Helplessness by knowing only our own Identities. But to be successfully helpless, one must integrate others' Identities as well. I failed to validate your fear; you failed to validate my fidelity. How could we possibly help each other? Reciprocity is a Policy behind all Laws of Nature."

The Historian nodded slowly. "You're right. You've found a truth despite your skewed Aliom approach." He pushed himself to his feet, regarding Krinata with an odd intensity. Then he nodded. "I wonder if Raichmat's knew what they were doing when they suggested a Dushau multicolony?"

Jindigar answered, "No, we didn't. But being right doesn't require foresight; it requires insight."

Threntisn grunted, then offered Jindigar a hand up. "Come, there can't be much time left."

Jindigar set the shellperson on Chinchee's shoulder with a few trills of explanation and accepted the Historian's hand. But as Threntisn turned to lead the way off into the red shadows, Jindigar bent to whisper to Krinata, "I apologize for saying you needed to develop an epistemology. Lelwatha couldn't have done better."

Bewildered, she watched him follow the Historian to the other end of the cargo bay. When they'd first met, he'd said she needed an epistemology, but she'd never followed his advice.

Darllanyu interrupted her. "We must attempt not to interfere. Do you know how to outfocus from a duad?"

She shook her head.

Darllanyu sighed. "The pentad can't accept you, or we'll drag Jindigar—and the Archive—in." Her eye lit upon a box of ration bars, and she seized it. "Here! Eat." She shoved the box into Krinata's hands, adding, "Get everyone to eat. Talk to them—" And she turned back to the pentad grouping, taking them away into the gloom.

Krinata felt the constant distraction of images from outside the fortress subside, and almost simultaneously the duad link shut down tight, leaving her with a sudden emptiness— a hole where she hadn't been aware of substance. She knew it took Jindigar a great effort to produce that effect, different from dissolving the link. Determined to cooperate even though she wasn't hungry, she took a ration bar and passed the box around, saying, "We may not get another chance to eat." She didn't want to tangle with that Archive again.

There was a stiff silence, then Viradel passed around a water bag, saying, "She's right."

Then the others were all asking questions about what had been said, and Krinata found it so much of a challenge to translate the concepts that she munched the bar and washed it down with the tepid, sterile water and never gave a thought to what was going on out in the cargo bay's shadows until the shock hit like a toothache that spread through all the nerves behind her face.

Gasping, she clawed at the pain, fending off queries until it subsided as suddenly as it had come on. Her nose was running, tears streaming from her eyes, her heart racing, and she wasn't sure if it was from the physical pain or the sudden overwhelming flood of bereavement that came in the wake of the pain: death, loss, endings, every parting she'd ever experienced. That, too, ebbed away just as quickly, to be replaced by an equally inexplicable joy, ecstasy beyond endurance. She was ready to prefer the grief when that burbling intoxication faded to be replaced only by darkness, void, emptiness, silence.

It was like stepping into an anechoic chamber—the constant feedback of living was gone. *Is there such a thing as a thought-echo?*

But before it became a horrifying sensory deprivation, Jindigar was bending over her, the duad link blossoming to full so she was bending over herself, and she was in desperate need of assurance that she wasn't hurt too badly. "I'm sorry, Krinata. I didn't know that would happen—"

Sniffing and blinking, she tossed her head back and managed to mutter, "It was nothing. Forget it." She could feel the tremors shaking his body. She had only felt the edges of what he'd lived through—the ripping asunder of the bonds holding the Archive to his mind at those strategic points of high emotion—the "scars" that ruined him for the Historian's functions. "I'm fine," she insisted.

He fingered the half-eaten ration bar in her hand. "Brilliant idea. You did beautifully." He straightened and went to lower himself beside Chinchee, moving as if he were afraid of becoming dizzy, but smiling freely now. His teeth seemed dark in the red light. They must be bluer than they'd been since the hive. He really was regaining his health, and if all it cost her was a few tears—it was worth it.

As he reached for the shellperson he glanced back at

Krinata. "Ready?" And suddenly she felt a new sharpness to her awareness of his perceptions, quickly swamping out the absence of a thought-echo. The hold was red-lit, and it was totally dark. It was filled with flat, odorless air, and it reeked of human sweat, Holot breath, and Cassrian acridity. And she understood the chirrup of the hivebinder.

"If you're finally ready," it was saying, "we must hurry, for the big ones cannot stop or turn quickly."

"We may begin slowly, not to touch Threntisn until he's ready. He has the Big Memory now. Let me guide."

Threntisn? She gulped. If he couldn't master the Archive—*I convinced him to do it....*

But there was no time to think. The hivebinder touched her through Jindigar, and a panorama of images returned. But this time it wasn't a wild, uncontrolled flicker-flash, nor the sickening whirl of the unSealed Archive. Stretching almost to the tearing point, her mind was able to interpret the pattern, perceived through vastly alien minds.

Below the cliff, the troopers held the settlement. The sun was setting. An Imperial banner made of photomultipliers was being raised on a pole in the middle of the settlement. It glowed the Imperial colors into the shadowed night, and every trooper turned to salute.

The settlers had been herded outdoors, under surveillance by the floating gun platforms and patrolling guards. Knowing nothing of the ground-blanketing swarm of insects coming toward them, they withstood defeat with pride.

She felt the first, tentative touch of the pentad—aching, hungering to complete itself again, but repelled by the taint of the Inverts. The hivebinder, relaxed and pleased, wound them all together, keeping the pentad a single entity—as if it were a hive all by itself, while she and Jindigar were a unit, with Jindigar holding the closest mental contact with the alien, Emulating the herald's role. He even walked with

Chinchee's gait as he rose to confront Terab. "Will you let the binder include you among us? It won't be like the last time, when the hive tried to swallow us. We're forming our own hive."

She recoiled, leery of anything so alien.

"It's not permanent," coaxed Jindigar.

Terab said, as if wondering if the Dushau had lost his grip on reality, "Jindigar, the herbivores are *not* intelligent—"

"No," he agreed. "They're not even self-aware as whole hives. So we must communicate on the lowest levels. Chinchee knows how. It's his role—Herald. But we need someone from each species among us." He turned to Irnils.

Terab reached toward the hivebinder tentatively. "Better me, then."

Krinata felt a wash of truly alien perspectives reshape the gestalt, realigning her concept of reality. And then Jindigar was kneeling before Shorwh.

Shorwh reached to touch the hivebinder. Suddenly he was in the link, too—a child's perspective, strange in its fragmented Cassrian view, yet vibrant with the essence of youth.

Jindigar turned to Storm. "You've been so close. Could a little closer hurt?"

The Lehiroh reached for the hivebinder with both shaking hands, and Krinata remembered her fascination for the Oliat linkages. What compelled a person to become an Outrider— always so close to the Oliat, yet never a part of it. Apparently Jindigar understood Storm's feelings. He took Storm's hand in his own and captured the Lehiroh's eyes, and Krinata was seeing the Lehiroh—so very human, even to the round black pupils of the eyes—through Dushau perception, handicapped by the darkness, so she saw only blotches enhanced by imagination and memory, augmented by the peculiar duad perception. But it was the hivebinder holding them, not an Oliat subform.

She suddenly knew something about Jindigar that had escaped her notice even through all their adventures and intimacies of shared memory; for all the good reasons he'd delayed taking Center, the real reason was that he loved working Oliat and didn't want it to end; he was too involved with experimenting. He wanted to offer others what Krinata had found. A peculiar stretching disturbed the duad, including Storm within its perceptions. But the harmony of triad couldn't solidify. There was a moment of painful discord, then she was on her knees, head spinning as Storm collapsed screaming.

Jindigar knelt, capturing Storm's hands, calming him. The hivebinder held the linkages out of sheer instinct. It was as shocked and bewildered as the rest of them. Jindigar finally got Storm's attention. "I shouldn't have allowed that."

But Storm struggled to his feet again. "No—I'm glad you did. Now I know I could never be part of even a subform." His eyes strayed to Krinata, but he said to Jindigar, "At least I can help with this." He touched the hivebinder again, apologetically, and the hivebinder brought him back into the group rapport. Now there was the pentad, the duad, a Holot, a Cassrian, and a Lehiroh—each a distinct entity, yet part of a whole. Krinata saw how exotic this seemed to the binder, but it was starved for its own function and willing to work even thus, to create what it must have to live.

With this multispecies core the hivebinder touched the group mind of the troopers, already resonating with a common patriotism, and brought them into light contact.

The settlers also had a united mind, a group opinion of the Imperial colors—a lifelong conditioning to upwelling patriotism overlaid by recent bitter experience. That, too, was brought into the overall resonance, though only the ones who'd touched the hivebinder seemed real to Krinata. The settlers and the troopers all seemed to believe they were imagining the images and sensations that flowed through their minds.

Among the minds joining now were many Dushau, adding depths and overtones as they grasped what was happening. They, led by the Aliom trainees, didn't reject what was happening but strove only to protect those who had no training with multiperception. Somehow, out of the swirling mists of Dushau memory, came the unmistakable trace of the Archive.

Oh, no!

But this time it was a multiplex stillness, warded round with a dynamic strength. Images flowed in connected sequences, with no compelling lure attached to them. Only one portal was open, and it was shrouded in a reflective grayness. Threntisn was in control—and recording.

Krinata's personal relief sent cascades of joy through the entire mind, and Jindigar's innocent wonder that she might have doubted cut off before it turned to confusion. //Look at what is truly threatening us,// he suggested.

The pentad, through the Outreach, brought a wide view into focus. Up on the plain, among the tall grass, huge mottled herbivores ran, half a dozen species, thousands of individuals. Heads down, hooves beating a hypnotic rhythm, they ran with their fellows, not the hive-bearers, nor the young, nor the providers—just the protectors, but from so many hives, so many species.

They ran. Under their pounding feet the ground turned to muck matted with pulverized straw. As far as anyone could see in any direction, humped backs pumped like waves of the sea, long necks poking up here and there, undulating in rhythm. Long, furred beasts beside scaled ones, curly

pelted beside sleek, a solid mass of living flesh moved as
one to their deaths. The hives would live. The hive was as
immortal as the plain itself.

At the edges of the stampede swarms of smaller creatures,
vermin and scavengers, hunters and hunted, ran together
toward the intruder crouched on the lip of the precipice.

On the lower plain, dusk did not halt the advance of the
swarm. Hundreds of varieties of insects, the warriors of
thousands of hives, some as big as a human hand, others
almost microscopic, flowed across the countryside, a living
blanket of destruction. But where they passed, grass and
leaves were uneaten, life undisturbed. This army was dis-
ciplined and dedicated to one target. The offworlders.

And then the beasts and insects of the plains saw a huge
native hive covering the fortress and spreading over the
settlement below—one such as the intruders destroyed so
routinely, one such as Chinchee visited in his eternal rounds
as Herald, binding the hives together, as this giant hive was
bound to all others.

The vision-hive covered the intruders, controlled them,
defined them, tamed them. Krinata was at once part of the
gestalt of the new hivekind, and on the periphery of the
lightly touching mass of plains hivekinds. The hives' mass
consciousness was infused with a red rage, energized by
instinct, driven by primal urges to defend the hives.

Desperate with how close the stampede was, Krinata
closed her eyes and summoned that natural ability Jindigar
had called being a natural Conceptor—conceptualizing the
dome of the hive over them.

The pentad flinched, almost shattering the multirapport,
and Jindigar caught her back against him. "No, that's Inverted. Come—be Receptor—like this . . ."

And they were suddenly cut off from the hivebound, and
deep into Raichmat's Oliat. Jindigar was Outreach, and she

was Receptor—full, functioning Oliat. It was as if they were standing with one foot supported by Jindigar's memory and another planted firmly on the deck of the fortress. She compared what she'd tried to do with how a Receptor functioned, seeing how to flip the function over with a topologist's disregard for essential differences.

Suddenly they were back among the hivebound, and she was Receiving the image of the monstrous hive covering fortress and settlement. It wasn't something she was doing, projecting outward. She simply looked and noticed the old moss on the mortar between building blocks, the weather curls in the plume of smoke rising from the chimneys, and the smells of cozy living. She didn't have to imagine it because it was real in its own way. Her Receiving made that level of reality available to everyone.

She became enraptured by the work, reveling in the sensation of being—having been—Officer to Raichmat's. She remembered how they'd discovered each of the species stampeding at them now and how they'd recognized the threat such a bound group would present to any settlement. They hadn't discovered the heralds, hadn't learned how to establish peace with the plain.

At some point the pentad re-joined them, giving them awareness of the movements on the plains, the mood of the stampede, of the pace slackening, the fury dissipating into confusion, the insectoidal programming disintegrating. The resulting chaos was perhaps more dangerous than true animosity. For as the pentad grudgingly began to trust Jindigar and Krinata again, the herds arrived.

Already, though, they saw a hive where they had expected to see a fortress and armored troopers. The leaders of the stampede could not stop with all the tons of hurtling flesh behind them—but they turned away from the "hive" as a river current cuts around a solid boulder.

Jarred out of the rapport, Krinata heard the hatch clang open, troopers' armor clattering into the echoing darkness. The Commander's reedy Cassrian voice called, "You can't stop them now! They're going to—"

The deck shifted hard under them as something hit the fortress, and Krinata tumbled off-balance into Jindigar.

TWELVE

Ad Hoc Oliat

Krinata was on hands and knees when the next impact jarred the unprotected fortress. Then they came thick and fast, the vibration reaching deafening proportions. Around them bulkheads deformed, stretching joints designed to withstand energy-bolt fire in space, the stresses of takeoff and landing, or the recoil of firing weapons—but not without cushioning energy screens.

Soon cracks opened, connectors parted, and sparks showered. Momentarily Krinata was gripped by déjà vu infused with a sense of horror. *Dying in agony. Malevolent sand dunes. Cry of betrayal.* "No!" she whispered, "it's not the same now." She crawled to a bulkhead where, using both hands, she made it to her feet.

Jindigar was sitting on the floor holding his head, the duad linkage bringing Krinata only a hint of his pain as the fragile boundmind gestalt shattered. The Cassrian Commander, even more dazed, stared at a cascade of sparks dousing a pile of his troopers.

"Commander," called Jindigar over the roar from without and the growing babble of voices within. "Can you deploy your auxiliary ground anchors? The mains aren't holding!"

Brought back to himself, the Commander made it to his feet in a virtuoso demonstration of suit armor handling. Swaying, he answered, "We lost them when the tornadoes demolished the other two fortresses."

Jindigar wiped a smear of blood trickling from his nose

and got to his feet, standing knees bent, arms flowing to keep his balance. "Then let's get the rim attitude jets going to keep us away from the cliff."

"Blew the circuits when we landed. My last technician is in sickbay, unconscious. Onboard Sentient has lost too much circuitry to help."

Jindigar swore, then glanced at the pentad. They were climbing to their feet by using the wall and each other, while the Outriders consulted in loud bellows. Jindigar called to them, "I have the fortress blueprints. If the pentad can locate the problem, maybe I can fix it in time."

The Commander began an objection while Darllanyu as Outreach consulted the others. Krinata grabbed at Jindigar's elbow to maintain her balance and captured the Commander's attention. "Jindigar can do it if you can find him the tools."

The Commander hesitated only a moment, then spoke into his communicator. But Jindigar was having less luck. He moved to the pentad, arguing in Dushauni Oliat jargon that Krinata couldn't follow. Then, in exasperation, he paced away from them, hissing something that sounded like, "Clumsy amateurs!" He turned to Krinata, summoning the duad. //Scan with me.//

It didn't come as words but as an urge to seek the integrity of the fortress—to reach for the gestalt that included the inanimate thing. Tantalizing, the perception hovered at the edge of knowledge, giving them only a few cryptic details of close-by functions. Just for a flash she realized what Jindigar had had with *Truth* and Arlai when he hosted an exploring Oliat aboard.

Jindigar hissed, frustrated, "No good. If a pentad can't make it, no duad could, either."

Cy had now rigged some kind of a line over a track that ran the length of the cargo bay. He handed the end to Jindigar, who absently accepted it. Keeping his balance by swinging from the line, Jindigar rounded on the pentad while the Outriders tore loose more cables and rigged more lines, the troopers picking up the idea and doing likewise.

"We're going over that cliff," said Jindigar grimly.

The Outreach replied dispassionately, "Animals have already plunged over. The people below are evacuating the area. There may be a pile of carcasses to cushion our fall."

Jindigar spat, "The fall will split this fortress open."

The swarm of insectoidals was not far beyond the river now, the lead flyers already flitting across the span of water in huge leaps, smaller mites carried on their backs. Krinata's flesh puckered in revulsion—but she thought the mass of tiny bodies was beginning to deflect its course.

"What do you propose, *Invert!*" It wasn't Darllanyu speaking—but the pentad, gripped by fear of what logic suggested.

Krinata staggered toward them and yelled to be heard, "Those poor beasts out there deserve to be *saved* as much as we do. If this is to be our world, we have to *act* like it. With just a small amount of power to the shields, maybe we could form a cushioning wall to keep them from going over the cliff!"

Jindigar looked from her to Threntisn, to Darllanyu, decision hardening his features. "Threntisn has earned his proof of the Archive's condition. I'll take your Center, with Krinata as my Outreach. I have the blueprints, you have the perceptions. Your hands can use my skills—we might be able to save a few hundred animals and ourselves—and this fortress for the community."

Jindigar's Oliat. Because he had a bare fifty years until Renewal, this would be one of the shortest-lived Oliats on record. She could be part of that—at least until a Dushau could take her place. Again he was asking her for a commitment without apprising her of the dangers. But this time she didn't mind. It would be worth her life if they could pull it off. Their eyes met as he added, "I renounce Inversion while bound to this Oliat, and so will Krinata."

Five pairs of dilated indigo eyes locked onto her. With the duad wide-open, she knew with Jindigar the factors they weighed with the swiftness only the Oliat linkages could achieve. They had grieved with her and survived it. But an Oliat link was closer. Would the tarnish on her soul rub off onto theirs? But she and Jindigar had turned away from Inverting when the hivebinder had constructed the vision of a hive over them.

She had things of her own to consider. *While I'm in the Oliat I can't have children or a husband.* If she fell in love, it might kill them all. She had to make up her mind to live celibate and helpless before the forces of this world. She'd never needed marriage, but celibacy wasn't her way of life, either.

Opening her mouth to say, *Surely you can find someone better than I,* she saw herself forever locked out of the awareness that had come to mean so much to her. The sensory deprivation frightened her more than the risks. *It won't be for a whole fifty years.*

Jindigar said, "We can't do skills-suffusion with less than an Oliat. Without that there's not enough time. We can't even abandon the fortress now. We're surrounded."

Suddenly Krinata was shamed at wasting time pondering her personal feelings. "I don't know what oath you'd accept from me—but—I renounce Inversion for as long as I'm part of Jindigar's Oliat, and I'll abide by the laws and customs of Aliom—even though I don't know what they all are right now."

After she'd said it Krinata waited, heart in her throat, hoping they'd accept her, and fearing it.

With the duad wide-open she felt the pentad examining

their balance. In the back of her mind there grew a bizarre image of ten separate Dushau eyes winking in a rippling pattern in rhythm with her own heart. Wispy Dushau fingers combed through her emotions. Her throat constricted around a scream, but she let them inspect—sensing they sought to discern her place in the scheme of things, even though as a mere pentad they couldn't be sure.

And then everything *changed*.

The world swam fluidly around Jindigar. Dimly she realized that the Officers were shifting function to accommodate a new distribution of talents and strengths, Jindigar's grip molding them, seeking a balance. They shifted and shifted again, randomly at first, then, under Jindigar's firming touch, purposively.

When she could see again, Zannesu stood between her and Jindigar—as Inreach—and Darllanyu, shaking with self-doubt, was at Krinata's right, Jindigar's Formulator. The others arranged themselves behind Jindigar, and she, herself, stood outside the organism that had assembled itself—Outreach. They were behind her, but she could see them clearly.

In front of her the Cassrian Commander was reaching to shake her shoulder, demanding attention, and Cy was forcing himself between them protectively while Storm bellowed orders to his co-husbands and the rest of Cy's team, proclaiming a new full Oliat in function.

Something buried within the back of Krinata's mind came to a solid equilibrium, the vision of the others faded, and she felt Jindigar, only slightly more intense than in duad. //Easy now, you can do it. Speak with us. Relax and let it happen—just as you learned to be duad-Receptor.//

In sudden panic she tried to find the Takora memories within her, but they seemed shriveled and gone. //I don't know how!//

//She can't do it!//

They're as scared as I am. The united panic threatened to rip them apart before they'd truly balanced.

But Jindigar wouldn't permit it. //She's done harder things. Krinata, turn—look at us.//

Petrified, she forced herself to twist around and look behind her. The world spun as she moved, and she knew she was failing the Oliat. Zannesu stood behind her, between her and Jindigar—only in his eyes, she saw also Jindigar—and Darllanyu—*I'm not crazy. I'm not.*

Dizzy with the composite views as the Oliat zunre looked directly at each other, Krinata finally reached a point of tension beyond which she couldn't go. As sudden relaxation struck her she thought she was fainting, too weak to live another moment.

But as her knees sagged another strength energized her body, and suddenly everything seemed normal. Her mouth opened, saying, "We know where the problems are." And she began to reel off a list of locations, ordering the Commander, "Send tool scurries—" The words choked off as a panic grabbed her guts. Her mouth had moved of its own accord! Horror gripped her. She had paid dearly to rid herself of Desdinda's compulsion. //No!//

//Easy,// came the soothing Central flavor of Jindigar as the others recoiled from her.

//She's conditioned against it,// argued Center. //We aren't properly tempered or balanced yet. Let's just see how long we can hold together.//

Krinata's body moved of its own accord—at the will of the Oliat, or maybe of Jindigar?—out across the cargo bay, pulling herself along on one of the lines. Outriders cleared the troopers away from them, calling loudly, "Oliat coming through! They know how to get the power going again!"

Forever after, the rest came to memory shrouded in the veils of dreamlike unreality. There were sharp images embedded in long blurs, and she suspected that the clear memories were shuffled out of time sequence. Jindigar, when pressed, assured her that this was because none of them had ever occupied the Offices they were now handling, and because, using such an impromptu assembly procedure, he could not be delicate with the skills suffusion. "But we didn't have six or seven days for the whole tedious business of stabilizing our form!"

At some point Krinata found herself bending over a nightmare tangle of circuitry hanging out of a buckled access hatch and tenderly snapping a wedge-shaped circuit element into place. A phrase drifted to the top of her mind on bubbles of laughter: *ad hoc* Oliat. //We're an *ad hoc* Oliat!//

Amusement at the absurd concept spread through their shared consciousness, and in its wake tension subsided. The work went faster. Her hands flew even though her eyes tended to see the work under someone else's hands in a far part of the fortress.

She staggered along a narrow passage, steadying herself against a bulkhead as repeated blows shook the fortress. She searched for a tubular access to a catwalk. Cy paced at her shoulder, keeping the troopers around them from demanding her attention. The thuds and shiftings had become muted because of carcasses piled against the hull and because the entire stampede was indeed slowing, more and more of the racing animals veering off before hitting the "hive." Chinchee and the hivebinder were still projecting a hive, and the animals' instincts screamed only, *Wrong, wrong, wrong!* as they hurtled into the symbol of ally, not enemy.

Suddenly a shudder slid the deck from under her, and a screaming of tearing metal filled the air. The thunderous sound of a million hooves pounding the turf redoubled as she smelled the reek of sweating animal bodies and freshly turned dirt on a puff of air. Her companions didn't need her announcement, "Hull's breached!"

The passage was inundated with small, brown-furred bodies, sharp teeth, beady eyes, short stubby tails, pointed ears. Carrion eaters, blood lust too aroused by the stampede to veer away from a hive—their natural prey,—swarmed into the fortress. And it wasn't just here—she sensed Darllanyu and Jindigar both wading through a sea of small bodies.

Large goose bumps formed all over her, and she felt her begrimed hair standing on end. Her physical reaction was mirrored among the Dushau, making them all acutely uncomfortable, echoing a derisive, *human*, around the circuit. Jindigar interceded, //That's not human sexual arousal!// Apology and curiosity swept them all, but she was at the panel Jindigar needed, and her hands flew.

How Jindigar managed to direct so many at once, she never knew. Later he only raised his hand, palm cupped, fingers pointing to the sky, and explained, "What must be done can be done."

She asked, "Is that a Law of Nature?"

"Maybe," he quipped. "Or maybe it's only a local ordinance."

But at the time, surrounded by a river of small, dirty, hot vermin nipping at her field boots with their sharp teeth until finally one of them actually hit flesh and made her yelp and dance, Krinata could only struggle against distraction, fight her natural inclination to resist the spooky *possession* that gripped her, and tell herself over and over that she couldn't afford a nervous breakdown yet.

Finally, Chinchee and the hivebinder convinced the vermin with hivelike projections of repelling horrors to stop chewing on wires and the crew's armored feet and find their meals *outside*. Then the board Krinata was working on came to life under her hands. Relief and a wild cheer rang through the Oliat linkages, infusing her with a warm glow unlike any other satisfaction she'd ever known.

The shuddering and jerking of the deck ceased. The roaring thunder, a vibration in the bones more than a sound, did not slacken, but the tone changed. The Oliat focus shifted so Krinata had a moment of nauseating vertigo followed by a horrid drop in the pit of her stomach as she *fell* into a seething cauldron of wide-angle Dushau visual fields. //Sorry,// Jindigar apollogised. //My fault. I've never done this before, either. Better?//

Krinata had both hands clamped over her mouth and her eyes squinched shut. Peripherally she felt Cy's hand on her shoulder, and his touch steadied her as much as whatever Jindigar had done. She got her muscles unknotted and fumbled for the communicator he carried for her. It was set on full shipwide and crew address, so her voice was heard everywhere as the Oliat announced, "//Lateral forcefields generating; attitude jets on minimum, vectored to hold our position. Observers below report if a jet oversplashes the edge of the cliff.//"

//What did that mean?// wailed Krinata, suddenly weary beyond endurance. She *knew* the Oliat was viewing the entire outside panorama, but she, herself, was cut off from it because, as Outreach, she was to be aware of their immediate environment, not bemused by the larger picture. Jindigar's fumble had given her too much information to process because when *he* functioned as Outreach, he was able to work inside the multiview contact as well. *After over three thousand years' experience!* And in her exhaustion she despaired of ever being a real Outreach.

Jindigar used her hands on the controls to shape the forcefield into a hyperbola, transforming the animals' forward momentum gently into momentum at right angles to the surface of the field where they hit, sliding them off along a vector pointing out into open plains. The terrified bellowing of the animals was louder than the rumble of their hoofbeats, and there was nothing the hivebinder could do to reassure them.

Hours and hours through the long night, the seemingly endless herd gradually slowed, gradually turned short of the "hive" forcefield and the cliff. As fewer hit the forcefields Jindigar diminished the power to the jets manually because they lacked the parts to give the Sentient control of those circuits. It was tricky work, balancing the forces to prevent the fortress from skidding into the stampede, yet not letting it slide over the cliff.

But at last, when Jindigar lifted the skills suffusion, the Oliat rejoined the gestalt the hivebinder struggled to maintain. With Chinchee's help, the binder integrated the new seven-way unit that now replaced the five-way unit. It seemed upset with the vanished five-unit and two-unit, but gradually it adjusted. Shortly after that, the frantic eruption of small, furred bodies through the rents in the hull ceased altogether. The vermin already running in frantic circles within the walls of the fortress had to be picked up by troopers in armor and put outside.

Their hunger sent them swarming over the carcasses heaped around the fortress, some of them finding their way down to the piles of flesh at the foot of the cliff. By the first graying of dawn, the grisly business of cleaning up was well under way.

As quiet descended, the evacuation of the fortress began. All the able-bodied went down to help those below. The Oliat was among the last to leave. They emerged onto a launch platform overlooking part of the cliff and part of the plain. Jindigar was trying to reduce the intensity of the Oliat contact, preparing to adjourn them—not to Dissolve, for once he'd Dissolved his Oliat, he'd be unable to Center another.

Jindigar's control was shaky, like a hand twitching uncontrollably from too many hours of clutching something. The scene of carnage she viewed around them alternated between the stark, revolting, but properly colored human vision; the dim, but semantically neutral, view seen by naked Dushau eyes; and the Oliat gestalt of a natural process proceeding in a healthy way.

Krinata was shaking all over with abating tension, too tired to celebrate properly, confused beyond endurance, nerves blasted, body aching. She barely remembered Cy urging her to step onto the largest weapons platform with Chinchee and the hivebinder. The rest of the Oliat crowded around her. The platform took off none too steadily with such a load, but as they moved out beyond the edge of the cliff, she ceased to worry about it.

The heaps of dead animals at the bottom of the cliff were crawling with scavengers and black with flying insects. The light of the rising sun gleamed off blood. Streams of animals carried chunks of meat and entrails away to their hives. But the sight that sent her groping for the railing to hang over open air and retch helplessly was the way the vermin attacked the dead settlers and troopers strewn about the battlefield. All over, surviving troopers still in armor teamed up with the settlers to fight the vermin off the bodies of their dead comrades.

She felt the Oliat react to her illness, but this time not with derision or contempt but a determined patience with her differences. She tried to open herself to their attitude— a joy that they had been fully accepted by this world—that even their dead would not be ignored but integrated into the natural processes. But she couldn't.

//Jindigar!// she protested through the fading Oliat linkages.

The Oliat embraced her, looking out at the scene through her eyes and her perceptions. The stark horror multiplied until she thought she'd fly to pieces. But then they moved as one, accepting her with all her differences. //Zunre.//

She spoke once more as Outreach, addressing Chinchee in his own language—scraping her throat raw in the process. Then the hivebinder's gestalt urged the scavengers away from the dead strangers, understanding suddenly that the renewed fighting was not a rejection of a kindness but a defense of a deep integrity.

As the platform reached treetop level Jindigar stood behind her, one long-fingered hand draped over her shoulder. //Now.// She felt a shifting, rending, straining realignment, the strange yet familiar compartmentalizing as when Jindigar loosened the duad or made it dormant. Only this time it was a pit-of-the-stomach bereavement, a needle-sharp shock, a wail that screeched along the nerves and made her hair stand on end and her teeth ache.

She gasped as the seven of them began to move and breathe in disconnected patterns. She hadn't noticed, before, how they had synchronized—even little things like blinking. Now it felt suddenly as if her *other* eyes blinked in spasmodic twitches that shattered her nerves.

Jindigar turned to each of them singly, making eye contact, somehow adjusting everything to ease. She thought she sensed him being critical of how roughly he performed this *adjournment*. At last he said to Cy, rather wistfully, "Consider us adjourned for the moment, though we may have trouble maintaining that."

Cy frowned at Storm, and then they both nodded agreement. Storm passed the word to the Outriders squeezed onto the platform with them: "Adjourned, then, but watch for sudden changes."

Below, people who had been fighting vermin off the bodies of the dead now stared after the retreating creatures. Some troopers began assembling the scattered bodies into neat rows. But Krinata noticed how they placed armored troopers beside settlers, making no distinctions.

As the Oliat platform passed overhead, aiming to land at the Dushau compound, troopers with their helmets off, settlers with their wounds bandaged, all stopped to gaze up at them. They'd been bound into the hive linkage. What did they think had happened? Would they keep the peace among themselves now?

She had barely thought the question when it was answered. In a single voice the people below raised a cheer that rang off the cliff and startled the busy scavengers into stillness.

Again the cheer, and again. Cy took Krinata's hand and raised it in a gesture of victory. Storm stepped to the forward railing and raised Jindigar's hand.

Trooper and settler together, at least five species, cheered louder and clearer, until she made out their words, "Krinata and Jindigar! Krinata and Jindigar!"

"But we didn't do it alone!" she protested, pulling her hand from Cy's.

Jindigar pulled his hand out of Storm's grasp and hugged the Lehiroh, though his voice was distant, distracted by the Oliat threads he still held. "No, we didn't. How could they have come by such an impression?"

Storm said, "Terab's been talking, I'll bet. And Shorwh. Even Viradel. They all went down hours ago."

Something caught Krinata's eye in the east, the sun clearing the horizon accompanied by a slice of new moon. "Look!" She pointed.

Above the rushing of the wind and the chanting cheer below she heard Darllanyu whisper, "Darllanyu again, but a good omen this time."

The Cassrian Commander, standing in the pilot's dock, bent over his instruments. "Good omen? For whom?"

"What do you mean?" asked Storm, craning his neck to see, but Cy pointed at the horizon again.

"A ship!"

"Can you identify it?" asked Krinata tensely, knowing Jindigar's wish that he hadn't adjourned them.

"I'm trying," answered the Cassrian working intently. "It's a lander—large one. Could be that privateer. This colony may be a short-lived one."

"Can you make voice contact at least?" asked Krinata.

The distant rumble finally attracted the attention of everyone on the ground, and cheering subsided as they scanned the sky. The silver-white dot grew as its impellers strained to dump velocity.

"Can the Oliat identify it?" asked the Commander, frustrated.

"We're adjourned," answered Jindigar, as if it were only of academic importance, yet she could feel his anxiety. "Can't dip in and out of Oliat as easily as a duad."

She remembered how much more difficult it was to assemble and adjourn a triad and realized that if she were pulled back into that deep seven-way contact again right now, she'd probably go into a screaming fit and drive them all beyond the ends of sanity. She shuddered. *Don't let it be necessary!*

The Commander announced, "It's going to land at the clay dig!"

Jindigar pulled the microphone for the platform's address system out and shoved it into Krinata's hand. "Tell them." Then he gently replaced the Commander at the controls, saying, "Let me see what I can do."

His fourteen long fingers danced over the controls as he spoke into the pickup in Dushauni. In moments he had an image on the tiny screen, an indigo face, and a voice came tinnily through the miniature amplifier. Krinata recognized the Dushau woman, exclaiming, "Ambassador Trinarvil!" Then she explained to everyone, "The Dushau Ambassador to the Emperor's Court!" Her voice boomed out over the crowd below, and she added, "It's a Dushau ship!"

Another cheer and everyone was running toward the clay dig to greet them.

Trinarvil was a small woman, stately, darker than Jindigar's deep indigo. Her voice was high and pleasant, and her face now unmarked by the intense anxiety Krinata had last seen there the night before Dushaun withdrew its embassy from the Allegiancy, breaking diplomatic relations. "Jindigar!" sang the Ambassador with obvious joy. "I should have known you'd get here before I could, but when we saw the Squadron leaving, we feared we'd find nothing here but pulverized ground. It looks like that from the air, you know, and your signal is being generated by Imperial equipment."

"Where's the Squadron?" asked Jindigar.

"That's the curious thing. They took one look at us and detimed." Trinarvil added to Jindigar, "I brought *The Organizer,* an unarmed passenger ship. Ripped out bulkheads so we've got three hundred aboard, with about fifty ephemerals. A good bit of cargo too. Couldn't have run from them as *Truth* could."

"They've gone for reinforcements," predicted Jindigar with that detached air, but he was gradually beginning to seem himself again.

The Cassrian Commander said, "I don't think so. They left expecting the stampede to wipe us and the settlement out. Our—objective—had been accomplished."

Trinarvil's eye had traveled over the armor with the neutrality of a trained diplomat, and Jindigar told her, "We both have long stories to tell. Can you land by the clay dig?"

"Jindigar," she answered with good-humored asperity,

"I've been piloting since before you were born. I could land *in* that dig if I had to."

They all laughed, and Krinata glanced down. They were over the dig now, and the small lake that had gathered in the center. The settlement was already experimenting with farming fish in the pond, and Krinata was unsurprised to see a piol waddling out of the water with a wriggling catch in his mouth.

Then she saw his destination—a mud-and-straw nest halfway up the slope. "Jindigar, look!"

Cy leaned over the forward rail, peering below. "Piol cubs! How many?"

Jindigar was working with the screens and brought a close-up onto the weapons target. "Four," he counted. He flashed an intimate, private grin to Krinata, then warned Trinarvil, "You'd better not land in the pond. The colony has begun to establish itself!"

In Outer Space!

__WHEN WORLDS COLLIDE
*by Philip Wylie
and Edwin Balmer*   (E30-539, $2.75)
When the extinction of Earth is near, scientists build rocket ships to evacuate a chosen few to a new planet. But the secret leaks out and touches off a savage struggle among the world's most powerful men for the million-to-one-chance of survival.

__AFTER WORLDS COLLIDE
*by Philip Wylie
and Edwin Balmer*   (E30-383, $2.75)
When the group of survivors from Earth landed on Bronson Beta, they expected absolute desolation. But the Earth people found a breathtakingly beautiful city encased in a huge metal bubble, filled with food for a lifetime but with no trace either of life—or death. Then the humans learned that they were not alone on Bronson Beta . . .

131